A Full Novel Written By: Danielle Grant

Altar'd

Altar'd

Altar'd: A Kalil And Chanae

Between Love Novel

Chapter 1

It has been six months after Nassir and Zariya's wedding. Everyone's lives was starting to get back on track and moving in the right direction. Chanae was trying to plan her and Kalil's wedding but it was starting to be harder than she thought. With taking care of their son who was now two years old and planning the wedding, it was a lot for her to handle all at once. She knew sooner or later she was going to need a wedding planner to help her with the vision she had planned over and over in her head for their special day.

Chanae was sitting on the bed reading Khalid one of his children's books when Kalil walked into their bedroom and kissed her on the lips.

"Ewww bae you sweaty and gross looking." Chanae laughed with her face frowned up.

"You know you like it sweaty. What's up little prince?" he said to their son before making his way to the bathroom.

"No correction I like to work up a sweat not you already sweaty that is just nasty." He poked his head out the bathroom door and laughed.

"When you go lay our little prince down for his nap you can always come in the bathroom with me and I will gladly help you work up a sweat." he said winking at her.

"Whatever playa. How are the guys doing?" she asked laying Khalid down under the covers. He had fallen asleep while she was reading to him.

"Well Nassir is going crazy because Zariya is having bad morning sickness. He said when she's not having morning sickness, she's going sex crazy." Kalil laughed as he turned the shower on.

"Well hell for some pregnant women they can't get enough sex and some don't want you to touch them. I say he should be happy that she's one of the sex crazed pregnant women... So who won the basketball game, I know you niggas made bets on who was going to win?" Chanae asked standing at the door admiring her man's naked body.

Catching her staring at him he grinned.

"You know you don't have to stand over there and stare like a pervert. I don't mind if you come and touch me." he joked stepping into the shower. Right when Chanae was about to take him up on his offer she changed her mind when she heard her stomach growl.

She thought about it for a second and realized that she

had not eaten since earlier that morning.

"Maybe next time freak." she joked before

walking out their room to go downstairs in the kitchen

to make herself something to eat.

"I heard that!" Kalil shouted before putting his

head back under the water.

"It was said for you to hear!" she yelled back.

Chanae walked into the kitchen and took the

ingredients out that she would need to make a deli

sandwich with. After setting everything on the counter

she stopped when she heard the doorbell ring.

Walking out of the kitchen and towards the front

door she looked through the peep hole before answering

it. She noticed that no one was standing there so pulling

the door open, the only thing she saw was an envelope

sitting on the porch. Picking up the envelope she then closed the door and locked it before she opened the envelope to see what was inside. Inside of it was a picture of her walking with Khalid at the park a few days ago with a red X across her face with the words DEAD BITCH written on the front.

Chanae wasted no time running upstairs to her and Kalil's bedroom. When she got to the room, Kalil was just putting on some basketball shorts and pulling them up.

"What's up you came back to take me up on my offer?" he smiled and then turned to face her. Once he saw the scared and worried look on her face his smile disappeared. "What's wrong with you?" he asked walking toward her.

Chanae handed him the envelope and the picture that came in it. Kalil took one look at the picture and saw nothing but red. Not only was someone following and taking pictures of his fiancé but they did it while she had their son with her.

"I swear it's like every time we start getting comfortable and living our lives there is always someone out to destroy our happiness" she began to cry out of frustration and anger.

"Baby do not worry about anything. I will take care of this." Kalil tried soothing her.

"How can you take care of this when we don't even know who is doing this? I bet it's the same person that has been calling the phone and not saying anything."

"Wait, somebody been playing on the phone and you didn't think to tell me about it?" Kalil could feel himself getting even more pissed.

"I didn't think anything of it at the time Kalil.

They would call and not say anything. If I didn't hang up first then they would just hang up. At first I just thought it was some kids dialing random numbers playing on the phones. Then the calls started coming more and more frequently as the days went by."

"Damn Chanae that is something you should have told me. What were you thinking; that the calls were just going to stop?!" Khalid started crying and Kalil realized he spoke louder than he had intended too. Chanae went to pat him on his back and try to get him to go back to sleep. When he did she covered him back up with the covers.

Kalil stood there watching his family and he knew he would do anything to protect them. Walking over to his dresser he threw on a shirt and quickly stepped into his shoes. Grabbing his keys off the nightstand with his cellphone he made his way out the door. "I'll be back."

"Where are you going?" Chanae asked following behind him.

"Out! Do not open the door for nobody; I will be right back." And with that he walked out the front door leaving Chanae standing there wondering if their relationship would ever be the same.

❧ ❧ ❧

Kalil drove around for fifteen minutes with no clear destination in mind. He just needed some time to clear his head and figure out who this person was that was threatening Chanae. He knew without a doubt he would kill and even die to protect her. Kalil was just pissed that Chanae did not feel the need to tell him about the phone calls she had been receiving. He felt like she thought maybe he couldn't protect her or something. That would be foolish thinking on her behalf because he had done so numerous times before.

11

Some of those times she knew nothing about and the others he had no intentions on telling her.

He was so lost in his thoughts that he was not paying attention to the car that had been tailing him since he pulled out of his driveway. He clipped his phone onto the dashboard and put it on speaker. "Call Nassir" he instructed. While the phone dialed Nassir's number Kalil continued to drive with no particular place in mind to go.

"What's up man?" Nassir answered the phone.

"I need to holla at you about something right quick. Is it cool to come through or no?"

"Yeah come through. You sound frustrated as hell I can hear it all in your voice." Nassir said while handing Za'kiya her snack and juice.

"Thank you daddy." she said skipping into the living room and sitting in front of the T.V.

"You welcome baby." he replied.

"Man I'm beyond frustrated. I'll be there in about ten minutes though." Kalil said bringing Nassir back to the phone conversation.

"Alright cool I'll be here." he said disconnecting the call.

Kalil was still thinking about everything that had happened within the last two years. He was starting to think their lives would never be normal or at least drama free. He was so focused on his thoughts and the road before him he never saw the car coming straight for him from behind. The impact of the car crashing into his forced him to bang his head on the steering wheel three times before finally passing out. Kalil's car went flipping over the medium rolling down the hill before the other car finally decided to pull off.

❤ ❤ ❤

Chanae had been calling Kalil's phone for over an hour now and still had not gotten an answer. She was really feeling guilty about not telling him about the phone calls she had been receiving. She had already left him three voicemails and was now in the process of leaving yet another one.

"Baby I know you're mad at me but please come home so we can at least talk about it. Kalil I love you and I know I was wrong for keeping the phone calls from you. It was never my intention to hide it from you. Look, just please come home." Chanae pressed end on her phone after leaving the voicemail.

Walking into their son's room where Chanae had taken him after Kalil left out the house, she decided

14

to call Zariya's house to ask Nassir if he had talked to his boy. While the phone rang she waited for someone to pick up.

"Hello, Williams house how may I help you?" Za'kiya answered the phone in her soft voice on the third   ring.

"Za'kiya?" Chanae asked trying to be sure it was her.

"Yes is this my te-te Chanae?"

"Yes it is. Za'kiya where is your mommy and daddy?" Chanae asked her.

"Well my..." Before she could finish her statement she was interrupted by Zariya.

"Za'kiya what did I tell you about answering that phone? You just asking for a whooping ain't you?" Zariya said taking the phone out of her hand. Za'kiya took off running to Nassir who had walked in the room right behind Zariya. Chanae could hear Zariya yelling in the background before she spoke into the phone.

"Hello?"

"Hey Zar, it's me I was just calling to speak to Nassir to see if he talked to Kalil."

"Well he right here - is everything okay?" Zariya could hear the worry in Chanae's voice.

"Not really but I will tell you once I talk to Nassir." Chanae said into the phone.

"Okay well hold up." Zariya walked up to Nassir and reached her arm out to hand him the phone while she rubbed her pregnant belly with the other. "Baby, Chanae wants to talk to you"

Nassir grabbed the phone and put Za'kiya down. "What's up Chanae I was just about to call over there and ask where your man at. He had me waiting for him and he never showed." Nassir said taking a seat on the couch in the living room.

"Wait he called you and never showed? I was just calling you to see if you heard from him but if he never showed up then I am worried. He would never just not show up if he told you he was on his way." Nassir was about to say something but Chanae told him to hold on because her other end just clicked and it could be Kalil.

"Baby?" Chanae guessed.

"No, Chanae this is Licia. I am at the hospital and Kalil was rolled in here a little while ago. I just got word of it and once I checked to make sure it was him I called you. He was in a bad accident; you should get up here at Barnes Jewish Hospital quick." Chanae didn't waste any time clicking back over telling Nassir what she just heard. She ran around the room getting herself and Khalid together before heading out the door.

Altar'd

Chanae strapped her son into the car and hopped in the driver seat pulling out the driveway and flying down the street like a bat out of hell. She never once noticed the car following behind her.

Chapter 2

Chanae, Nassir, and Zariya were in the waiting room waiting for the doctor to come out and tell them what is going on with Kalil. Their attention was drawn to the door when Kalyah and her mother Karla walked in. They made their way over to them both with tears in their eyes.

"How is he? What did the doctor say? What happen to him?" Karla asked question after question. She kept thinking in her head over and over again that she would not make it if she had to bury another child of hers.

"I was told that he was in a real bad accident. No one has come out to update us on anything else just yet." Chanae said in a shaky voice as she held on to Khalid tight. He was just sitting there on his mother's lap quiet. His young mind didn't know what was going on.

Kalyah escorted her mother to the seat next to Chanae. She could tell that she was on the verge of a nervous breakdown. She was praying that Kalil made it through whatever his injuries might be. She knew if not then she could not only lose her brother but her mother as well.

"Kalyah, did everything go well when you dropped Kamyra off at the house?" Zariya asked. They had asked Zahyir and Qadir to watch the girls. Since

Kamira and Tara were already at the house with them when Zariya and Nassir had left, they agreed to watch the girls for them.

"Yes as soon as she saw Za'kiya she ran in the house and closed the door. Her little butt didn't even say bye." Kalyah laughed even though her heart ached for her brother.

"Yeah when those two are together no one else matters to them." Giggled Zariya.

Chanae was just about to say something when she saw the doctor walk out into the waiting room. She stood to her feet when he asked for the family of Kalil Barber.

The doctor walked over to them and explained the injuries that Kalil had suffered. By the time he was finished they learned that Kalil had endured a concussion, three broken ribs, and his left leg was broken. He would have to wear a cast for a few weeks in order to let it heal properly. Other than that the doctor told them that he would be just fine. He also expressed to them how lucky Kalil was to be alive because of how bad the accident was – he informed them that a lot of people would not have made it out still breathing.

❧ ❧ ❧

Chanae was seated in the chair next to Kalil's hospital bed. He was still asleep and had not woken up since she came into the room about thirty minutes ago. Khalid started making noises with his lips and trying to reach for Chanae's diamond necklace she had around her neck. Karla and everyone else offered to get him while she came in the room to check on Kalil but she declined. She told them that Kalil needed to see both of their faces when he finally decided to wake up. Khalid started getting frustrated that he could not reach

Chanae's necklace so he began cry. She knew he was only fussing because he was sleepy.

"Shhh stop all that unnecessary fussing mommy's little prince." She said while bouncing him on her lap and trying to soothe him.

"What you over there doing to my little man?" Kalil said in a raspy tone.

"Daddy!" Khalid said pointing to his father.

Chanae hopped up out the chair carrying Khalid and walked up to the bed. "You scared the hell out of me Kalil. Was it my phone calls that caused you to have an accident?" she asked him with tears in her eyes. Ever since she got the news that he was in a car accident she blamed herself for him even being in his car. Then she kept calling his phone so she thought maybe he tried answering and crashed his car in the process.

"What? Why would you ask me something like

that? No it was not your phone calls. I know what you over there thinking, get that shit out your head this was not your fault."

"But bae if you would not have got mad at me then you would not have been in the car. Then none of this would be helping." Chanae cried.

"Chanae listen, none of this was your fault. I was forced off the road. Someone wanted me dead and they came really close to doing just that today." He stated.

"Oh my god Kalil someone really tried to kill you? Do you think this is connected to the phone calls?"

"I don't know but I plan on finding out." Kalil said with nothing but anger in his voice. At that time Khalid made a loud spitting sound like he was trying to make bubbles.

Chanae popped his little hand and told him to stop. He didn't even cry he just had a sad little frown on his face.

"I want you and our little prince to go stay with Nassir and Zariya until I get out of this hospital."

Chanae looked at him as if he lost his mind she was not leaving this hospital until he was discharged.

"I'm not..." she started to speak but he interrupted her.

"Chanae I need you and my son safe. The only way that I will be able to get well is if you two are somewhere that I know you will be protected at all times. With Nassir and Zariya I know I won't have to worry because Nassir will never let anything happen to you." He explained to her hoping she understood where he was coming from. If not, oh well because that is where they were going and he was going to make sure of it.

She stood there staring at him wondering why they could not just be happy for a change. Every time they got comfortable something or someone always tried to come along to bring them harm or just plain ole drama. Chanae was sick and tired of the same things.

"Okay fine Kalil we will go but as soon as you are discharged we are coming home with you." she said finally agreeing to go.

Chapter 3

Three days later…

Kalil had just hung up the phone with Chanae and his son. She was still a little in her feelings about not being up there at the hospital with him. He needed her to understand that if something was to happen up there he would not be able to protect her like he would want to. He was just about to cut the TV back up when Charles came walking through his room door.

"How are you feeling today son?" he asked

Kalil as he took a seat in the chair next to the bed.

"Better than I was yesterday. I miss my family though. Chanae mad that I won't let her come up here and stay with me until I'm discharged." Kalil shook his head because every time she would say she understood his reasoning, he knew that she didn't.

"Chanae is stubborn you know that. She has a point though Kalil." Charles could tell by the expression plastered on his face that he didn't agree with what he had just said.

"What you mean she has a point? Me keeping my family safe is my first and most important priority, Charles. Chanae don't understand that but right now she has no choice because I will do anything to make sure no harm comes to her or my son." Even though Kalil spoke calmly when he spoke those words, Charles knew by the stern look on his face he was serious about what he said.

"All I am saying is that Chanae feels as if her place as your woman should be by your side when you need her most. I know what you are saying and yes I do understand your position in the matter. What I am asking you to do is understand her position - put yourself in her shoes for second." That was the last thing Charles said before leaving Kalil in the room alone with his thoughts.

👄 👄 👄

At the Williams' house...

Chanae and Zariya was in the kitchen getting everything ready for the dinner that they are going to be cooking tonight. Za'kiya was in the family room playing with Khalid. She was so excited when she found out that they would be staying with them for a few days. They were playing doctor and Khalid was the patient. He loved himself some Za'kiya so every time he saw her he was down to play whatever she wanted, even dress up.

"Okay Mr. Barber we have to give you a shot to make you feel better." Za'kiya said as she took the toy needle and stuck it gently by his arm.

"All better now?" he asked her while she now looked inside her doctor bag for something else.

"Yes all better now. I have to find you a band aid." When she couldn't find any in her bag she stood to her feet before speaking again. "I'm going to go in the bathroom and get you a band aid you stay right there okay?"

"Okay." Khalid said as he laid there on the floor waiting for her to come back.

"What you in here laying on the floor for little dude?" Qadir asked as him and Zahyir made their way into the family room.

Khalid was caught off guard from hearing his voice that he jumped a little. Qadir went and picked him up off the floor.

"I playing doctor with my Kiya" he said in one of the sweetest and most innocent voices they had ever heard.

"Aw yeah little man?" asked Zahyir and Khalid replied with a head shake.

"Hey, put my patient down!" Za'kiya yelled with her hands on her imaginary hips. She had a frown on her face as she walked all the way into the room.

"What you going to do if we don't?" Qadir asked messing with her.

Za'kiya raised her left eyebrow and folded her arms across her chest. "I'm going to tell my daddy on you! You better put my juicy cheeks down now or it's going to be a problem up in here." she said waving her hands all around.

Zahyir and Qadir busted out laughing. They loved messing with Za'kiya because you never knew what was liable to come out of her mouth.

"Nassir not even here bighead. Now what you going to do?" Zahyir said as he stuck his tongue out at her. Qadir had just put Khalid down when Za'kiya ran up on Zahyir swinging. Her hits were landing on his legs but they were powerful for her only to be five years old. Khalid saw that and started hitting on Qadir. No matter what he had his Za'kiya back so if she started swinging so he was too. Zahyir and Qadir was trying hard not to laugh while they tried to get them up off of them.

❖ ❖ ❖

Nassir was just walking through the front door when Za'kiya and Khalid came running towards him with Qadir and Zahyir not too far behind them.

"What the hell you two in here doing to my baby and nephew?" Nassir asked them when Za'kiya and Khalid came and stood right next to him.

"Naw you should be asking what they do to us." Zahyir said.

"Daddy they tried to take my patient from me. They always messing with my juicy cheeks." She said rolling her eyes at them.

Nassir laughed and then looked down at Khalid. "Little man are they messing with you too?"

"They mess with my Kiya. I don't like that." he said pointing at them with a frown on his face.

Zahyir and Qadir just stood there and looked at one another while shaking their head. Nassir laughed at them before letting them know he going to kick their asses if they kept on messing with them. Za'kiya followed behind her daddy as Khalid followed her. She turned around and stuck her tongue out at them before

running after Nassir.

Chapter 4

"What was all that noise out there?" Zariya asked Chanae as she came walking back into the kitchen.

"Girl that's just Khalid and Za'kiya out there beating on Zahyir and Qadir again." Chanae laughed as she took her seat back at the kitchen table and continued picking the greens.

Zariya shook her head at the thought of those two. "They better stop before Zahyir and Qadir end up kicking their little asses."

"They better be prepared to get fucked up too!"

35

Nassir yelled walking into the kitchen with the troublesome duo following close behind him.

"Boy ain't nobody scared of your ass." Zariya said turning around from the stove to look at her husband.

"Yeah okay keep lying to yourself and others." he said walking up to her and kissing her on the lips.

"Ewwwww." Za'kiya and Khalid both said at the same time.

"Nasty stuff." Khalid said waving his hands at them. Everyone broke out in laughter.

Za'kiya stood there with her arms folded across her chest while tapping her right foot against the floor. "Daddy you know that you and mommy said a bad word right?" she started.

"You ain't getting no money from me little girl so you can go have a seat somewhere." Zariya said turning back around to check on the food before Za'kiya could even start trying to ask for money.

"Daddy, everybody keep saying that all the time. They always say a bad word and don't want to pay up. I can't deal with this stuff all the time." she said with a frown on her face. Khalid saw her frown so he started to frown his face up too.

Chanae and Nassir busted out laughing while Zariya just ignored her little spoiled ass as she called her all the time.

"Not funny!" she shouted before storming out of the kitchen.

"Now look what you two did. Done went and made my baby mad." Nassir laughed as he walked out the kitchen in search of Za'kiya.

"Boy bye." Zariya said taking a seat at the table to help Chanae pick the greens.

Altar'd

Khalid walked up to Chanae and tapped her on the leg. "Mommy." he said just loud enough for her to hear him clearly.

"What's wrong baby?" she asked him wiping her hands off on a napkin before reaching down to pick him up. She sat him on her lap and saw the sad look appear on his face all of a sudden.

"I want daddy. Mommy, go get daddy." he said. Chanae looked over at Zariya whose face looked just as clueless as hers did on what to say.

"Khalid, you just talked to daddy a little while ago. Remember daddy is getting better so that he can come back home to us." He looked up in her eyes and Chanae could see the tears threatening to fall from his little brown eyes.

"I want my daddy." he cried with his bottom lip sticking out.

"Do you want mommy to call daddy so that you can talk to him again?" she asked as she wiped the tears that spilled out of his eyes. Khalid shook his head yes.

Chanae got up from the table with him still in her arms. She walked to the guest room where she and Khalid had been sleeping. Sitting him on the bed, she grabbed her phone off the charger that was sitting on the nightstand. Chanae pushed Kalil number and sat on the bed next to her son as the phone rang.

"Hello?" Kalil answered on the first ring when he saw that it was Chanae calling.

"Hey bae it's me" she replied.

Laughing, Kalil shook his head at Chanae's response. "Yeah, I know it is you baby. What you need?"

"Well I was calling because your son is over here crying for you."

"I just spoke to him and he said he was going to be a big boy for me." Sighing Kalil knew this had to be hard for his little prince. He wasn't used to not seeing his father's face every day.

"Okay baby put him on the phone." Kalil said into the phone.

Chanae passed him the phone and told him his daddy was on there. "Daddy you come home now?" Khalid asked his father and Chanae tried hard to keep the tears from falling but one single tear had managed to escape. She turned her head so her son wouldn't see her cry but it was too late because he already had.

"No little prince daddy not coming home just yet but soon I will be there, okay?" Kalil found it hard trying to explain to his son why he was not there with him and his mother.

"Daddy, mommy sad she cry and I'm sad too. I

want to go home with you." Khalid pointed to Chanae as if Kalil could see him.

Kalil sat up in the bed and rubbed his free hand over his face. "Why is mommy crying Khalid?"

"Her sad daddy. She want you too" he replied in an innocent voice. He really did not know what was going on but he knew his father never stayed away from him and his mommy for this long before.

"Okay this what I want you to do. I need you to try and be a big boy for me. Make sure mommy is okay and I promise I will be home soon. Can you do that for me my little prince?"

"Yes you come home now daddy?" he asked smiling.

"No not today but soon okay?"

Putting his head down with the saddest facial expression anyone has ever seen, he responded in a sad and low tone. "Okay daddy." he handed Chanae the phone and hopped off the bed walking over to the corner with his arms folded across his chest. He turned towards the wall so no one could see him cry as the tears started pouring from his little eyes. Chanae's heart broke watching her baby cry for his daddy. Her heart truly ached for him and at that moment she made a decision.

Putting the phone to her ear she spoke with confidence and a calm tone. "We will be up there tomorrow to see you Kalil and I don't want to hear nothing else about it." she spoke into the phone.

"Chanae I already told you that..." before he could finish his statement Chanae interrupted him.

"Kalil, we will be there tomorrow so see you then. Goodbye." With that she ended the call as she walked over to the corner of the room where her son was crying his little heart out for his father. She comforted him and let him know that everything will be just fine.

"We're going to see daddy tomorrow so stop crying baby everything will be okay."

Chapter 5

The following day...

Kalil was sitting up in the hospital bed getting checked out by the new nurse they had assigned to his room. Every so often the nurse would look up at him and smile. He thought she was a cute chick with her short spiked haircut. She was a little on the flat side when it came to breast but her huge ass made up for that. Right when she was about to flirt with him, Khalid came running into the room.

"Daddy!!!" he yelled running full speed to the side of Kalil's bed.

"My little prince what's up with you?"

Chanae came walking into the room and her beauty took Kalil's breath away. She wasn't wearing anything special - just a pair of skinny jeans, a purple tank top, and some sandals. Her hair was in a neat bun on the top of her head. Nevertheless, he thought she was gorgeous.

"Hey baby how are you feeling today?" she asked as she walked up to him, leaned over and kissed him on the lips.

"Better than I felt yesterday so I can't complain." He was starting to notice that that was the answer he always gave when asked that question.

"Well that's good to hear." She said picking Khalid up and placing him on the bed with his father. Chanae could have sworn she saw the nurse roll her eyes at her out the corner of her eye.

"So let's talk about you doing the opposite of what I asked of you." Kalil said looking Chanae dead in the eyes. She knew he was going to ask that, just not right out the gate.

"Look Kalil you didn't have to watch our son cry himself to sleep because he wanted his daddy. What was I supposed to do? He wouldn't stop crying for you and it broke my heart to just stand there and watch."

"I understand that baby but I asked you not to come up here for a reason. If something was to pop off right now how would I be able to protect you and our son?" He'd been trying hard to get Chanae to see where he was coming from but so far it was going in one ear and out the other.

"Daddy you come home now with me and mommy?" Khalid asked trying to play with the remote control but Kalil put it out of his reach.

"Daddy got something for you and mommy. Baby can you come over here and hand me that folder out of that top drawer?" Chanae did what she was asked and handed Kalil the folder.

"What is that?" she asked curious.

"Here read that" he commanded handing her a piece of paper from out of the folder.

Chanae began reading off what was on the paper and a huge smile spread across her face when she read the word DISCHARGE.

"Oh my god, baby you're being discharged today!" she shouted excitedly while jumping up and down.

Khalid, not understanding what they were talking about, was starting to get upset. He folded his arms across his chest with a frown plastered on his face.

"Daddy I don't want no paper I want you to

come home. No stupid paper." He said a little angry.

Chanae looked at him and shook her head. "Khalid, what I tell you about saying that word? I better not hear you say nothing else is stupid." She disciplined.

"But mommy…" he stopped when he saw the look on her face.

Kalil laughed as he hugged his son. He really missed his family and he couldn't wait to get out the hospital to be home with them.

"Little prince that paper says that daddy can go home with you and mommy. But since you said you don't want that paper I can give it back to the doctor and stay here." He joked.

"Noooo I want paper please. Mommy I want paper." Chanae and Kalil busted out laughing.

"Sorry to interrupt you, Mr. Barber but I need to

check your vitals one more time before you leave." The nurse said walking back into the room.

"Go ahead, I was just about to get up and get ready." He responded.

The nurse came over to the side of the bed and did her job. When no one was looking she slipped something in Kalil's jacket that was hanging off of the side of the table by the bed.

"Okay Mr. Barber you are all set to go. You definitely been one of my best patients." The nurse stated before exiting out of the room.

Chanae looked at Kalil and tilted her head to the side. "What?" he asked

"Nothing at all play boy. Are you ready to go?"

"Let me go throw my clothes on and I'll be ready to roll." He grabbed the crutches that was next to the bed and got up. All Chanae could think about while

Kalil got ready was who this new nurse bitch was. She was definitely going to find out though. She knew when she saw a thirsty look in a chick's face they meant nobody any good. She grabbed Khalid's hand who was on his way into the bathroom to go get his daddy. Chanae had this gut feeling that something else bad was going to happen. She just prayed it wasn't anything that they couldn't bounce back from.

Chapter 6

A month later…

Everything was going good with Chanae and Kalil. He finally got the cast off his leg and was moving around on his own a lot better now. They still hadn't figured out who it was that was calling Chanae and hanging up but they changed all of their phone numbers and Kalil had set up cameras in and around the house.

Chanae had just put Khalid to bed when she walked into her and Kalil's bedroom and saw him lying on the bed watching TV. All he had on was a pair of basketball shorts. They made eye contact as she walked

51

over to her side of the bed and started stripping off her clothes.

"You see something you like?" Chanae asked with a raised eyebrow.

"Nope." Kalil tried to keep from laughing but once Chanae's pillow connected with the side of his head he couldn't do anything but laugh.

"Keep laughing just make sure you keep your hands to yourself tonight." Chanae said as she slid into bed with nothing on. She planned on sleeping in her birthday suit tonight. She knew Kalil wasn't going to be able to keep his hands off of her like always.

Kalil turned the TV off and got under the covers. Once Chanae felt his hands slide up and down her thigh she knew she had him where she wanted him.

"Um Mr. Barber what are you doing?" she asked never turning around to face him.

"What you mean what am I doing?" he said now sliding his hands between her thighs and massaging her clitoris.

"Mmmm" Chanae moaned. She was mad at herself for enjoying the feeling of his fingers rubbing on her sweet spot.

Kalil figured he had her once she spread her legs open wider for him to get better access to her treasure. He turned her over on her back before getting on top of her kissing her soft lips. He then started to make his way down her body leaving a trail of wet kisses behind. Once he got to her pussy lips he began tongue kissing them as if it was the first time.

Chanae started gripping the sheets tight as she felt her body temperature rise. Kalil was eating her pussy as if it was his first meal in weeks.

"Uhmmm   baby   I'm   aboooout   to

cu…cu…cummmm!" Chanae screamed out as her honey cream squirted in Kalil's mouth. He made sure he lapped up every drop before lifting up out the bed.

Kalil pulled his shorts and boxers off kicking them to the side. He reached for the comforter and snatched it off the bed tossing it on the floor. Chanae smiled because she knew that she was in for one hell of a night. She can see his dick standing at attention and she was ready for him or so she thought.

Climbing between her legs Kalil slowly entered her inch by inch. They both let out a moan once he was all the way in.

"Damn baby you'd think you was a virgin with how tight this pussy is." Kalil moaned as he started moving in and out of her at a slow pace.

Chanae pulled Kalil down to where his ear was only inches away from her lips.

"Baby, I want you to fuck me." she whispered. Kalil didn't say a word as he got on his knees pulling Chanae with him never pulling out of her. He lifted her legs up resting them on his shoulders as he started pounding in and out of her.

They went at it for hours switching from different positions before they finally fell asleep. They both knew they were going to be feeling the aches from their love making fuck session when they finally decided to get up and start their day.

❤ ❤ ❤

"Damn she is one lucky bitch." Andra said to herself as she sat in her living room watching Kalil and Chanae make love. She had personal front row seats courtesy of one of her tech savvy friends who had been able to tap into the security camera Kalil had installed. So whatever it was that they saw, she would see too. She lucked up when she got Kalil as a patient after his car accident. She thought he was one of the finest men she had ever laid eyes on. She was ecstatic when the transmitter she dropped in his jacket worked. Andra knew she had to play this out carefully she don't want what happened last time to happen again.

"No, this time I will play my cards right. I will have to find a way to turn them against each other. Whatever I do he will be mine and their son will be calling me mommy." Andra laughed at what she planned to do to them.

Getting up off the couch she made her way to her bedroom. Taking off all her clothes she laid across her bed and began to pleasure herself. She filled her mind with thoughts of Kalil doing to her the same things he did to Chanae in the video.

Andra planned to wipe Chanae out completely

and take over her life. She had no idea that many had already tried this same thing but they all had failed. If she handled her plan correctly she just might be the one to succeed at what they all died trying to do; all she had to do was succeed in killing Chanae and she'd be out of the picture once and for all.

Chapter 7

"So how is everything between you and Kalil going?" Zariya asked taking a bite of her sandwich.

"Everything is great I couldn't be any more happier and in love." Chanae smiled.

"Oh shit I know that tone, you got you some last night!" Zariya laughed.

"I sure in the hell did. Girl, I'm surprised I was able to get out of bed to meet you for lunch." She joined in on the laughter.

"You so nasty, you better slow up before you be

pregnant again. My baby Khalid going to kick you and Kalil's ass then watch."

"Girl please I am not getting pregnant again no time soon. Khalid little bad ass is already a handful. Did I tell you his ass went and poured a whole bottle of lotion on my damn living room couch the other day?"

"What? No you didn't tell me that. Did you whoop his little ass? I'm still pissed Za'kiya poured a whole damn thing of baby powder on my couch and living room floor. Talking about she was trying to make it snow." Zariya said rolling her eyes at that memory.

"Yes I popped his ass and I remember that, you was mad as hell that Nassir was protecting her from getting an ass whooping." Chanae chuckled.

"Girl yeah he always trying to protect her bad ass. She can go rob a damn bank and he will be at the police station saying she was with him the whole day so it couldn't be her who did it." Zariya laughed at that. Nassir was so protective of Za'kiya no one can tell him she did anything wrong.

"That sound just like something he would do too." Chanae laughed as she picked up her ringing phone to answer it.

"Hello?" Chanae answered but no one responded. She could hear breathing and a radio playing in the background. The person on the other end of the phone wasn't saying a word and this made Chanae nervous.

"Hellooo?" Chanae asked again which caused Zariya to look over at her with a frown on her face.

"Who was that?" Zariya asked once Chanae hung the phone up.

"I don't know no one said anything. Remember I told you someone was playing on the phone and I didn't say anything to Kalil?"

"Yeah I remember you telling me that. I thought you got the numbers changed though?"

Chanae gave Zariya a worried look before responding. "Zar we did change all the phone numbers. That's why this is suspicious to me. I don't know how they got my new number."

"It may be listed and they looked it up the same way bill collectors do. Who do you think it might be playing on your phone?" Zariya asked a question Chanae had been asking herself since the phone calls first started. Only one person came to mind.

"Honestly I think it's Janice who keeps calling and not saying anything. I mean I remember her being upset that you and I were closer than me and her. One day she just stopped calling or coming by the house. I haven't heard from her in about a year and a half. It's like she just dropped off the face of the earth." Chanae shook her head at how Janice came back in her life asking for a second chance. The part that was confusing Chanae is that when she got that second chance she just up and pulled a disappearing act.

Zariya looked at Chanae and knew she had to tell her the truth about Janice.

"Chanae I have to tell you something." Chanae saw the look in Zariya's eyes and knew it had to be something really serious she had to tell her.

"Okay go head what do you have to tell me? From the look on your face it must be serious."

"It is serious and first I want to say that we would have told you but we felt that it was better if you didn't know."

"If I didn't know what Zariya? What are you talking about? Chanae asked with her face scrunched up.

"I know for a fact that Janice is not the one calling your phone." Zariya spoke softly she really didn't know how to tell Chanae this.

"How you know it's not Janice that's calling me Zariya? You seem so sure about this." Chanae could tell that Zariya was fighting with herself on how to explain this to her.

"I know Janice isn't the one who is calling you because she is dead Chanae. Janice isn't calling anyone from where she is." she blurted out.

Chanae looked at Zariya as if she was crazy. "Zariya what the hell are you talking about? Why do you think she is dead?"

Zariya went on to explain to Chanae how Janice only came back in her life because she was broke. She told her about Janice's plan on trying to kill her in order to collect the money her mother left behind for her. She let her know that the guys caught wind of it and made it so that Janice would never try to harm her again. When she was done explaining she sat there and waited for Chanae to say something.

Chanae was trying to wrap her mind around what she just heard. She always knew Janice hated her and was jealous of her for some reason. Now she know why that was. What was messing with her head though is that all this time the people who claimed to love her the most kept something this important from her.

"Why did you all keep this from me? Zariya, I had a right to know" Chanae said more hurt than mad.

"I'm sorry Chanae..." that was all Zariya got out before Chanae got up and left out of the restaurant they were eating at.

Now not only was Chanae hurt from all the

people she trusted keeping a huge secret like this from her. She was now even more worried because now she really didn't know who was harassing her and out to get her. She thought of anyone who could have any hard feelings toward her but her mind was pulling a blank.

"Maybe I'm not meant to be happy or enjoy life. Every time I turn around something or someone is out to get me. I keep to myself and don't bother anybody but apparently that don't matter to folks. Well now they pushed me too damn far so whoever it is that is out to get me this time they ass better come prepared to for a fight. I'm tired of being the nice Chanae so now everybody is about to meet the bitch that ain't to be fucked with named Chanae Walker!" Chanae said to herself out loud as she pulled off headed to her home. She and Mr. Barber had to have a little chit chat.

Chapter 8

At Forest Park...

"Man it's hot as hell out here. These kids better be lucky I love they asses." Kalil laughed.

"Who you telling? Shit if my princess didn't beg me to bring her we would have our ass in the house playing with all those damn toys in that toy room." Nassir chuckled.

"Za'kiya got your ass wrapped around her tiny little finger." Kalil cracked up laughing while they watched Za'kiya, Kamyra, and Khalid play on the slide. They were sitting on top of the picnic table joking around.

"Nigga I know you ain't talking? Not only do she have you wrapped around her finger but so does Khalid and Kamyra. You should be the last one to laugh at me." Kalil stopped laughing and stared at Nassir stone faced before they both burst into laughter.

"Man these kids be having us looking like some straight suckas."

"Hell yeah! I had to protect my baby from Zariya a few days ago when she poured powder all over the living room."

"Aye I remember Chanae telling me about that she said Za'kiya told Zariya she was trying to make it snow." Kalil couldn't stop himself from laughing.

"She wanted to beat the hell out of Za'kiya for that, man." Nassir joined in on the laughter.

They looked over at the kids who were standing

on the side of the slide looking as if they were having a discussion. "Look at them," Kalil nudged Nassir.

"Kamyra, I want you to spend a night at my house tonight. We can play with my new tea set and my Zahyir and Qadir having company too." Za'kiya said in a hush tone.

"Ohhh is Kamira and Tara coming over? I like them, they nice too." Kamyra said and Za'kiya shook her head.

"Mira and Tara my girlfriends." Khalid said matter-of-factly.

"Un un juicy cheeks those are Zahyir and Qadir girlfriends. You have to find another girlfriend when you get big okay?"

"Un unnnn those my girlfriends. I don't want to hear it, I don't want to hear it." he said waving his hands from side to side.

"Oh whatever boy." Za'kiya said as she smacked her hand across her forehead.

Kamyra just stood there laughing until someone caught her attention.

"Who is that nasty lady in front of my uncle Kalil?" she asked with her hands on her imaginary hips.

"Where?" Za'kiya asked turning around in the direction of where her daddy and uncle were sitting at.

"Nasty lady." Khalid said repeating what Kamyra had just said. His face was curled up in a frown as if he smelled something stinky.

"Oh naw she tripping now." Za'kiya said as she made her way over to where they were with Kamyra and Khalid following right behind her.

When they made it over to them Za'kiya stood in between the lady and her Uncle Kalil.

"Hi, my name is Za'kiya and I'm six." she said

looking up at the lady.

"Hi Za'kiya my name is Andra. You are so cute."

"Thank you. I get that a lot because I look like my mommy and she look good." Nassir and Kalil were trying their hardest not to bust out laughing. They knew Za'kiya could be a little pistol at times; she stayed ready to pop off just like her mother and aunts.

"Well I bet she is. What is your name?" Andra asked looking at Khalid and Kamyra who just stood off to the side and eyed her like she was funny looking to them.

"Those my cousins and this my daddy and my uncle." Za'kiya said pointing at everybody.

"You all are so adorable." Andra smiled at them. She secretly wish they had of stayed over there where they were. She wanted to talk to Kalil and they were messing up her plans.

"Again thank you. You know my daddy married and my mommy don't play that mess." Za'kiya said with her arms folded across her chest.

"Za'kiya!" Nassir yelled.

"Yes my daddy." she turned and smiled at him sweetly.

"I'm not here to get into any mess with your mommy or anyone else sweetie." Andra chuckled but inside she wanted to smack the shit out of the little girl standing in front of her.

"Okay good. Just so you know my uncle Kalil go with my Te-Te Chanae and she really ain't to be messed with either." Za'kiya said now giving Andra the stank face.

"Za'kiya that is enough so go finish playing because it's almost time to go." Nassir ordered in a stern tone.

"Okay daddy, can you and uncle Kalil come push us on the swing please?" She said giving off the cutest puppy dog eyes.

Kalil and Nassir both prepared to walk them over to the swing. "It was nice talking to you um?"

"Andra." she answered.

"Yes, Andra nice seeing you." Kalil said before following Kamyra and Khalid who was pulling him by the hands.

Za'kiya turned around to find Andra staring at her uncle and she frowned before speaking, "Bye Miss Lady!" she yelled smiling and waving at her. Za'kiya flipped her hair over her shoulder with her right hand and smirked at Andra one last time before running to catch up with everyone else.

Chapter 9

"Ughhh that little bitch knew exactly what she was doing!" Andra yelled out in frustration as she slammed her car door shut. She started her car and pulled off.

"That little girl is going to be a problem and I can't have her messing up my damn plans." Andra stopped at a red light and began thinking about how she was going to make sure her plan went off without a hitch.

At the exact time that the light turned green

Andra had a plan to make sure that little girl didn't mess up what she had planned for her Te-Te Chanae. She laughed as she drove off to her next destination for the day.

❧ ❧ ❧

Kalil and Khalid had just walked into the house when he heard Chanae yelling at someone. He walked in the kitchen where he followed her voice with Khalid following right behind him.

"There goes my little prince!" Chanae squealed as she went to pick Khalid up and sit him on the counter in front of her.

"Mommy I have fun at the park with my Kiya and Myra." he said still hyped about spending time with them.

"You did that's good baby." she kissed him on both his cheeks.

"Baby who was that you was yelling at on the

phone." Kalil asked as he went in the fridge and grabbed a bottle of water.

"I don't know somebody is back to playing on my phone. I received another one of those phone calls today with someone just breathing and not saying anything." she explained.

"Damn we changed the numbers how the hell…" Kalil stopped what he was about to say and rubbed his left hand over his face. He had been trying to figure out who this could be but he couldn't think of anyone.

"I was thinking that maybe it was my sister Janice calling." Chanae said looking directly in Kalil's eyes. She wanted to see if he was going to tell her the truth about Janice.

Kalil didn't look fazed or nervous at all when she mentioned her sister. He knew that this day was going to come eventually.

"Look Chanae we need to talk about your sister Janice but I won't do it in front of our son." Kalil said making sure she understood as long as Khalid was in ear shot he was not discussing Janice.

"Okay cool let me take him to the play room and we can talk about whatever it is you have to say." Chanae opened the fridge to grab him a juice. She pulled out a green juice and Khalid frowned his face up and shook his head from side to side.

"Oh that's right you say the green juice is nasty. Sorry, mommy forgot."

"Mommy nasty lady at the park." Khalid blurted out and Kalil damn neared choked on the water he just drank.

Chanae turned around and looked down at him before looking over at Kalil who was now coughing.

"Who is the nasty lady?" she asked Khalid but she was looking directly at Kalil.

"Nasty lady at the park talk to my daddy and my Kiya said noooo her don't." Khalid said replaying the story in his own version while shaking his hands out in front of him.

"Oh yeah daddy got nasty ladies talking to him at the park, huh?" she said never taking her eyes off Kalil.

"We were chilling at the park with the kids and the nurse from the hospital spotted us. She came over to say hi I guess but Za'kiya nipped all that shit in the bud." He chuckled as he remember how Za'kiya acted towards the chick.

"What nurse from the hospital, Licia?" Chanae asked confused.

"No the chick that was my nurse before I left."

he corrected.

"Oh the chick with the eye problem." she said nodding her head.

"The chick with the eye problem?" now it was Kalil's turn to be confused.

"Yeah, she got an eye problem because every time she looked at me, her eyes would roll so I said the trick must have a damn eye problem."

Kalil started laughing because he knew the nurse was feeling him and although she was cute, she damn sure wasn't worth losing his family over.

"I don't see nothing funny. Every time these skanks grow some type of feelings towards you they quick to throw me shade and jump stupid." Chanae said rolling her eyes.

Kalil watched as she took their prince into the play room and prepared himself for this talk they were about to have. He knew Chanae was going to be pissed off that he didn't tell her. He just hoped she saw why and understood that he did it to protect her.

Chapter 10

Chanae walked into the family room where Kalil was sitting on the couch with his head buried in his hands. She figured he was trying to get his mind right before telling her that Janice was dead and he was one of the people responsible for her death. She wasn't mad that she was dead, she was mad that he of all people kept something like this from her.

She sat down next to him and stared at him.

"Damn I love this man" she thought to herself as he lifted his head up and turned to face her.

"Look, I'm going to get straight to the point. Janice ain't making those phone calls because she dead." Chanae was about to say something but Kalil held his hand up signaling for her to let him finish.

"Janice planned on having you killed and collecting the money your mother left behind for you. I couldn't let that happen baby. One time when you were pregnant and we went to grab something to eat I noticed a car that was parked up the street from the house. I did some researching and found out that the car belonged to your sister. Why she would be staking out the house I had no clue until Demarco started following her around."

"Demarco knew too?" Chanae shook her head now she was beyond pissed. "So everybody *but* me knew about what Janice had planned *and* about her death?" Kalil didn't respond he just looked at her and that answered her question.

"This is some straight bullshit!" she shouted standing up. Chanae began to pace the floor while Kalil just watched her for a good minute before speaking again.

"Chanae I knew you wasn't going to be able to handle that shit. It was so much that was going on at the time that if I told you about how shady your sister really was you probably would have had a damn nervous breakdown." He said getting up off the couch and walking towards her.

"A nervous breakdown? Really Kalil; you couldn't come better than that?" Chanae yelled with her right hand on her hip.

"Yes a damn nervous breakdown. So you trying to tell me you would have been cool finding all that out and knowing that you almost destroyed your relationship with Zariya for her?" Once Kalil said it he wanted so badly to take it back. That was still a soft spot for Chanae and he knew it. He just wanted her to understand why he did what he did. The hurt look in her eyes said it all; his words had hurt her.

"Look baby I'm sor..." Chanae stopped Kalil before he could finish because she didn't want to hear shit else he had to say.

"Fuck you Kalil!" Chanae stormed out of the room ignoring Kalil calling her name.

"Chanae!" he shouted before slumping down on the couch shaking his head.

❤ ❤ ❤

"Ha! This could work for me too. Aww she is so upset with him." Andra laughed watching the screen with footage of the cameras in Kalil's house.

She got up off her couch and walked into her bedroom. Looking in her closet for something sexy to put on, she settled for a skin tight off the shoulder red dress that barely covered her ass. She dropped the robe she was wearing revealing that she had nothing on underneath. Without a second thought she slipped on the dress and some six inch red heels. Walking over to her dresser that was covered in different kinds of perfumes. She picked up her Victoria Secret Angel fragrance and sprayed a little over her body.

Grabbing her clutch, Andra made her way out of the front door and hopped in her car. Tonight she was on a mission to put her plan into motion.

Chapter 11

Forty-five minutes later she was pulling up to the 54th Bar & Grill. Finding a parking spot she turned her car off and got out. Walking into the place she turned a lot of heads because of her outfit of choice for the night.

"Hi, I'm here for the Banks party." Andra said to the waiter.

"Name please?"

"Andra Banks." she responded.

"Oh yes ma'am right this way." the waiter led

her to her table that was located in the back of the restaurant.

"Has the rest of my party arrived yet?" she asked the waiter as they made their way through the restaurant.

"Yes ma'am they have." the waiter answered.

"Here you are ma'am someone should be with you shortly." the waiter said handling Andra a menu before walking off.

"I'm glad you finally decided to make it here." The person sitting across the table from her said while giving her the once over.

"My bad, I had to take care of something first and it took me longer than I intended for it to." Andra said finally looking up at her dinner party for the night. *"Damn that is a face only a mother could love."* she thought to herself.

"So you called me down here; now what do you want?"

"Like to get right down to business I love that. Well for starters I been watching you watch the Barber family for some time now..." Andra took a sip of her water that was placed in front of her.

"Okay, what do you want?" the person asked irritated with Andra and the way the conversation seemed to be going already.

"I just figure we could help each other. You were extremely sloppy with how you handled the whole situation with the car accident. With my help you can get what you want because it's the same thing that I want." Andra said leaning on the table resting her hands under her chin.

"What is it that you think we both seem to want?"

Laughing a little, Andra responded calmly.

"We both want to rid the world of Chanae Walker." this caught the person sitting across from her attention quick.

"I'm listening." Andra begun breaking the plan down. She knew if they both worked together they could get the job done without a problem.

After an hour of laying everything down play by play they both agreed to keep in touch. Before Andra got up to leave, she asked the person their name.

"Just call me Mo." Andra shook her head to show that she understood.

"Okay Mo I'll call you so that we can handle the rest of the details." She was half way out her seat when she sat back down. "Oh yeah one more thing" she said reaching into her clutch and pulling out a folded up picture.

She slid the picture over to Mo. "What is this?" Mo said looking at the picture that had a little girl on it.

"Before we do anything we need to get rid of her. She will be a huge problem if we don't."

"What kind of problems can a little girl make for us?" Mo asked confused.

"A lot. She is a smart little girl in every sense of the word." Andra replied rolling her eyes.

"So you want me to *kill* a little girl?" Mo asked trying to confirm what was being asked of her.

"Yes we need her out of the way if we want to succeed with what we have planned."

"Okay - done." Mo stood to her feet and prepared to leave but Andra stopped her.

"One quick question, Mo. Why do you want Chanae dead? I mean I know why I want her gone but why do you?" she asked curious to what the answer may be.

"Because of her my sister is dead so it's only right that that bitch join her in the afterlife." with that Mo walked out of the restaurant leaving Andra there with her thoughts.

"Damn mama was right it really is a cold world out here." she said to herself before exiting the restaurant. Andra knew she was playing a dangerous game but in her sick twisted mind, she felt that she was only doing what needed to be done in order to get what she wanted.

Chapter 12

Two weeks later…

"So have you talked to Chanae?" Kalyah asked sipping on her glass of wine.

"No, every time I call she either sends me straight to voicemail or rushes me off the phone saying she's in the middle of doing something. I'm tempted to do what she did to me and get mommy involved." Zariya said shaking her head.

"Well you ain't the only one she not speaking too. Kalil keeps calling me begging me talk to her for him." Kalyah chuckled a little.

"Wait they are still in the same house right?" Zariya asked confused.

"Girl yeah you know Kalil ain't letting his family go."

"Wait, so she's giving him the silent treatment too?"

"Yup he said only time they talk is when they're discussing Khalid." Kalyah felt bad for her brother. She knew how much he loved Chanae and was willing to do anything for her.

"Oh wow that is crazy. I am about to call her and force her to talk to me - if not I'm calling mommy on that ass just like she did me." Zariya declared as she picked her cell phone up off the table and dialed Chanae's number.

Chanae picked up the phone on the third ring.

She saw it was Zariya calling and knew that she had been avoiding her long enough. She actually missed her and during times like this when she and Kalil weren't exactly seeing eye to eye, she needed her sister and best friend.

"Hello?"

"Hey Chanae, I thought you were going to call me right back when you finished doing whatever it is you were doing?" Zariya asked happy that she actually answered the phone this time.

"I know Zar I had forgot"

"Chanae, that was three days ago. You know just like I do we talk every day."

"I know Zar I really been having a hard time dealing with this." she confessed.

"How about you come over and have some wine with me and Kalyah? We can talk about whatever is bothering you." Zariya suggested.

"That sounds like a good idea. I'll be there in an hour." Chanae agreed.

"Great! I know the girls will love to see Khalid." They ended the phone call and Zariya couldn't stop smiling.

"So she's coming?" Kalyah asked with a raised eyebrow.

"Yes! Let's go tell the girls their juicy cheeks is coming to play with them." They got up from the table and made their way to the family room where the girls were playing.

When they walked down the hall to the room, they saw Zahyir and Qadir standing at the door laughing at something.

"What are you two knuckleheads laughing at?" Zariya asked with her hands planted on her hips. She and Kalyah were now standing in front of them.

"Za'kiya and Kamyra doing a concert but they are charging people to see it." Zahyir said unable to hold his laughter.

"What? Oh my goodness what are they charging?" Kalyah asked curious.

"Go 'head see for yourself." Qadir said stepping to the side.

Kalyah tried to step foot inside the room and was stopped by a little hand on her stomach.

"Not so fast mommy you have to pay to get into our concert." Kamyra said folding her arms across her chest.

Kalyah looked back at Zariya who was shaking her head and the boys who were damn near falling all over each other laughing. Turning back around to face her daughter she tried hard not to laugh herself.

"How much do it cost to come to the concert?"

"That will be twenty dollars please." she said putting her hand out to receive the money.

"Twenty dollars? Oh, you two done lost your damn minds if you think somebody is about to pay you twenty dollars to sit in the family room." Kalyah responded.

"Right; who do you two think you are?" Zahyir cosigned.

"Beyoncé charge more than that so you just being cheap." Za'kiya said rolling her eyes at him.

"That's where you confused because you ain't Beyoncé." Zahyir laughed.

"She a diva and we divas too little silly little boy. I'm going to tell my daddy you keep laughing at us. That's why I don't like nobody no more." Za'kiya said running past them and down the hall. When they heard a door slam they knew she was mad and her feelings were hurt.

"Ohhhh my husband going to kick y'all's asses. It was really nice knowing you. I really did enjoy the time we got to know each other." Zariya laughed knowing Nassir was going to fuckup them up for messing with his princess.

"That ain't funny Zar, we was just playing with her we didn't know she was going to get mad." Zariya and Kalyah both laughed at the faces they were making.

"What y'all in the hallway laughing at?" Nassir asked damn near scaring all of them.

They all looked at each other. When Zariya and Kalyah looked at one another they both shrugged and at the same exact time pointed at the boys.

Altar'd

Chapter 13

Nassir was ready to fuck Zahyir and Qadir up. He had been standing outside Za'kiya's toy room door for a good thirty minutes trying to convince her to come out. She locked herself in the room and vowed never to come out ever again.

"Princess, please open the door and come out." He asked for what seemed like the hundredth time.

"Daddy I'm not coming out I'm going to stay in here forever and ever." she said kicking a toy ball across the floor with her arms folded.

"Za'kiya you cannot stay in that room forever. Plus Zahyir and Qadir wanted to say they were sorry for laughing at you." Zariya said trying her hand at convincing her.

"Mommy I don't want their stupid sorry! I'm not ever talking to them again!" she yelled.

"Kiya if you don't talk to us how you going to see Kamira and Tara then?" Qadir asked thinking that would work.

"Daddy can you tell him that I don't need them to talk to my Kamira and my Tara?" she said rolling her eyes as if they could see her.

"Then how you going to talk to them if we don't call them?" Zahyir asked curious as hell to know the answer to the question.

"Mommy, can you tell him that I have the number I got it out their phones." Za'kiya said sticking her tongue out at the door.

"You did what!" they both yelled and Kalyah started cracking up.

"Uncle Nassir can you get my cousin out the room please?" Kamyra said mean mugging Zahyir and Qadir.

"I'm trying baby girl but she won't come out." Right when he was about to try again there was a knock at the front door.

"I'll get it that's probably Chanae and Khalid." Zariya said walking to the door and confirming that it was them.

"Hey you came just in time for the ass kicking show." Zariya laughed letting them in and locking the door behind them.

"What's going on?" Chanae asked looking at everybody standing in the hallway by a door.

"Your big cousin is about to fuck your little cousin and brother up for messing with his princess who locked herself in the toy room. Oh yes you came just in time for the crazy show." Zariya said shaking her head.

Khalid walked over to where Kamyra was standing. "Myra where Kiya at? He asked looking around for her and not seeing her anywhere.

"She locked herself in the room because of the big head meanies over there." she said pointing to Qadir and Zahyir who just shook their heads.

Khalid walked over and stood right in front of them. "You mess with my Kiya?" he said with an angry look on his face.

Nassir saw Khalid and an idea popped in his head. "Come here little man. Uncle need you to do something." Khalid walked over to him but not before mean mugging Zahyir and Qadir.

"Princess, someone here to see you." Nassir said through the door.

"Who daddy? Did you get Nelly to come to the house?" Za'kiya asked excitedly.

Nassir chuckled at her question. She swore up and down that he and Nelly were twins because they looked just alike. She told him all the time that she was not going to believe that they were not twins until she talked to Nelly for herself.

"No Nelly not here baby but another one of your favorite people in the whole wide world is."

"Daddy, my juicy cheeks out there?" She put her ear to the door to see if she could hear him.

"I'm right here Kiya open the door." he yelled banging on the door.

Za'kiya unlocked the door and opened it.

"Boy don't be beating on my door like that you crazy or something." she said with a huge smile on her face.

"My uncle said open the door then girl." everybody started cracking up because they went back and forth for a good ten minutes before they finally stopped.

"Guess what princess?" Nassir said picking her up.

"What my daddy?" she giggled when he started tickling her.

"Everybody is going to come to you and Kamyra's concert." he declared and looked around daring anybody to say otherwise.

"Yayyy daddy put me down. I have to go get ready for show time." she said taking off running to the family room as soon as he let her feet touch the floor.

Chapter 14

Showtime…

The lights were dimmed as everyone was seated around the family room waiting for the girls to start their show. Once the music came on, Za'kiya and Kamyra stood up in front of their audience.

Both girls had microphones in their hands and Za'kiya begun to sing the lyrics to 'Love and War' by Tamar Braxton.

"Somebody said every day, was gon' be sunny skies,

Only Marvin Gaye and lingerie, I guess somebody lied

Altar'd

We started discussin' it to fightin' then "Don't touch me,

please."

Then it's "Let's stop the madness, just come lay with

me."

And truth be told I'm wavin' my flag before it goes bad

yeah yeah

'Cause we made it this far on for better or worse

I wanna feel it even if it hurts

If I gotta cry to get to the other side, let's go 'cause

we're gon' survive oh"

Everyone in the room sat there with shocked expressions plastered on their face. They thought for sure that the girls were going to start singing off key. To their surprise, Za'kiya and Kamyra had beautiful singing voices that would give anyone on *American Idol* or *The Voice* a run for their money.

Altar'd

Once the second verse started, Chanae started having thoughts about her and Kalil's relationship. She found it ironic that Love and War was the song the girls chose to sing. She'd been giving Kalil the cold shoulder lately and to be completely honest with herself, the truth was she really missed him and the talks they used to have. She listened as Kamyra and Za'kiya both sang the ending of the song.

"As long as we make up after every fight when it's over

You know I'm comin' home right there where I belong

I'm takin' off this armor oh-oh-oh-whoa-ooh-oh-oh"

"And we stay on the front lines

Yeah but we're still here after the bomb drops

We go so hard we lose control

The fire starts then we explode baby

When the smoke clears we dry our tears

Altar'd

Only in love and war

Only in love and war

Only in love and war"

Chanae listened to the words and when they hit that last note she made up her mind on what she was going to do. She was going to talk to Kalil and tell him that she forgives him. She planned on telling him that she loves him more than life itself and without him her life would forever be incomplete.

She got up out of her seat and turned to walk out of the room to go call and talk to her man. When she looked up she saw that there was no need to call him because she was now standing face to face with the love of her life. She walked up to Kalil and grabbed him by the hand leading him out of the room and out towards the backyard.

❧ ❧ ❧

Kalil and Chanae sat in the backyard just staring

at each other not speaking a word for five whole minutes. Kalil took Chanae's hands in his palms and rubbed them with his thumbs.

"I love you Chanae." he said looking her in the eyes.

"I love you too Kalil." she responded.

"When I did what I did, I thought I was doing it to protect you. I never thought I would risk losing you for it." Kalil admitted.

"I wasn't mad that you did it Kalil. I mean the Janice thing that is. I was mad because you kept it from me. Bae, we don't keep secrets from each other so to find out that you did hurt. I thought we were better than that." Chanae confessed looking deep into his eyes. She knew that she loved Kalil and that she couldn't see herself being with anyone else.

"Chanae I'm sorry for keeping it from you this

long but I'm not sorry for what I did. I did it for you and I will gladly do it again without a second thought. Now right here and right now I need to know if we still stand a chance. I won't keep staying in the same house with the woman I love for her not to even speak to me." Kalil said dead seriously. He was tired of being in the same house but not speaking. He was tired of being punished for looking out for her wellbeing. She had to decide right now if with him is where she really want to be.

"I believe we can get pass this. I love you and I want to be with you. I can't see myself with no one else." Chanae confessed.

Kalil leaned forward and kissed her soft lips gently.

"Good because you stuck with me. I'm it for you baby girl. There is no one else, you are my one and only as I am yours. You the reason my heart skips a beat when you smile. The reason my soul feels free because you are my soul mate and with you I see an everlasting love. I love you Chanae with ever fiber in my body and that will never change."

"I love you too." Their lips met with a passionate kiss. A kiss that spoke volumes to their heart letting each other know they will forever be connected as one.

Chapter 15

Two months later…

Chanae and Zariya were at the bridal shop for Chanae to try on her wedding dress that is being customized to her liking. They were sitting in the waiting area flipping through bridal magazines when Zariya turned to Chanae with a concerned look on her face.

"What's wrong, Zar?" Chanae asked sitting the magazine down on her on lap.

"You know we never got a chance to really talk." She said looking her in the eyes.

"Talk about what?" Chanae asked confused at what Zariya could be talking about.

"You know, about the whole Janice thing. I mean we were going to talk but you were trying to get back right with Kalil. After that we kind of forgot about it and fell right back in step to talking every day and hanging out all the time so it sort of slipped our minds. I just want to know if we are really straight and to make sure you are not holding anything against me deep down inside." Zariya chuckled nervously.

"Oh Zar of course we're straight. I didn't say anything else about it because I forgave you already for not telling me. Kalil helped me understand why you all never told me. Trust me we are good sis." She said smiling.

"Alright, that's good to know. Now where the hell did that sales rep go because we've been sitting over here for damn near twenty minutes?" Zariya said as she and Chanae started looking around to see if they could spot the sales rep who was supposed to be assisting them.

"I don't know…Oh there she go over there talking to another customer." Chanae said pointing over in their direction.

"She should've taken care of us first. I mean we were here first." Zariya said as she eyed the representative and the customer she was servicing.

"Wait, I think I seen that chick somewhere before." Chanae said trying to jog her memory on where she had seen the customer at.

"I don't know but um Miss Thang over there is about to bring her ass back over here and do her damn job." Zariya snapped.

Chanae chuckled a little. She knew Zariya was

about to show her ass in this store if the sales rep didn't get back over to them soon. Now she could see where Za'kiya got her spoiled and bossy ways from.

"Excuse me." Zariya yelled out to the sales rep, who turned to see Zariya waving at her. She had forgotten all about them for a moment and hoped it didn't cost her the commission she was looking forward to.

"Would you please excuse me miss; I will be right back with you soon?" she said to her customer.

"Okay I'll just look through some of the dresses you brought out for me and try them on." The customer said going through the rack of bridal dresses. The sales rep walked back over to Chanae and Zariya with an apologetic look on her face.

"I am truly sorry for the wait. I lost track of time getting the new customer settled. Now where were we?" she asked with a nervous smile.

Chanae and Zariya looked at one another before both returning their attention back to the sales rep.

"Kelly right?" Chanae asked reading the nametag that is pinned to her shirt.

"Yes."

"Well Kelly before you abandoned us; you were going to get my dress so that I can try it on again and see if it's now to my liking. Remember last time I came it seemed a little off and you guys were going to fix it for me?" Chanae reminded her. She thought about giving her a hard time but she had other things to do today and sitting in this shop all day was not part of her plans.

"Oh yes let me go and get the dress and again ladies I am truly sorry for the wait." Kelly said turning around just in time to hear the other customer trying to get her attention.

"I found the dress I want Kelly it is beautiful!" she yelled sliding her hands down the side of the wedding dress she was now wearing.

"That's my damn dress!" Chanae yelled catching everyone's attention. She was now all the way pissed off and she now knew exactly where she knew the chick from. *"The bitch with the eye problem."* she thought to herself.

The sales rep Kelly knew that nothing good was about to come out of this situation. She could now chuck her huge commission that Chanae was giving up as a total loss.

Chapter 16

Chanae was so pissed she started cursing everybody out and telling them how unprofessional they are. Zariya was trying to keep her calm but she was not trying to hear any of that. The sales rep Kelly went over to the other customer explaining to her that the dress belonged to someone else. The problem really got worst when the customer stated that she wanted the dress and it should not have been on the rack with all the other available dresses.

"Ma'am, we can't sell you the dress because it

117

was made special for another customer." Kelly knew she was on the verge of losing her job now. Two upset customers was not a good look.

"I don't care this is the dress I want. It was given to me with the rest of these dresses to look at for purchasing. I would advise you to go and tell her ass to pick another damn dress." Andra spat with one foot planted firmly in front of the other while shaking it and her arms folded.

Kelly was about to speak up but she was stopped by Chanae words.

"The fact that you standing there letting those dumb ass words come out your mouth tells me you are a trifling ass female." Chanae laughed but there damn sure wasn't anything funny.

"I tell you what - I want my money back *with* interest seeing as how that is *my* dress design." She said looking straight at Kelly. Turning to Andra she chuckled some before speaking again.

"Congratulations you will be wearing a Chanae original you should be grateful that I don't whoop your ass up in this shop."

"I would love to see you try bitch!" that was the wrong move to make on Andra's behalf. Chanae's fist connected with her mouth so quickly that no one had any time to react. Andra's body went knocking into the rack of dresses she was standing in front of. Her mouth was now split open and starting to swell up quick. The blood began to pour from it ruining the front of the dress.

"And this is for being so damn unprofessional and stupid!" Zariya said before slapping the shit out of Kelly.

"Come on let's get out of here." Zariya said

pulling Chanae by her arm as they walked out of the bridal shop. She was smiling inside happy to finally see the side of her sister that had been begging to come out for years now. *"The bitch has finally arrived!"* she thought to herself as they drove away leaving Kelly and Andra back at the shop looking stupid and shocked.

Chanae dropped Zariya off at home and then made her way home as well. Kalil had called her and she filled him in on the incident that occurred at the bridal shop. He could tell that she was mad as hell so he decided to do something really special for her. He dropped Khalid off at his sister Kalyah's house earlier in the day and he planned to make the night all about Chanae.

When he heard her car door slam shut he hurried to put the finishing touches on his surprise. Chanae walked into the house shutting and locking the door behind her. When she turned around a smile spread across her face. *"Aw my bae did this all for me?"* she whispered to herself as she walked down the candlelit hallway leading her to the stairs. The candles were flameless so they didn't have to worry about the house catching fire.

Once she got to the stairs she noticed her favorite kind of white and pink rose petals leading a path up the stairs. There were also candles on every other step helping to guide her way. Chanae followed the path to their bedroom and opened the door. The bed was covered with the same white and pink rose petals. The only difference was there was a huge heart made out of them with a Tiffany's bag sitting in the center. She was about to open the bag until she realized that she hadn't seen or heard Kalil since she had been in the house. She made her way to the bathroom and opened the door to find him sitting on the edge of the tub as if he been waiting for her.

"Hey beautiful." he smiled at her and got up and stood directly in front of the woman he would give his life for.

"Hey bae…You did all this for little ole me?" she asked smiling sweetly at him. He responded with a head nod.

"Let me help you undress. I made us a bubble bath." She let him do just that. He then got undressed and stepped into the tub helping her in also. Chanae laid her head back on Kalil's chest as she closed her eyes and enjoyed the peace and quiet with her man.

Kalil and Chanae made passionate love in the bath tub before bathing each other and getting out. Once in the bedroom Kalil gave Chanae a full body massage with some edible oils he had picked up from the store. Once done, they made love into the wee hours of the morning before both falling asleep exhausted and satisfied with big smiles on their faces.

Chapter 17

The following afternoon…

Being the first to wake up, Kalil decided to go and make them both breakfast or better yet lunch seeing as it was now three in the afternoon. He knew they were going to need it to get some of their energy back after last night. When he was finished cooking he went back upstairs to the bedroom to find Chanae still knocked out on her back. He was about to shake her awake until he thought of another way to get her up.

He climbed into the bed after sliding the covers

off of her and throwing them on the floor. He smiled when he saw that she was still naked. He gently opened her legs licking his lips before diving into her creamy cave.

Chanae's eyes popped opened as she felt a big orgasm wash over her entire body. Kalil felt her body tense up which caused him to lick until he got every drop of her sweet cream.

Lifting his head up to look at her he wiped his mouth and smiled. "Did I wake you?" he chuckled getting up off the bed.

"You kno…kno…know that you was wrong for that right?" Chanae asked trying to catch her breath.

"Wrong for what baby I didn't even do anything." he smirked.

Chanae threw a pillow at him and got out of the bed. She walked into the bathroom with Kalil watching her every move. She smiled knowing his eyes were on her. She turned the shower on before stepping in and closing the shower door behind her.

Chanae was too busy with her head under the water that she never heard Kalil open the shower door and call her name. He slid his index finger down the center of her back causing her to jump, scream, and almost bust her ass in the shower.

Right when she was about to hit the floor he stepped in and caught her. "You scared the shit out of me!" she yelled hitting him on the arm as she got out of the shower wrapping a towel around her dripping wet body.

"My bad I was calling your name but you didn't say anything. I wanted to let you know that the food was ready." He said stepping out of the sweats and boxers he had on that were now soaked.

"Okay you still could have gotten my attention another way I almost busted my ass in there." she said frowning at him.

"Yeah I know. You gone have to work on your reflexes baby." he laughed smacking her on the ass as he walked out of the bathroom butt naked. They both got dressed still talking shit to each other.

They ate and joked around for a few hours before heading out the door to go pick up Khalid from Kalyah's house. Chanae and Kalil enjoyed their time together alone but they treasured the times when their family was together as one whole unit.

❖ ❖ ❖

Andra had been lounging around her house since she came in yesterday after the bridal shop incident. When she saw her face she was pissed. She planned on making Chanae suffer for what she did to her. When she turned on the T.V. last night she had plans on catching up on her Lifetime movies but she had forgotten she left the cameras on from Kalil and Chanae's house. The sounds of their love making had filled her home. She was going to turn it off but she was fascinated with the way Kalil was with Chanae. How he made sure to satisfy her wants and needs before taking care of his own.

Now it was mid-day and she was right back to watching their home. When she saw them get into the car and pull off, that is when she made her move. She called up her tech guy and had him shut the cameras off to the house so she wouldn't be seen.

Quickly making her way up the street and to their home she went through the side of the house to the backyard. She silently thanked God they didn't have any dogs or she knew she would have been screwed. She used the key she had another friend of hers make for her. She laughed at how perfectly the bridal shop plan played out. When Chanae walked over to confront her, she had her friend get the keys out of her purse and make a clay mold of the keys before returning the keys and making her exit.

"Yeah that bitch is dumb. He definitely needs a woman like me by his side." Andra said making her way inside the house. Walking straight for the stairs she knew she didn't have much time because there was no telling when they would be returning back home. She walked into their bedroom and over to their dirty clothes hamper. Reaching in her pocket, she removed a pair of her panties that she had taken off last night and a letter. She pulled out some jeans she believed to be Kalil's and put the panties in his pocket. After doing that, she then grabbed his shirt and pulled out a bottle of her perfume spraying his shirt with a few squirts.

She replaced everything before walking out of the room and back downstairs to the kitchen. She opened the fridge and grabbed the three bottles of flavored water she saw that Chanae drank all the time. She removed the caps and poured a white powdery substance that she had in her back pocket into all three bottles. She then took out the small tube of Super Glue she had and began gluing the caps back on making it look as if they had never been opened. Shaking the bottles good until the substance has dissolved completely; she placed the bottles back into the fridge and made her way back out the way she came.

Once she made it back home she fell out on the couch laughing hard. "Now let's see who gets the last laugh bitch!" she was laughing so hard she had tears running down her face.

"Oh and how could I forget about my man? I

will be taking her spot real soon and Kalil will be making love to me while her son will be calling me mommy." Andra laughed until she couldn't laugh anymore. Now she had to sit and play the waiting game; she just hoped Mo did her part so that her plan wouldn't be sabotaged in any way.

Chapter 18

Ring...Ring...Ring...

"I'm in the middle of something - now is not a good time." Mo spoke through clenched teeth as she gripped the phone tight.

"You don't have to talk to me like that I was just calling to make sure you do your part of the plan without fucking up!" Andra yelled as she sat up on the couch.

"I don't need you to check up on me! Let's get something straight sweet cheeks. I do not work for you. We only working together because we want the same thing and that is Chanae buried six feet in the dirt. If I was you I would think twice about how you come at me because it will be no problem for me to have you and that bitch sharing a body bag!" with that Mo disconnected the call and got back to what she was doing before she was interrupted.

Parked up the street from St. Andrews Academy, Mo was waiting for four o'clock to hit so she could make her move. Mo had been watching Za'kiya and her family's every move for quite some time now. She knew their schedule and had it down to where she knew their every move during the week.

Ten minutes later she saw the crowd of kids running out of the school to their awaiting vehicles whether they took the school bus or parked cars with their parents waiting. Mo got out of the car and walked the short distance to the front of the school.

Altar'd

Taking out the picture she had of Za'kiya out of her pocket she looked at it and scanned the crowd of kids until she spotted her. Za'kiya was walking out of the school talking to another little girl.

Mo knew today was Wednesday and on those days Za'kiya got on the school bus. She looked around to see if anyone was watching her. Seeing that the coast was clear she walked up to the two little girls.

"Hey, are you Za'kiya?" Mo asked her still checking her surroundings.

"We not allowed to talk to any strangers." the other little girl said with her face scrunched up in a frown.

"Good thing I wasn't talking to you little girl." Mo replied giving her the same look she was giving her.

"Are you a man?" Za'kiya asked looking at Mo

with a look plastered on her face as if she smelled something stinky.

"No, I am a woman and your parents wanted me to pick you up today." she smiled.

"If you a woman then why do you have a mustache on your face?" Za'kiya asked looking as if she were trying to figure it out.

"I am not a man sweetheart. I'm a woman, trust me and we have to get going so I can get you home to your mommy and daddy." Mo said but she was thinking about snapping the little girl's neck right now in front of everybody.

"Ewww, if you a woman you sure are ugly. You can't be a woman walking around with a man face that is not healthy. Your mommy should take you to the doctor so you can get that fixed." Za'kiya said while the other little girl covered her mouth to try and hold her laughter in.

Mo was now getting pissed and right when she was about to snatch Za'kiya up she heard a guy call her name. When she turned to get a better view she saw that the two dudes were her uncles. When they saw her they started walking faster and this caused Mo to panic. Next thing she knew she had snatched Za'kiya up by the waist and took off running to her car.

When she made it to the car she reached for the door handle and noticed that the door was locked. She now had people running her way and Za'kiya was kicking and screaming. She had to make a choice and she did just that by throwing Za'kiya on the sidewalk. She didn't even watch her hit the ground as she ran over to the driver side of the car and hopped in. She pulled off right when Qadir and Zahyir made it to where Za'kiya was laid out on the ground crying with a bloody leg.

Mo knew she had fucked up, she just didn't know how badly. This one single act would cost her everything; the main thing being her life.

◔ ◔ ◔

Zariya and Nassir were in the car driving home from a doctors appointment when Nassir's cell phone rang. Nassir told Zariya to answer the phone for him while he ran into the gas station to grab her a cup of ice and a bottle of water.

Zariya saw Qadir's name pop up on the screen and answered it on the second ring. "What's up big head?"

"Zariya something happened at the school today." he solemnly said into the phone.

"WHAT?!" Zariya sat up in her seat and listened to every word that Qadir spoke.

Once Nassir came out the store and got in the car he noticed the tears running down his wife's face.

"Baby what's wrong?" he asked her with concern in his voice.

She yelled that they needed to get home because someone tried to snatch Za'kiya. That was all Nassir needed to hear before speeding out of the gas station parking lot. Zariya was now shaking as the tears continued to run down her face; all she could think about was when Jaylin kidnapped her baby. Now someone else tried to do the same thing.

"Baby I need you to try to calm down before you end up in the hospital. You said Za'kiya is with Qadir and Zahyir right?" he asked looking from the road over to her every so often.

"Yes but they said her leg is scraped up really bad." Zariya cried into her hands.

"Zariya everything will be okay I am going to make sure of that but I need you to calm down." he said putting his hand on her thigh and noticing that it was wet.

"Baby, did you waste something on yourself?"

Zariya looked down and noticed that the bottom half of her Maxi dress was soaked.

"Baby, I think my water broke." she said making eye contact with Nassir.

Nassir grabbed his phone and immediately started making calls. He not only had to prepare for his son to enter the world but also prepare to take someone out of it for trying to touch and harm his daughter.

Chapter 19

Kalil and Chanae had just got back home from picking Khalid up from his sister's house. They ended up bringing Kamyra along with them since Kalyah had a date later on tonight. Things were heating up for her and her new boo and they were happy she was finally enjoying this new chapter in her life. As soon as they stepped foot in the door his cell phone started ringing.

"Talk to me." he said into the phone as he watched Chanae and the kids walk into the kitchen. He

140

listened intently as Nassir explained what was going on and what he needed him to do. After ending the call he went into the kitchen to inform Chanae of what just happened.

"Mommy, I want some." Khalid said reaching out for some of the water she was drinking. Chanae drank half the bottle before giving him some. Khalid took three sips and gave it back to her.

"Kamyra do you want some sweetie?" she said looking over at her reaching for an apple that was in a bowl in the center of the table.

"No te-te I'm going to eat this apple." she replied taking a bite out of it.

"Okay baby." Chanae finished the water off before throwing the bottle in the trash.

"We have to get to the hospital. Zariya's water just broke." Kalil said grabbing Khalid an apple and handing it to him.

"Oh my god my nephew is coming! Come on kids let's go!" Chanae yelled excitedly but her excitement was cut short with the next words out of Kalil's mouth.

"Someone also tried to snatch Za'kiya from school today and Qadir and Zahyir is on their way with her to the hospital too. Something about her leg being messed up."

"Who tried to snatch her?" Chanae asked but Kalil just shrugged his shoulders. No one knew who this person was. They all filed out the house en route to the hospital with heavy thoughts on their minds.

❖ ❖ ❖

"We need one more big push Mrs. Williams!" The doctor yelled preparing to bring the next Williams child into the world.

"No this shit hurts! I swear Nassir if you ever

touch me again I will kill you!" Zariya shouted in pain.

The nurses in the room tried hard not to laugh at some of the things Zariya would yell out when her contractions hit but they were finding that hard to do. Nassir looked at his wife and smiled. He knew she was going to talk shit through the whole birthing process especially since she decided to take the route of having a natural birth.

"Baby if you give us one more big push I promise to keep my hands to myself even when you the one trying to feel up on me." Nassir joked but Zariya didn't see anything funny.

"If I was not in so much pain right now I would punch the shit out of you and those bitches over there that seem to think everything is so fucking funny!" she yelled as a another big contraction hit. She pushed with all the strength she had left.

"Wahhhhhhhhhh!" they all heard one of the loudest cries come from such a small little person.

"Well Mr. and Mrs. Williams you two are now proud parents of a healthy baby boy!" the doctor announced holding the baby up. The nurse got the baby and got to work on cleaning him up before handing him over to his mother who looked to be exhausted.

Once they were alone Nassir's phone started ringing and he knew it was his boy calling him.

"Come up to Room 308." he spoke into the phone before hanging up. Within five minutes everybody was walking into the room. But Nassir and Zariya's minds weren't put at ease until Qadir walked into the room carrying Za'kiya in his arms. They had just got her to stop crying ten minutes ago. She had a sad look on her face with a big bandage wrapped around her leg.

As soon as she saw her daddy she started to cry all over again. Nassir grabbed her out of Qadir's arms and walked her over to the bed with Zariya. He tried to calm her so that she wouldn't scare the baby with her cries.

"Daddy, the man lady tried to take me away." she cried onto his shoulder. Nassir and Zariya looked at each other then looked to Qadir and Zahyir. He didn't know who tried to pull this stunt but he knew they fucked up when they came for his little girl. He gave Kalil a look to let him know what time it was. Kalil responded with a head nod letting his boy know he was down for whatever.

Chapter 20

Chanae was sitting next to Zariya's bed holding baby Nassir who they had already started calling NJ. He had fallen asleep so she laid him down in his bed. When she turned around to go sit back down she felt a little dizzy like the room was spinning around her. Everyone else was talking to Nassir who still held Za'kiya in his arms so they didn't notice. Zariya on the other hand was paying close attention.

"Are you okay?" she asked her as she watched

146

her sit back down.

"Yeah I think I turned around too fast or something." Chanae replied as if she was fine but Zariya saw right through it. She really was convinced that she wasn't okay when she noticed her head was swaying from side to side with her eyes halfway closed.

Next thing everyone heard was a little scream coming from Kamyra as she watched Khalid pass out on the floor next to her. Kalil turned and ran over to his son to see what was wrong. Once Chanae got up out of her seat to see about her son, she took two steps before passing out on the floor herself.

Zahyir and Qadir ran to get some nurses or doctors - whoever could help them see about what was going on with Khalid and Chanae. Three nurses and a doctor ran into the room and told everyone to step away from them. Kalil was about to protest but Nassir told him to let them do their job.

They brought two gurneys into the room placing Khalid on one and Chanae on the other. Rushing them out of the room Kalil followed behind them. Zahyir walked out too while calling his dad on the phone for him to get to the hospital ASAP.

❤ ❤ ❤

Once Chanae and Khalid came back around the doctors had been running test after test on them. When they felt that they were stable, they let Kalil in the room with them. Chanae was in the bed staring over at her little prince in the bed across from her with IVs sticking out of his little arms. Her head was hurting really bad and she couldn't understand why.

"Chanae...Chanae!" Kalil called out to her while looking over at her from the side of Khalid's bed. He looked down at his son and got pissed all over again because he couldn't help him.

"Kalil, what happened?" Chanae asked him trying to sit up in the bed. He walked over to her and helped her sit all the way up.

"I don't know. The doctors ran some test to try and figure out why you and my little man passed out all of a sudden." Right after he finished his statement the doctor walked back in the room.

"Doc what happen to them why did they pass out like that?" he asked and noticed the confused and concern look on the doctor's face.

"Well we ran every test we could think of. When the blood test came back it showed that they both have traces of Synthroid in their systems. What caused them to get shortness of breath and pass out is an active ingredient in Synthroid called Levothyroxine." Kalil and Chanae both looked at each other and then back to the doctor.

"What's that?" they both asked in unison.

"Levothyroxine is a liquid or powder substance that if not used properly could cause very dangerous side effects." The doctor went on to explain to them what some of the side effects were. He also told them it was a good thing that they both were at the hospital at the time because the longer they would have went without medical attention the deadlier it could have been for them.

"So what happens now? Are they going to be okay?" Kalil asked looking over at his son then over to Chanae before giving the doctor back his full attention.

"First we need to figure out how the drug got into both of their systems. They will both be fine because we were able to catch it in time but if we don't find out how it got there in the first place then we could possibly end right back up in this same predicament or worse."

"We haven't taken any medicine that would have that drug in it and all we drink is juice and water…" Chanae's mind started to drift off as she thought about everything her and Khalid ingested that Kalil didn't since he was the only one not sick.

"Well I will leave you two to make a list of things that you could have ingested. I'm glad that we were able to get to you guys in time this could have killed all three of you."

"You mean the two of them, doc I'm fine." Kalil corrected him.

"Oh no sir I wasn't speaking of you I meant her, your son, and the baby that she is now carrying. She is pregnant and this could have really harmed the baby if we didn't get to her in time." He said finally looking up from his paper and making eye contact with Chanae then Kalil.

"Pregnant!" Kalil and Chanae shouted at the same time. Chanae looked as if she was about to pass out again.

"Yes I will send the nurse in to make sure everything is still perfectly fine with the three of you. If you have any questions please don't hesitate to call me or have me paged." He said before walking back out of the room leaving Chanae and Kalil with their thoughts.

Chapter 21

"How the fuck could you mess that up?!?" Andra yelled into the phone. She was steaming mad and only had one thing on her mind; MURDER.

"Wait a minute, who the fuck are you yelling at like that? I told your ass once already that I don't work for you so bitch you need to lower your fucking tone!" Mo shouted into the phone while peeking out of the hotel window that she staying in.

Andra sat on her couch rocking back forth while

153

gripping the phone tight in her hand. Her breathing became heavy as her body temperature started to rise. She was trying hard to calm herself down. The last time she got this worked up she had to up and relocate to St. Louis; all because she wanted what she couldn't have. Being told no was something she does not take kindly.

"Mo, we need to find a way to make her disappear now more than ever. She knows your face! I'm just trying to make this work out good in the end for the both of us. You get what you want and I get what I want but to do that we have to work together." Andra spoke while still gripping the phone tightly. She needed Mo to see things her way so that her plan would still work. Andra wanted Kalil badly; she was just dying to feel him inside her and doing the things he did to Chanae every other night to her.

Mo thought about it for a minute and realized

that she was right.

"Okay. So what is the new plan then?" she asked ready to get this over with so that she could get the fuck out of the STL; there was nothing left here for her anymore.

Andra took a sigh of relief before speaking again.

"Meet me at the address I'm about to text to you. We will go over our next set of plans there." Andra instructed and then disconnected the call so that she could text the address to her.

❧ ❧ ❧

Mo pulled up to the address Andra sent her. It was a rundown house on a quiet residential street. She got out the car and looked around checking her surroundings before making her way to the steps that led to the front door.

"She's here. You remember what needs to be

155

done, right?" a person spoke into Andra's ear as they watched Mo make her way to the front door.

"Yes I have to correct the mistakes that were made." Andra responded nonchalantly.

"Exactly and I will be watching you." And with that the person disappeared into one of the empty rooms where cameras were set up to watch every angle of the house from the inside out.

Knock...Knock...Knock...

Andra looked to make sure the coast was clear before opening the door for Mo.

"Did you get lost or something? It took you a while to get here." she asked when she opened the door and came face to face with her next victim.

"No I had something else to do before getting here." Mo replied walking all the way into the house. The house had no real furniture, only a table in the center of the empty room with two chairs arranged around it. Mo assumed it had to be the living room and dining room.

"What else did you have to do?" Andra asked with a raised eyebrow after shutting and locking the front door.

"That's none of your business. Let's get this show on the road and run the game plan down. This house creeps me the hell out." Mo said looking around before taking a seat at the table.

Andra rolled her eyes and walked over to the table. Still standing, she asked Mo if she would like something to drink.

"Can I get you anything a drink or something?"

Looking around the room again Mo was feeling uneasy about something but she couldn't put her finger on what exactly that something was.

"Yeah if you got something strong up in this raggedy muthafucka I will take a glass of that."

Andra smiled and walked into the kitchen to make them both a drink. When she walked back into the room Mo was in, she handed her a glass and sat down across from her at the table. Mo looked at her as if she was crazy.

"Hold up baby girl I ain't the fool you think I am. Let me see your glass." she reached her hand out for Andra to hand her the glass she had sitting in front of her.

Still holding the same smile she had before making the drinks she handed Mo her glass. At the same time Mo slid her glass across the table for Andra to drink. Her smile got bigger as she picked the glass of vodka up and took it straight to the head. She slammed the glass back down on the table shaking her head from side to side to subdue the burning sensation as the liquor slid down her throat.

"Trust me sweetie I am not about to waste no good liquor on you." Andra said laughing.

Mo smiled at her before taking her drink to the head too. She sat the glass back down on the table. She started to speak but instead grabbed her throat as a burning sensation traveled through her throat down to her chest. Mo began to bang her fist on the table as it started to become hard for her to breathe.

"Are you okay? Would you like me to get you something else to drink?" Andra asked as if she were concerned.

Mo started shaking her head viciously up and down. Andra got up and went to the kitchen when she returned Mo was now on the floor grasping for air.

"I'm sorry Mo all I have left to drink is the same

thing you already drank." Andra held up a clear glass bottle that had the words acid plastered across it. She broke out into a crazed laugh as she watched Mo fight to breathe. Reaching behind her back she pulled out a gun and placed it to the center of Mo's head when she rolled over on to her back.

Mo's throat looked as if it was burned to a crisp. Her eyes were pleading with Andra to help her.

"I'm going to help you don't worry. I bet now you wish you would have just went along with what I said huh?" she laughed again before shooting Mo in the center of her forehead. She watched her brains splatter on to the hardwood floor.

The person that was watching everything from the other room walked over to where Andra stood grinning at the dead body.

"You did well today but now that she is no

longer with us we have to find another way for our plan to work. I will contact you in a few days make sure you are available." They walked to the door and stopped to get one last look at Mo who now lying lifeless on the floor.

"Do something with this mess and leave no traces." Andra nodded her head as she watched the person she always looked up to walk out the front door.

Chapter 22

Three hours later…

"You are late!" Licia stated to an exhausted Andra. She was rushing trying to make it to work on time but she still somehow ended up being thirty minutes late.

"I know and I am truly sorry. I promise it will not happen again." Andra replied apologetically. She walked over to the patient board they had posted against the back of the nurses' station wall.

"I had to cover for you this time and Stacey the

other time. Please do not make that a habit because that is the quickest way to find yourself in the unemployment line." Licia said rolling her eyes as she walked off to go do her rounds.

"What a bitch! She must need some good dick in her life or something." Andra mumbled to herself. She grabbed her notepad and started making her rounds to meet her patients.

She was about to walk into the room that her first set patients were in until she heard the conversation that was going on inside. Standing outside of the door out of eyesight she looked down at her notepad and read the names of the patients. Her eyes got big when she saw who it was. Andra listened intently to the conversation because it could possibly be some important information they were discussion that she could later use.

"I don't give a damn who you are no one is taking my son from me!" Chanae shouted at the top of her lungs as tears ran down her face.

"Baby, calm down and let me talk to them." Kalil said trying to keep her from getting sicker than she already was. He definitely didn't want his son to see her like that.

"Sir, we are only doing our jobs. When something this serious occurs we have to take immediate action. There is now a case open on you both. We have to investigate and find out how your son got sick like this. The drugs that were found in his and his mother's system are not something you could easily get your hands on." One of the two case workers that were standing in front of Kalil stated. He felt bad for having to take a child from his parents but all they knew is that it could be for his own safety.

"You think I would drug myself and my son - is that what you're trying to say?" Chanae asked two seconds away from throwing the pitcher of ice that sat on the table beside her at them. She could not believe what was happening.

"You're not taking my son and putting him in no damn foster care. I don't give a fuck what your jobs say for you to do. If you even attempt to touch what is mines and place him in the care of the state there is not a rock in the world you will be able to hide under." Kalil was so calm when he spoke it sent a surge of chills searing through both of the case workers bodies and Andra who was still listening outside of the room.

"Sir, this is not neither yours nor our decision to make. If you in any way interfere with our investigation you will be arrested." The female of the two case workers finally said, speaking up for the first time since they stepped into the room.

"We will take him because ain't no way in hell my nephew is going to be a ward of the state." Kalyah said walking into the room with her mother in tow.

"I know that's right!" her mother yelled walking over to Khalid's bed. He had the saddest look on his face as he lay with his head on Chanae's chest. She had went and climbed in the bed with him right before the case workers entered the room.

"And you are?" both of the case workers asked at the same time.

"That is my sister and mother." Kalil answered for them both.

"Only way either of you would be able to get temporary custody of him is if you signed some paperwork and agreed for him to have no contact with either of them."

"That will keep him from becoming a ward of the state?" Kalil's mother asked them.

"Yes."

"This is only temporary until the investigation is over and you find that neither parent is responsible for this. Once that's done and over with, he goes back home where he belongs with his mother and father?" Kalyah asked to get clarification.

"Yes ma'am."

"I'll do it. Where are the papers I have to sign?" Kalil looked at his mother then to the look on Chanae's face before she broke down.

"We will have everything ready for you before he is released from the hospital. We also ask that he be moved across to the Children's Hospital next door. He cannot be in the same room with his mother. He should have already been taken over to that hospital when he was mobile. Why wasn't he?"

"I have here that the parents ask that he stay in the room with the mother and for some reason the hospital agreed to it." Andra said causing everyone to turn and look at her.

"You have to be fucking kidding me?" Chanae shouted locking eyes with Andra.

"Who the hell are you? Why were you standing outside the room like you were looking over some paperwork?" Kalyah said stepping closer to her with her arms folded across her chest.

"I *was* looking over some paperwork and I'm the nurse assigned to this room." she smugly responded.

"Oh and don't forget the chick who tried to steal my wedding dress!" Chanae spat staring Andra down as if she was about to jump off the bed and whoop her ass again.

"Wait, this is the chick you told me about with the incident that happened at the bridal shop?" Kalyah asked looking at Chanae while referring to the punch she gave Andra for not wanting to give her the dress back.

"Yes, that is her and I want her removed as my nurse ASAP." Chanae stated matter-of-factly.

"I'm on it. I'll be right back." Kalyah said mean-mugging Andra as she walked out of the room to tell them that Chanae requested a new nurse.

"I'm just doing my job that's all." Andra quickly defended herself.

"I am so tired of hearing that shit today. Get out!" Andra gave her the stank face before turning around and leaving out of the room.

Kalil looked over at Chanae and knew she was about to have a mental breakdown at any given moment. Their lives were falling apart right before their eyes and there was nothing he could do to prevent it from happening or so he thought.

Chapter 23

It was four hours later and Chanae was a nervous wreck. She was crying so hard that she literally began to shake when the doctor and nurses came to remove Khalid from the room. It got so bad they had to sedate her just to get her to calm down because she had started to run a high fever. They didn't want to risk her miscarrying from all the stress she was under so they put her on around the clock watch.

Kalil stood in the doorway and watched his fiancé struggled in her sleep while tossing and turning.

He felt like his heart had been snatched out of his chest when they came to take his little prince away. Watching Chanae and Khalid cry out for one another was enough to bring him down to his knees.

"This can't be life right now." he thought to himself trying to shake the murderous thoughts he had flooding his mind. He needed to find out how the drugs got in their systems and get his family back together.

"How is she?" Charles asked walking up to Kalil and breaking him away from his thoughts.

Turning around to face him, Charles could see the worry written all over his face.

"She and the baby will be okay if they can keep her from stressing and her fever down. But under the circumstances it's hard not to stress the fuck out. I mean they took our fucking son from us! Even had the nerve to make assumptions as if we would do something to harm him. MY FUCKING SON!" Kalil pounded on his chest as he let out the frustration that had been fighting to be released for quite some time now.

Looking around, Charles noticed a few people were staring at them. "This ain't no free show. What the fuck is you looking at?" He stated before putting his attention back on Kalil. The people quickly turned their attention somewhere else.

"Kalil, my daughter and grandson need you to be the strong backbone they depend on. Especially Chanae - if she sees you like this she will surely lose it." Charles had a look on his face as if something just hit him. "Did you say her and the baby? What baby?

Kalil washed his hands over his face.

"The baby that she's carrying. We just found out that she is pregnant again."

"Who is pregnant?" Zahyir asked as him, Nassir, Zariya, and Za'kiya came walking down the hall to Chanae's room. Well Nassir was pushing Zariya in a wheel chair while Zahyir carried Za'kiya. Zariya insisted on coming down to help comfort her sister/friend in her time of need.

"Zariya what are you doing down here? You just had my nephew you should be resting." Kalil chastised her.

Zariya rolled her eyes as Nassir stopped right in front of him and Charles.

"You already know that I am going to be here for my sister so hush it. Plus Qadir is up there watching NJ making sure those heifers up there don't try anything slick with my baby." Nassir rolled her in the room next to Chanae's bed. He went back to the door to check on his boy and knew Kalil was battling with what his next move should be.

Zahyir walked in the room and stopped at the foot of his sister's bed still holding Za'kiya in his arms. Zariya watched him walk over to the other side of the bed lean down and kiss Chanae on the forehead. He then sighed deeply before taking a seat in the empty chair placing Za'kiya on his lap. She was quieter now then she had ever been after the kidnap attempt. It obviously scared her.

"She's going to be okay Zah. Chanae is stronger than we give her credit for." Zariya said giving him a small smile.

"I hope you right Zar. My sister already been through a lot in life as it is and I hate seeing her go through stuff like this." Zariya could really see the protective nature Zahyir possessed for his older sister. She smiled at him again and shook her head agreeing with him.

Thirty minutes had passed and the guys were still outside the room having a conversation in hushed tones. Zariya was about to prepare to leave and go back upstairs to her baby when she looked at the T.V. and saw a news broadcast of yet another murder that happened on the West side area within the last two weeks.

"Hey Zahyir, can you turn that T.V. up right quick for me?" she asked. He reached over and picked up the remote that was lying on the side of Chanae. He turned the volume up and he and Zariya listened as the news reporter came on to the screen.

Hi, I'm Sidney Curry and we are live on the scene at Fairground Park where two afternoon joggers called police about reportedly coming upon a severed head. We have just been informed that the severed head belongs to a 28-year old woman named Morena Stagmen from the St. Louis area who was just released from prison six months ago. It is not yet clear what happened to Stagmen but by the brutal attack, I think it is safe to say that Stagmen's murderer or murderers are still at large and dangerous. If you have any tips, please do not hesitate to call the tip line at the bottom of your screen.

Once the jail mugshot of Morena Stagmen popped up on the screen, Za'kiya started screaming at the top of her lungs startling everyone. Nassir, Kalil, Charles, and Demarco who had just got to the hospital a few minutes ago all ran into the room. Being the closest one to her, Zahyir turned her around on his lap and asked her what was the matter.

"What's wrong short stuff?" he asked her calling her by one of the nicknames he gave her.

"That's the man lady that tried to take me away! I want my daddy!" she cried aloud reaching for Nassir who had come over to see what was wrong with his princess. Everyone else stood in shock at the revelation that was just made. Nassir and Kalil both wondered what their next moves would be now.

Chapter 24

Out in the hallway at the nurses' station Andra sat staring at the T.V. with a wide smile spread across her lips. The news broadcast of Morena Stagmen aka Mo's head being found in the park excited her. In her own sick, twisted way she enjoyed severing her body parts and spreading them all over the St. Louis area. That was the real reason why she was so late to work today.

"I wonder when they will find the other body pieces. It probably take them awhile though; I made

sure to spread them out." She thought to herself but laughed aloud. She looked around and made sure no one had heard her.

"*I wonder what my little friend is doing now?*" she mumbled before grabbing her cell phone out her shirt pocket and sending out a text.

Me: Did you see the news report yet?

Silent Partner: Yeah I saw it you did well that was

some shit I wouldn't have even thought to do.

Me: Thanks I had a lot of practice remember I told

you my daddy was a hunter. Hahaha

Silent Partner: Don't forget I will be contacting you

with our next set of plans.

Me: I will be waiting for the call.

They concluded their conversation through text and Andra got back to work. She laughed to herself at the name she gave them on her phone. *"Silent Partner,"* she mumbled to herself.

"Well hell in a way this person is like a silent partner because no one knows that the person helping me destroy Chanae's life is someone that hates her even more than I do." Andra laughed and continued her work shift thinking about what their next set of plans could possibly be.

❧ ❧ ❧

The St. Louis air hit his face as he inhaled deeply while looking around at his surroundings. He didn't know how truly homesick he was until he crossed the "Welcome to St. Louis, Missouri" sign. He felt and heard his phone ringing in his pocket and reached in to answer it.

"Hello?" he answered on the third ring.

"Daddy why you leave me?" a sweet little voice asked.

He chuckled a little before speaking.

"Little mama I told you I had to come and take care of some unfinished business. Where is grandma?" he asked his daughter.

"Ummm my granny is in the kitchen cooking food daddy. Are you coming to eat with us?"

"No baby I'm not coming back for a minute until I handle some business." He could hear the sadness in her voice when she responds with a simple "okay".

"Guess what though?"

"What daddy?"

"When daddy comes back I'm going to bring you a big surprise."

"Ohhh daddy what is it? Tell me tell me tell

me!" she said jumping up and down excited about what he would bring her back from his business trip.

"You sure you want to know?" he asked teasingly.

"Yesss tell me pleeeease!"

"Well daddy came here to get your mommy and bring her back so that we all can be a family."

"Daddy you going to bring mommy here to live with us?" her little mind was working overtime. She always wanted her mommy to be with her and her father. Every time she would mention her to him his response would always be that her mommy was away on some business trip helping the less fortunate. Her little mind would wonder why she never physically saw her mother face to face and only had pictures of her.

"Yes little mama I'm going to be coming back home with mommy. We are going to be together as a family and I will make sure of that."

"I love you, daddy!" she shouted through the phone.

"I love you too baby. Now go help your granny cook and I will call you tonight when it is time for bed to say goodnight." They said their goodbyes and hung up the phone.

Von sat and thought about how he was going to bring Chanae home with him and get her to help raise his daughter. He wanted them to be a big happy family. But he knew that was going to be easier said than done. He first had to set his plans in motion to get rid of his biggest problem that could halt any plans he may have. That one single problem went by the name of Kalil Barber.

"Yeah he has to die this time around! I am about to let these muthafuckas know I'm back and ready to take back what the fuck is rightfully mines." Von stated

to himself. The games were about to be turned up to the

max. This time around he was out for blood and the

woman he loved. Von didn't plan on stopping until he

got exactly what he came back for.

"Let the games begin muthafuckas!" he got in

his rental car and pulled off.

Chapter 25

A week later...

Kalil had just helped Chanae get settled into their bedroom. She had been released from the hospital today but she was still very much depressed. The doctors wanted her to get as much rest as possible and to try and relax. Kalil had called Kalyah and asked her how Khalid was doing since he had been released the day before in their mother's care. He had the phone on speaker thinking it would at least put Chanae's mind at ease knowing he was somewhere safe. He didn't know how wrong he would be with that move.

186

Chanae's exact words when Kalyah finished telling them that Khalid was doing fine other than keep saying how he wanted his mommy and daddy were; "He not supposed to be anywhere but with his parents! I want my damn son back home where he belongs!"

"Kalyah, thanks for the update. I'll call you later." Kalil said staring at Chanae.

"Okay I will be there to check on you all tomorrow." Kalyah said before ending the call.

Kalil pushed the end button on his cell phone and gave Chanae his full attention. "Look. I'm hurting just as much as you are. I want our son home with us where he belongs just as much as you do but spazzing out on people over something we can't control at the moment is a waste of time." He calmly stated.

"Of course you would say something like that." Chanae said rolling her eyes. She got up out of bed and was about to walk pass him but was stopped by Kalil grabbing her gently by the arm.

"What the hell is that supposed to mean?" he said trying not to spazz the fuck out on her for the statement she had just made.

"You wasn't the one who got sick and still don't know how the hell it happened. Then to find out that our son could have died too and now he was taken from us and you basically saying let's do nothing about it!"

"That is not what the fuck I'm saying Chanae and you know it! What the fuck can we do? Please tell me and I will go and do the shit right fucking now!" he shouted back at her. Chanae said nothing because there really wasn't anything she could say to that. She was not mad at Kalil - she was mad because like he said there wasn't anything they could do right now to get their son back. Not to mention the pregnancy had her hormones all over the place.

"I just want things to go back to the way it was Kalil. We were finally happy for a change and this just literally ruined our lives. Now we have another baby on the way and I don't know what to do. What are we going to do while our family is split apart?" She cried burying her face into his chest.

❤ ❤ ❤

After that night, things in Kalil and Chanae's household had been shaky. Chanae cried most of the time and Kalil spent most of his time away from home. He hated being there knowing his family was not complete. The man in him felts as if he didn't deserve to share a bed with Chanae if he couldn't even keep his family together.

Chanae was in Khalid's room lying on his bed crying for what seemed like the hundredth time that day. It was three in the afternoon when she decided it was time for her to get up and stop all this moping around seeing as it wasn't helping anything. Right when she climbed off the bed and stood to her feet she heard the room door open.

"I wiped the entire kitchen down and threw away everything in the refrigerator and cabinets. I'm about to run to the grocery store and restock the food. Is there anything else specific that you want?" Kalil asked her standing in the doorway. She had been holed up in Khalid's room all day. She didn't even hear him when he came home.

"No I don't have any special requests." she said in a low tone. Kalil could tell by the red and puffiness in her eyes that she had been crying again. He felt helpless seeing her like this and knowing there wasn't anything he could do to help ease her pain hurt his pride.

"I will try not to be long okay?"

"Okay."

He turned to walk away but stopped when he remembered something.

"I'm going to go and pick up your prenatal prescriptions while I'm out too."

"Thank you."

"Chanae, you don't have to thank me for doing what is required for me as your man to do. Oh yeah and before I forget, remember we were trying to figure out who were sending you the notes and ran me off the road that night?" That caught Chanae's full attention.

"Yes, did you find out who did it?"

"Yeah it was the same person who tried to snatch Za'kiya and one of the people who you had that fight with when you got arrested that night at the hospital. We sent someone to dig up some information on where she was staying. They found the car she was driving the day she tried to snatch Za'kiya over on the Eastside in a vacant lot. They took the car to the chop shop and stripped it down. The dumb ass broad had all the evidence under the driver seat of the car. There were pictures of you, our son, and Za'kiya. It was some pictures of another person too but I'm looking more into that person myself." Chanae took in everything that Kalil just said and all she could do was shake her head. Every other person she came into contact with lately ended up trying to either kill her or the ones she loved the most. She decided right then and there that enough was enough and she was not going to sit around being anyone's damn victim any longer.

Chapter 26

Chanae was cleaning the house from top to bottom and feeling like a brand new person. Even though Kalil had just done it a few days ago, she wanted to do it again. It was helping her keep herself busy and it distracted from her current problems. She decided tonight she would cook her and Kalil a nice little dinner and talk about their situation. They barely touched each other anymore and she knew part of that was her fault. Tonight she planned to fix all of that by spending some much needed time with her man.

Altar'd

Walking into their bedroom, she went to grab their dirty clothes hamper so that she could wash the clothes.

"Damn look at all these clothes. You can definitely tell we ain't washed shit in weeks." She picked up the hamper and carried it downstairs to the laundry room. Once there, she started separating the whites from the colored clothes. She made sure she checked all the shirt and pants pockets so that nothing important would get washed and damaged.

Chanae picked up one of Kalil's shirts from out of the hamper and scrunched her nose up at the smell radiating off of it. "This shit smells like an old woman's perfume. What the hell he been doing?" she asked herself out loud. She brushed it off as nothing and threw the shirt in its own separate pile.

"That shit is getting washed by itself smelling

like a damn old folk's home ewww." she said as she continued to separate the clothes. She then picked up a pair of Kalil's jeans and started emptying out the pockets.

Pulling out a wad of money she smiled as she counted out three hundred dollars.

"Well, look like this is going in Khalid's piggy bank. Thanks bae." she laughed to herself. She reached in his other pocket and damn near had a heart attack at what she saw. She threw it across the room as if it was on fire or crawling with spiders.

She ran upstairs to their bathroom and grabbed some of the latex gloves she used when she did her hair. On her way out of the room she picked up her cell phone off of the nightstand. Walking back into the laundry room she walked back over to where she threw it.

Chanae put a glove on her right hand and reached down to pick up what she wished was something other than what it actually was. Holding up a pair of silk panties in her hand she swore her mind had to be playing tricks on her.

"What the fuck is this bullshit?!" she shouted her voice echoing off of the laundry room walls.

She pulled her phone out of her pocket and dialed Kalil's number so fast it felt like the screen was going to crack under the pressure from how hard she was pounding on the numbers.

"What's up baby?" he answered once he saw it was her calling.

"Where are you?" she asked in a semi calm tone.

"I'm at Nassir's house discussing some business. Why, what's up?" he asked catching on to the tone she used. It was a little too settled for him and he could feel that something wasn't right.

"We need to talk. Can you come home please? It is very important." Kalil was curious as to what could be so urgent about what they had to talk about.

"Okay I am on my way now and should be there in like twenty minutes." He confirmed.

"Okay good. I will be waiting" she ended the call before he could get another word in. She stared at the panties while shaking her head. If she found out Kalil was sleeping around on her, she was calling the engagement off.

❧ ❧ ❧

Kalil pulled up to the house and got out of the car. He walked into their home and spotted Chanae sitting on the couch with her hands clasped together under her chin while leaning forward with her elbows on her knees.

Walking over to the couch he sat down next to her. "So what was so urgent that you needed me to rush home? Are you okay?" Kalil asked with concern.

"No I'm not okay. I was getting ready to do some laundry when I started sorting the clothes and checking the pockets for anything non washable and I found these." Chanae explained holding up the panties to where Kalil could see them.

He looked at them and shrugged his shoulders. "Okay, I'm confused you found a pair of your panties in your pants pocket?" he asked for clarification.

"No these are not my panties. I don't wear this cheap shit! I found these in *your* pants pocket!" Chanae shouted now standing up in front of him fuming.

"I don't know what the fuck you talking about or where those panties came from!" Kalil shouted just as loud as she was and stood up. They were now standing face to face both pissed off. Chanae was mad that Kalil would step out on her and Kalil was mad that Chanae was accusing him of something he didn't do.

"So you don't know how another bitch's panties got into YOUR pants pocket?" Chanae asked pointing at him.

"Come on now Chanae you know me better than that. What the fuck would I be doing with another woman's underwear in my pocket?" Kalil was now steaming mad at the bullshit she was throwing his way.

"I don't know Kalil that is what I am trying to figure out but hold on maybe this will help both of us out little bit." Chanae said reaching in her back pocket and pulling out a folded piece of paper. A piece paper that could damage everything they fought so hard for.

Chapter 27

"What is that?" he asked more confused than before.

"Oh this is the letter I found in the back pocket of your jeans. Should I read out loud what your lover wrote to you or no?" Chanae waved the letter in Kalil's face trying to fight the tears back from falling from her eyes. This letter would definitely be the reason their relationship came to an end in Chanae's eyes.

"Chanae you better gone somewhere with that bullshit. What the fuck you in here sipping on? I ain't fucking nobody so you tripping right now and you need to sit your ass down some damn where!" Kalil yelled in her face. He had enough of the bullshit today.

"Fuck you Kalil I hope like hell that bitch you fucking makes you happy because the next man I fuck will damn sure make me…" Chanae never got to finish that statement before Kalil was up close in her face. They were so close she could feel and smell his warm honey scented breath on her nose.

"You can muthafucking play with me if you want to Chanae but I swear to God you will regret pulling some shit like that. You done lost your damn mind and I suggest you go find it ASAP! Like I said from the gate, I am NOT fucking nobody else and you already know you better not even think twice about another nigga!" Kalil stood there staring hard at her daring her to say some stupid shit like she just said. Chanae didn't say anything she was too scared to even blink. She had never seen this side of Kalil before.

"I don't know where that shit came from but I didn't put it there and I damn sure ain't out here fucking other women. I might not always be home but I am out taking care of business and trying to figure some shit out. I never once thought about another woman or even thought about stepping out on you." Kalil took a step back and shook his head at Chanae before walking out of the door never looking back.

Chanae fell to her knees and cried letting all the tears fall wherever they may. She never felt this much pain in her entire life. Her life was falling to pieces and she didn't know if it would even be possible to put it back together again.

❤ ❤ ❤

"Yes...yes...yessss!" Andra yelled jumping and down in her living room in nothing but a tank top and a thong. She just finished watching the whole scene at

Kalil and Chanae's house go down.

"That's right bitch send my man this way where he REALLY belongs. She didn't know how to handle all that man anyway little stupid bitch!" she laughed to herself.

"It will only be a matter of time before I will be riding that dick all night long. Ummm, I can just imagine how it would feel to have him inside me. Shit I might even give him a couple more babies." Andra laughed even harder and then stopped abruptly.

"Shit that reminds me I really have to get rid of this bitch and the little bastard that she got the nerve to be carrying now. My man doesn't need any more kids from her dumb ass!" Andra's mind started working up different ways to rid their life of Chanae.

"Oh maybe I could use the poison again but this time use a little more than before." She said pacing the floor tapping her chin with her finger while in thought.

"Naw I can't do that it will definitely draw some kind of attention and more so to my man and I can't have that." Andra never once realized that she was having a full blown conversation with herself. Not even when her phone started ringing.

"Damn who is this I am trying to figure out how to get my man sooner rather than later shit!" she yelled marching over to the table where her cell phone was and snatching it up.

"HELLO?" she yelled with much attitude.

"You must have lost your damn mind. Who the hell you yelling at like that?" the caller shouted with just as much attitude as her on the other end of the phone.

Andra took the phone away from her ear and looked at the screen. Her eyes got big once she saw

'Silent Partner' across her screen. Placing the phone back to her ear she began to apologize.

"I am so sorry I didn't know it was you on the phone." she said apologetically.

"Look we ain't got time for all that I need you to focus. We need to figure out a way to get Chanae away from Kalil. As long as he is near her it will be impossible to touch her with him around."

"Oh that won't be a problem anymore. I have a feeling that he will be leaving that little stupid whiny bitch very soon." Andra said confident.

"How you figure that?" Andra begun to explain with a smile plastered on her face what just went down between the couple. Without even knowing, Chanae helped her enemies with their plans in making her a permanent resident of one of the many cemeteries located across the St. Louis area.

Chapter 28

Kalil sat outside the house in the car trying hard to wrap his mind around what just happened. He couldn't believe Chanae would even think to accuse him of some shit like cheating. He never thought about another woman because he knew the treasure he possessed at home. He had to catch himself because he was two seconds away from snatching Chanae's ass up for coming at him about another nigga.

"I got to get my damn head right and there is only one person I can talk to about this shit." He said himself starting the car up and pulling out of the driveway.

Twenty minutes later Kalil was pulling back up in front of Nassir and Zariya's home. He sat there in the car for five minutes before getting out and walking to the door. Ringing the doorbell he waiting for someone to come and answer the door. He could hear the voices that were coming from the other side. The door slowly opened to reveal a smiling Zariya with Za'kiya peeking out from behind her leg.

"Uncle Kalil you back already!" Za'kiya shouted running into his arms. She was still limping a little from her sore leg but you couldn't tell unless you paid close attention to it. He scooped her up and kissed her on the cheek.

"Hey itty bitty!" she giggled at him.

"Uncle Kalil I'm not itty bitty I'm a big girl but my NJ is itty bitty." Kalil and Zariya both laughed at her. She was always claiming somebody as hers.

They walked into the house and Zariya informed Kalil that Nassir had just left.

"Your boy just pulled off before you got here. He said he was on his way to your house to talk to you about something he forgot to mention before you left earlier. Do you want me to call him and tell him that you are here?" she said taking a seat on the couch.

"Actually I came to talk to you about something." He said taking a seat on the loveseat across from her with Za'kiya on his lap.

"Oh okay then you came back at a good time because I just put your nephew down for a nap." She replied a little thrown off because she and Kalil never had a one on one talk before and she was curious to know what this was all about.

"Za'kiya, go and see what uncle Qadir is doing

in the family room." Za'kiya frowned as she jumped off of Kalil's lap.

"Mommy, where did my daddy go? Is he coming back soon?" Zariya gave her the *"I'm not playing with you little girl look"* and she hurried up and ran out of the living room.

"I swear every time somebody tell her something and she don't like it she start screaming she want her damn daddy. Ugh!" Zariya stated shaking her head while Kalil laughed.

"Nassir got her little ass like that. He loves that little girl." Kalil said as if he was lost in his thoughts.

"Yeah he spoiled her little badass and then yell don't whoop his baby when she do something wrong. Anyway what did you want to talk about?" she asked leaning back on the couch.

"Okay so here's the rundown: Chanae and I got

into a big ass argument today. She accused me of cheating and finding some woman's panties in my pants pocket with a letter. The shit is all fucked up to me because honestly I don't know what the fuck she's talking about." He explained.

Zariya leaning forward on the couch and looked him dead in the eyes. "Are you out cheating Kalil?" she asked straight up no chaser.

He looked at her like she lost her damn mind with his face scrunched up in a knot.

"Zariya when would I have time to cheat? Every day if I'm not at home trying to get her to eat or talk to me, I'm here."

"That is true. Ever since we left the hospital you've been here which is why when I call Chanae to make sure she's okay I get no answer. I guess she didn't want me to know you were barely home not knowing you're here with us." Zariya shook her head. She didn't understand why they were distancing themselves from each other during the time when they needed one another the most.

"You know her better than anybody Zariya. I need to know why she keeps pushing me away. I honestly don't know how the fucking panties got there or that damn letter." Zariya could see that Kalil was sincere with what he was saying but the mystery still stands how did it get in his pocket if he didn't put it there.

She then got a look on her face as if something finally hit her. Kalil noticed it and asked her what she thinking about.

"What's up Zar? Why you looking at me like that? What are you over there thinking?" he asked leaning forward in his seat.

"What exactly did this letter say? I mean maybe it could help us figure out who wrote it and is trying to destroy you and Chanae's relationship."

"I don't know what the letter says. I didn't wait around for her to read it. I had to hurry up and get away from her before I ended up snatching her ass up talking about another nigga." Kalil was getting pissed all over again. He didn't even want to think about another man touching his woman.

"Oh God you two done lost your damn minds over there. Do you have any kind of idea who might want you two to separate?" Kalil looked as if he was in deep thought before mumbling something.

"There is only one person I can think of but we haven't heard a peep out of him. You know what, let me get back to this house and see this damn letter. You're right it could definitely be a clue or something.

"Okay and Kalil?" Zariya said as she walked him to the door.

"Yeah what's up?" he said turning around to face her after opening the front door.

"Chanae loves you. I've never seen her love someone as much or as hard as she loves you. Right now she's confused and hurt with everything that is going on. Don't give up on her Kalil. She needs you now more than ever whether she wants to admit it or not." Kalil nodded his head and kissed Zariya on the cheek before getting in his car and pulling off.

Altar'd

Chapter 29

To My Lover Man,

If you are reading this then you found the letter I slipped in your pants while you were in the shower washing the scent of our love making off of you. I really enjoyed last night. (giggles) You definitely know how to make a woman feel good from every touch and kiss you gave to my body I felt as if I was in heaven. I still can't believe you got me to put on my uniform and role play the naughty nurse while you pretended to be my little bad sick patient. (Lol) I still find that funny seeing as how that is exactly how we met because at one point

214

you actually were just that to me.

On a serious note I know you said to give you time to end things with your son's mother but a part of me wants you here with me now. I get that you feel obligated to her because of him but baby you can still be a part of your son's life without being with that bitch. Just give it some thought okay? I can't wait to be in your strong arms again. I love you...

Sincerely Your Naughty Nurse XOXO

Chanae read the letter out loud for what seemed like the thousandth time. Every time she read it she got even more furious at the words another bitch wrote about her man.

"Can you believe this shit?! Then this letter smells just like his shirt with that stinky old lady perfume scent!" she shouted flopping back down on the couch next to Nassir. He came over to talk to Kalil but instead found a heartbroken and crying Chanae.

"Wow! That definitely is some crazy shit. Now listen I am not picking sides but in your heart do you truly believe that Kalil is fucking whoever that woman is?" he asked the question she knew he was going to ask. Chanae honestly didn't know what to believe. Her heart was telling her that Kalil would never do anything like that to her but her mind was telling her that all the evidence was pointing to him sleeping around on her and that's exactly what she expressed just that to Nassir.

"My heart is telling me that he loves me and would never risk what we have for some ass on the side. Then there is the evidence staring me dead in my face. I don't know what to do and I am tired of fucking crying about it."

Nassir knew how much his boy loved Chanae.

With that being said he knew there was no way in Hell he would cheat on her and risk losing his family. *"The letter,"* he mumbled but was loud enough for Chanae to hear him.

"What about it?" she asked a little confused at what he was getting at.

"The letter tells us who this person is. It says *'I still can't believe you got me to put on my uniform and role play the naughty nurse while you pretended to be my little bad and sick patient. I still find that funny seeing as that is how we met because at one point you actually were just that to me.'* Meaning that whoever this person is was or still is a nurse and at some point in time Kalil was their patient." Nassir said now in deep thought.

Chanae thought about what he was saying and agreed.

"Wait didn't the chick you hit at the bridal shop for trying to take your dress used to be a nurse for Kalil after his accident? The same chick we saw at the park when we were with the kids?" Nassir asked turning to look at her. Chanae's eyes got huge at the mention of the chick from the hospital, bridal shop, and park all being the same person.

"Yes! She was at the hospital the day the case workers came to take Khalid away. She seemed excited about putting her two cents in for them to take my baby away. Damn I forgot what her name was." Chanae was now up pacing back and forth in front of Nassir.

"I think she mentioned it before at the park but I can't remember at the moment. Wait I think it was something like Andra. Yeah that is what it was; Andra! Look I'm going to have somebody look into who this chick really is." He said getting up and making his way to the door.

"Oh yeah Chanae?" he turned around to face her.

"Yes?" she walked over to the door where he was now standing with his hand on the doorknob.

"Before you go making any life changing decisions, which will not only affect you but my nephew and the baby that you are carrying, I want you to think long and hard about what kind of man you are in love with. Knowing that, do you really think he will do some messed up shit like cheating on you when he worked hard to get you to be his woman?" Nassir turned around and opened the door. Chanae was about to respond but when the door was opened up all the way they both came face to face with Kalil. He looked as if he was about to use his key to open the door before it opened.

Even though Nassir was standing directly in front of him the first person he locked eyes with was Chanae. He could tell from her red and puffy eyes that she had been crying.

"Let me talk to you right quick man." Nassir said stepping around him and walking to his car.

"Alright hold up." He said with his eyes never leaving Chanae's. "I'm about to see what he needs to holler at me about. We will talk as soon as I'm done. No arguing just talking, okay?" Chanae nodded her head but from the frown on his face she knew that that was not the response he was looking for.

"Okay we will talk." she said giving him a more satisfying response. She watched him walk over to Nassir's car before closing the door shut.

"What's up man? I was just at your house talking to Zariya. She said you had something you wanted to tell me but forgot." He stood in front of Nassir as he leaned up against his car.

"I got word that our boy is back in town. He hasn't made a sound yet but you know just like I do it's only a matter of time before his dumb ass tries to make a move." Nassir revealed.

"I had a feeling he might have been back. All this shit that is going on probably has his fingerprints all over it." Kalil shook his head in frustration.

"Naw man, with the shit that is going on we think it might have something to do with that one chick from…" Before Nassir could finish his statement a series of gunshots rang out. They both ducked down in front of the car. Nassir and Kalil pulled out their guns from under their shirts and started shooting back. The person or people shooting must not have been expecting them to react so quickly because they stopped shooting back in drove off.

"Who the fuck was that?" Nassir asked. When he didn't get a response from Kalil he looked over to his left where he last saw him. He damn near had a heart attack at the sight of his boy laid out on the ground.

Chapter 30

After hearing that the gunshots had stopped Chanae opened the front door. She ran outside towards Nassir's car but almost fainted when she saw him kneeled down in front of Kalil.

"Noooooooooooooo!" She screamed at the top of her lungs with the tears that were falling almost clouding her vision. She ran over to him dropping to her knees.

"Baby get up! Please get up Kalil, don't do this to me. Don't leave me baby get up!" she cried burying her face into his chest begging for him not to die on her.

"Shit!" he groaned in pain reaching up grabbing his head.

"Baby are you okay? Where are you hit? Chanae started searching his body for wounds. She noticed blood coming from his side. She lifted his shirt up and saw that it looked as if a bullet had grazed him on his side.

"I'm fine it was just a graze. My head is what is killing me though. I hit it on the ground when I fell." He explained. They all could hear the police sirens in the distance. The neighbors were starting to come out of their homes to see what was going on.

"Come on, help me get him up on his feet." Nassir said as the police started pulling up. He grabbed both his and Kalil's guns and stuffed them in his pocket. Once Kalil was on his feet they all turned to the officers who were now walking towards them.

"Is everyone over here okay?" the first officer that made it over to them asked.

"No we need…" Chanae started to speak but was stopped by Kalil.

"We are fine and before you ask no we don't know who was just shooting." Kalil said cutting Chanae off.

They stood there for thirty minutes giving the police their statements. Once everyone cleared out Kalil, Chanae, and Nassir went back inside the house.

"Kalil, you need to go to the hospital and get that checked out." Chanae pleaded with him.

"I will be fine. I'll call the doc up and have him come check me out. Right now I need you to go and pack a few things so that you can go with Nassir." He demanded rather than asking her.

"What? No Kalil I am not going anywhere if you not going with me." She said crossing her arms and staring at him. At this moment all the thoughts of him cheating went out the window. When she saw him laid out on the ground in the driveway her heart damn near stopped. She couldn't picture her life without him.

"This really ain't up for debate Chanae go get your things." Kalil sat on the couch holding his head in his hands. His head was pounding and he was not in the mood to go back and forth with her.

"No Kalil you always want to shield me from shit and that is probably the main reason these bitches and bitch made niggas always make me their damn target. I am so fucking tired of being the one everybody has to walk on pins and needles around when some shit goes down. So you know what, I will go pack a few of my things but wherever the hell you lay your head I will be laying mines right next to it." With that, she turned on her heels and went upstairs to grab her things. She was going to show everyone that she was not the same weak person they may have thought she was.

Kalil and Nassir sat on the couch in shock. They never saw or heard Chanae act like that before. They looked at one another then back at the stairs she had just gone up. Kalil didn't want to admit it but that shit turned him on to see his woman go from calm to straight bitch mode in two seconds flat.

"So what's the plan man?" Nassir asked him breaking him out of his thoughts.

"Man I'm going to check us into a hotel and then call you so we can figure out who the fuck was just shooting at us." Kalil replied shaking his head.

"You sure man because you two can come and stay with us. You know that shit ain't a problem." He looked at his boy and could see the stress building up.

"Naw we going to go to the hotel plus we have to get some shit squared away." Kalil stated right before Chanae walked back into the living room.

"I'm ready I packed a few of my things and a few of yours so where are we going?" she asked while they both shook their heads and stood to their feet. Things will never be the same after this.

Chapter 31

"Damn, I wish I could have been there to see the looks on their faces." Von said to himself taking the mask off as he walked into his motel room.

"Yeah I bet now those muthafuckas know that they and their people can be touched at their home at any time. Bitch ass niggas." Von grabbed a beer out of the mini fridge he had in the room and plopped down on the queen size bed.

"Tomorrow I will make my next move. They probably think a nigga still MIA so I would be the last person they suspect." He laughed as he screwed the top off the beer and took a drink.

"Oh shit!" he hopped up off the bed quick throwing the bottle across the room. It was a huge cockroach crawling up his arm. He jumped up and down waving his arms wildly until it fell off. He hurried up and smashed it by stepping on it.

"That is some nasty shit. I have to hurry up and get the fuck out of here. Once I get what belongs to me we are out of St. Louis for good." Von said out loud to himself still twitching from the roach crawling on him.

❤ ❤ ❤

Kalil and Chanae had just checked into the Marriot Hotel. Walking into their suite neither one had said a word to the other since they got into the car and were on their way there. Kalil popped the top off of the bottle of Tylenol and placed two pills in his mouth. Grabbing the bottle of water out of one of the

Walgreens bags he drank half of it.

Chanae sat on the bed and watched him. She couldn't stop thinking about how much she loved this man but something wasn't right with them. She had to talk to him about everything that had been going on in their relationship for the past few months. When he came and sat down next to her on the bed she knew now was the time for them to put it all out on the table.

Turning around on the bed to face him she sat Indian style. "Kalil we need to talk about us and all this shit that keeps happening." He looked at her ready to have this talk and to get it over with but before he could respond his cell phone started ringing.

He looked at the screen before answering it. "What's up sis?" he answered.

"Kalil I need you..." Kalyah sniffled before speaking. "I need you to get here now!" she cried into the phone.

"Kalyah what's wrong? Where are you?" He hopped up off the bed and started pacing back and forth in front of Chanae.

"Kalil, I'm at my house now but I just left Mom's house and someone had broken in and destroyed the place. I was dropping Mom and Khalid off after we left Incredible Pizza with the kids. When we walked in and saw someone had vandalized the whole place we got back in the car and came here. What if they would have been home when it happened? Kalil they could have been hurt or even worst killed!" Kalyah was talking a mile a minute and wasn't hearing anything Kalil had said to her.

"KALYAH!" he shouted not only scaring Kalyah but Chanae too.

"Yes?" she whispered.

"I said that I am on my way. Do not call the police until I get to you, okay?" he started searching for his car keys and couldn't find them.

"But I told you we left mom's house and now we at my house and what about the investigation with Khalid?"

"I know where you said you were and I said I am on my way there. Oh and don't worry about that bullshit, my son could have been hurt tonight so I don't give a fuck what anybody has to say I'm coming to see him." As soon as Chanae heard the words 'my son and hurt' in the same sentence she hopped up and threw her shoes on.

"Look I will call you when I am outside." Kalil ended the call and turned around to find Chanae standing in his face.

"What happened?" she asked him ready to go

see her baby.

"Have you seen my keys? Kalyah said someone had broken into ma's house."

"Are you serious? What the hell are we still standing here for?" she said walking to the door and opening it.

"I can't find my keys have you seen them? And you are not going Chanae. You are going to stay here and I will call you when I get there."

"Again Kalil where you go I go so let's go!" Chanae said holding up the keys in her hand as she walked out the door. Kalil couldn't do shit but sigh heavily while following behind her out of the hotel room door.

Chapter 32

"How the hell did they connect me to all of this shit just that quick?" Andra had just gotten home and turned on the video surveillance from Kalil's house. She was shocked to see Chanae and Nassir discussing the letter and how she may be connected to it.

"Fuck! This could be all bad for us. I have to stop them from telling him if they haven't already done it." Andra grabbed her keys and was on her way back out of the door when the voices from the TV caught her attention.

"She saw Kalil, Chanae, and Nassir on the screen. A minute later she just saw Nassir and Kalil having a conversation. Having listened to what they had said her blood began to boil. She was beyond pissed.

"Shooting? Who the fuck tried to kill my man? Oh see now this shit done got real personal! They can kill any of those other fuckers but Kalil is NOT to be harmed in any fucking way!" Andra called up her inside man who she got to place a tracker on Kalil's car. All she had to do in return was give him a little ass.

"What's up baby you ready for some more of this good stick already?" he asked once he answered the phone.

Andra felt like she could vomit. Just the sound of his voice and the corny stuff he said made her skin crawl but she needed him.

"Hey baby, I need you to tell me where Kalil

is." She felt sick to her stomach because she knew what he was about to ask her.

"If you let me taste you I will tell you anything you want to know." He said. She could picture him smiling on the other end of the phone.

"Where do you want to meet?" she walked out of her door and out towards her car.

"Let's meet at the motel we always meet up at and in the same room you gave yourself to me for the first time." Andra agreed and hung up the phone.

"I swear if I didn't need him I would have killed his ass by now." She got in her car and pulled off.

❧ ❧ ❧

Andra arrived at the Motel Inn down on South Broadway within twenty minutes. She parked her car all the way on the far end of the parking lot and got out. Walking swiftly through the parking lot she knocked on the door twice once she stepped in front of it. After a two minute wait, the door opened up and she came face to face with her secret helper.

"For a minute I thought you changed your mind." He smiled as he stepped aside granting her entrance to the room.

"Would you have been disappointed if I had of changed my mind?" she asked walking into the room and turning to face him as he closed the door and locked it.

"I would have been very disappointed." He said as he walked up to her and grabbed the back of her neck tilting her head to the side before slithering his tongue down her throat.

Gently pushing him off of her she took a few steps back.

"Aggressive today aren't we?" she said walking over to the bed and taking a seat at the end of it.

"I missed you that's all baby." he said stepping in front of her dropping to his knees.

He started sliding his hand up her leg and under the mini skirt she was wearing. Once he reached her panty line he started to tug at it trying to pull it down. Andra slid her hand on top of his and pushed it back down her thigh and off of her.

"You know I don't like to be handled like that. Now first things first, where is the information I asked you for?" she asked with a raised eyebrow.

"Oh yeah of course business first, pleasure later." he said getting up off the floor to fetch the paper with Kalil's location written on it. He walked back over to the bed and handed her the paper. She unfolded the paper taking a quick look at it before looking back up at him.

"Are you positive that he's still at this

location?"

"Yes, I checked again right before you got here. That is his sister's address but if for some reason he leaves there when you leave from here I will call you with the new location." He said getting back on his knees between her legs.

"Why are you helping me? Do you hate Kalil or something?" Andra caught him off guard with her questions. He knew why he was helping her it was really simple. He chose pussy over loyalty.

"I don't hate him. In fact, I really have nothing against him. He's a great man and all but he ain't you. I helped you because the first time I laid eyes on you I fell in love with you. When you told me he was an ex who hurt you and you just wanted to get evidence that he was probably hurting his fiancé too, I wanted to help you. I had to." He looked up into Andra's eyes.

Andra smirked at the lie she told him to get him to help her. At the time she didn't think he would really believe her but once she put it on him one good time he was willing to do whatever she said.

"I almost feel bad about this." She said still smiling at him.

"Feel bad about what?" he asked a little confused.

"About this." With the quickness she brought a gun with a silencer attached to it from behind her back. He never got a chance to react before she placed it to the left side of his head and pulled the trigger. She watched as his brain matter came splashing out the right side of his head.

Pushing his upper body backwards she watched as he hit the floor still on his knees. She got up and changed into the extra clothes that she had brought into the room with her. She then wiped down any and everything that she may have touched and made a quick exit.

Chapter 33

Andra tried to make a mad dash to her car but she was not really paying attention to her surroundings and didn't know that she was being watched. She kept having a bad feeling that someone was following her but she was too afraid to turn around to be sure. Right when she reached her car she reached in her pocket for her keys and realized that they weren't there. Turning around she bumped face first into someone's chest.

"You dropped these, baby girl." A man said holding up her keys in his hands. She grabbed her keys and looked at him like she seen him somewhere before.

"Thank you. I didn't even realize I had dropped them at all." She said still staring at him. He gave her a small smile and she returned it.

"No problem, little mama. I saw you walk out and noticed you dropped your keys so instead of you walking around the parking lot looking for them I decided to help you out by bringing them to you." Andra thought he was a little cute, not as fine as Kalil; but cute nonetheless.

"That was very nice of you..." she hinted for him to tell her his name.

"Javon...the name is Javon and yours is?" he said still grinning at her.

"Andra...it was nice to meet you Javon but I really must be going now." She started unlocking her car door to get in.

"Okay cool well can I at least get your number

so that I can maybe take you out sometime?" All he was thinking about was taking her back to the room he was staying in and fucking the shit out of her with her legs in the air. His smile got even bigger at the thought.

Looking around the parking lot, Andra was tempted to shoot him for holding her up but it was something about him that intrigued her.

"Sure let me see your phone?" he handed her his phone and she quickly dialed her number and waited for it to ring. When it did, she hung up the phone and handed it back to him.

"Bye Javon." She said before getting in her car and pulling off getting far away from the murder scene she had just created. She reached in her pocket for the paper with Kalil's sister's address written on it.

"Now let me go see what is up with my future husband. Maybe they will lead me to the assholes that were dumb enough to shoot at my man." Andra smiled at the thought of Kalil being her husband one day. She just had one *huge* problem in her way.

"That bitch Chanae has to go now! I'm tired of waiting; my partner will just have to understand that there will be a slight change in plans."

Andra was completely clueless to the fact that her partner was across town thinking the same exact thing. Andra continued to drive and think of a way to rid her and Kalil's life of Chanae once and for all.

❤ ❤ ❤

Kalil and Chanae sat next to each other on Kalyah's couch in the living room while she explained to them everything she saw when they walked into their mother's house.

"It was a mess, Kalil and I took pictures with my phone too." Kalyah said handing him the phone.

"Mommy can I go home with you and daddy
246

since granny house messed up?" Khalid asked Chanae as he sat on her lap looking her in the face. Chanae looked over at Kalil because she honestly didn't know what to tell their son. She was so close to saying fuck the courts and taking their son and leaving town.

"Little man, soon you will be able to come home with me and mommy but right now we are just getting everything together for you." Kalil hated not having his son but he knew if they didn't at least somewhat do what the courts said they could lose him for good and he wasn't trying to risk that.

"I'm going to play with my Myra now." he said sadly jumping down off of Chanae's lap and running down the hall to Kamyra's room.

Chanae and Kalil looked at one another both heartbroken from seeing their little prince so hurt from not being able to go home with them. Kalil then tried to focus his attention back to the pictures in Kalyah's phone. He thought his eyes were playing some kind of trick on him when he saw a picture of the wall in the living room area.

"This can't be possible." He said more so to himself than anyone else.

"What is it? What can't be possible?" Kalyah asked what everyone else in the room was thinking.

"On the picture of the wall in the living it says, 'I'M BACK TO CLAIM WHAT'S MINE'." Kalil read out loud.

"What does that mean?" Chanae asked confused.

"It's a warning to me. He's letting it be known that my family is not untouchable and also that he is back in town. He's coming for what he thinks belongs to him or better yet WHO he thinks belongs to him."

Kalil stated locking eyes with Chanae.

"Who the hell is he?" Kalyah and her mother both shouted at the same time.

"Von…" Kalil rose up off the couch and started pacing back and forth.

"I thought he left town for good or something" Kalyah was now sitting down next to Chanae on the couch.

"If he was out tonight vandalizing mom's house then who the hell was shooting at me and Nassir tonight in front of the house?" Kalil mumbled to himself but again everyone in the room heard him.

"Shooting in front of the house?!" Kalyah and their mother yelled at the same time. Kalil cursed himself for speaking louder than he intended too. His mind had a million thoughts running through them all at once. The main one was who was shooting at them if

249

Altar'd

Von was across town at the same exact time.

Chapter 34

The Following Morning...

Javon had awoken to the sounds of gruesome screams coming from outside of his motel room door. He jumped up out of the bed and threw on his jeans he had on yesterday. Opening the door he stepped outside and looked to his left at the group of housekeepers standing in front of the room door he saw the chick come out of last night. Walking down to where they were he pushed them aside to see what they were screaming about. When he looked inside of the room and saw a man laid out on his knees on the floor with a gaping hole on the side of his temple he damn near throw up his dinner from last night.

He ran back to his room and locked the door behind him. He started pacing back and forth in front of the bed.

"Damn little mama is a fucking killer. I stood there talking to her and the whole time she had just blown a nigga head the fuck back." Javon stopped dead in his tracks when an idea popped in his head.

"I could use somebody like her to help me take care of these niggas so that I can get my girl back and go home to my daughter." Javon smiled at how he was going to get Andra to do exactly what he wanted her too.

"If she don't want to sit in jail, she'll do whatever I say whenever I say do it." He started patting himself down as if he was looking for something. He turned around and walked over to the nightstand picking up his phone off the charger. He scrolled through his call log and dialed the last call made from his phone.

"Hello?" she answered on the fourth ring.

"Hey, Andra. It's me Javon, I was wondering if you would like to join me for lunch today?" he asked hoping that she accepted his offer, if not he was going to have to find a different approach.

Andra looked down at the clothes she had on yesterday and then back up at the Marriot Hotel that she had been camped out at all night. She had followed Kalil and Chanae there after they left Kalyah's house. Unbeknownst, to her she had been spotted way before they even pulled off away from the curb.

"How about we do dinner instead? I know the perfect restaurant." She said looking up at the hotel again.

"Aight dinner it is. I'll call you back later to get the details of our dinner date." Javon stated grinning from ear to ear.

"Okay that sounds like a plan then."

"Aight then, I will talk to you later little mama." Andra cringed when he called her that. She hated to be called anything other than her given name.

"Okay bye." She quickly said then hung up the phone. Looking up at the hotel one last time, she sighed before pulling off.

"Maybe I can use Javon to help me get my man and when I get what I want I can just dispose of him the same way I did the rest." She laughed as she drove home to change clothes. She made a mental note to call her partner and have a little talk about the new plans she wanted to set in motion as soon as possible.

Kalil watched from the balcony at Chanae laid in the bed trying to get some sleep. He noticed that she was tossing and turning all night again. He had to wake her up a few times when it seemed as if she was having a nightmare. He still hadn't been to sleep himself. He picked up a napkin with the license plate number of the car that was tailing them last night. He had a feeling about who it might be but then again he could be wrong just like he was with Von being the one shooting at them.

"Are you going to have someone check that out to see who it is or are you going to just stare at it and hope the answer pops into your head?" Chanae asked while yawning and stretching in the bed.

"I already called up one of my boys down at the DMV to check it out. You were over there snoring so that could be why you didn't hear me at the time." He joked.

Chanae laughed and threw one of the pillows from the bed at him. When it hit him upside the head she laughed even harder.

"That is what you get you know I do not snore." Kalil walked over to the bed and leaned down in her face as if he was about to kiss her.

"You do snore baby and you even have a little drool right there on the side of your mouth." He laughed when she went to wipe her mouth and didn't feel anything.

"Just kidding."

"Ugh I can't stand your ass sometimes." Chanae tried to hit him with another pillow but this time he caught it.

"Now why are you lying to yourself? You know you love me just as much as I love you." Chanae smiled at him but not for long. Her smile quickly turned into a frown in a split second.

Kalil was about to ask her what was wrong when he noticed that she wasn't looking at him but instead behind him. He followed her eyesight to the T.V. where there was a picture of a man flashing on the screen. He grabbed the remote from the nightstand and turned the volume up on the television. He was just in time to catch the ending of the news broadcast.

"The murder of Jared Benison was taken place sometime around 10 o'clock last night authorities would like to believe. They believe he may have been here with a prostitute for sex and something went wrong. There are no leads on whom the suspect or suspects may be at this time so authorities would like for you to contact them if you have any information on this case..."

Kalil turned the T.V. off while he tried to make sense of who would kill Jared.

"Wait, isn't that your manager at the restaurant?" Chanae asked pointing to the blank screen on the T.V she was still in shock from the news.

"Yes." That was all he could reply with because he too was in shock at the news. Kalil began to mentally put pieces of the puzzle together. When he finally figured out the final piece, it just might be too late for either him or Chanae. Maybe even both of them.

Chapter 35

Listening to the phone ring he waited for someone to pick it up on the other end.

"Yeah man I just saw it so what you want to do?" Nassir said into the phone when he picked it up already knowing who it was from what he just saw on the news.

"Let's meet up at the restaurant. I know I have to talk to some of my staff about what happened." Kalil replied from the other end of the phone.

"Aight cool give me an hour and I will be there. Oh yeah I wanted to ask you wasn't he the one that set

259

up the cameras in your house when Chanae was getting

those threatening letters?"

"Yeah man that's why I'm over here trying to

make sense of this shit. I will get at you in an hour

though."

"I'm going with you." Nassir could hear Chanae

say in the background.

"Man, tell Chanae her pregnant ass needs to get

some rest my little cousin she carrying needs some

too." He said causing him and Kalil to laugh. He

listened to Kalil relay the message and Nassir could

hear her in the background telling him to shut the hell

up before she gets Za'kiya on him.

"Tell her she can't turn my princess on me. She

daddy's little rider. We stick together over here in the

Williams household."

Chanae grabbed the phone from Kalil before

speaking into it.

"Yeah that's until you tell her 'no' for the first time then you going to be in the same boat with the rest of us. I can't wait until she gets older and starts dating so I can laugh at your ass because I know you going to be stalking all the dances and dates." It was now her turn to laugh while she hung up the phone in his face before he could get another word in.

"I know her pregnant ass didn't just hang up on me?" Nassir said looking at the phone.

"Daddy is breakfast ready yet? Mommy said you probably in here burning the house down." Za'kiya laughed as she ran into the kitchen where Nassir was.

"Oh yeah mommy said that huh?" he said swooping her up in his arms.

"Yup that's what she said." She shook her head up and down.

"I will be sure to give her the burnt parts then."

"Mommy not going to eat it if you burn it daddy you have to turn it over so she doesn't see the burnt side." Za'kiya burst into laughter at her own comment.

"You couldn't wait to run in here and tell your daddy what I said huh little snitch." Zariya said coming into the kitchen holding NJ in her arms.

"Nassir, you better tell her snitches get stitches and end up in ditches." Qadir said laughing as him and Zahyir made their way into the kitchen.

"Naw my baby ain't no snitch she supposed to tell me when people talking shit. Don't you two got school today?" he asked sitting Za'kiya down in a chair at the table.

"Nope it wasn't any school today." Zahyir said taking a seat at the table.

"So what you two have planned to do today

then?" Nassir sat the food down on the table and took a seat at the head of the table.

"I'm going to just chill here I don't feel like doing nothing today." Qadir responded.

"What about you Zah?" Zariya asked putting NJ down in his swing before taking her seat at the other end of the table.

"I was going to see what my sister and pops is up to today. I feel like I haven't spent much time with them especially Chanae with everything she been dealing with."

"I think that's a great idea. I have to meet up with Kalil in a little while you should call your sister up then so she won't be alone."

"What you and Kalil got planned? Don't think you slick, we still haven't talked about what happened last night over there." Zariya said giving him the *'nigga don't play'* look.

"Chill out, we have to talk about some things." He said looking at Zariya giving her the *'you don't run shit'* look.

While they took turns giving each other the stare down, Zahyir left out the kitchen to give his sister a call. He had some things of his own he wanted to get her advice on.

❤ ❤ ❤

"Hey little brother." Chanae greeted Zahyir getting into the car.

"Why do you have to say the little part all the time? You do know I am almost a grown ass man right?" he said pulling off into traffic.

Chanae looked over at him and bust out laughing at his comment.

"Boy please; you're eighteen but that sure as hell don't make you no man. Stop it, you making my

264

stomach hurt."

"Yeah whatever biscuit head girl. How you feeling today and how is my niece or nephew doing in there?" he reached over and rubbed her baby bump. She was now starting to really show, it was as if she had gotten bigger overnight. Her clothes were starting to feel smaller as they days went by.

She pushed his hand off of her belly and started rubbing it herself.

"Honestly Zah, I am not doing so well. I miss my son, I miss Kalil, and I just miss us as a family. We're supposed to be preparing for our wedding right now but yet we are damn near at our breaking point. It's like I love him but every time we turn around there is someone trying to come in between us. I'm just really tired of having to fight for something that is already mine." Zahyir didn't say anything at the moment; he just let her get everything off of her chest. They pulled up to Sweetie Pies and got out the car.

Once they were seated at the table, Zahyir looked over at his sister. Just a few years ago he didn't even know he had any siblings. He and Chanae had become real close over the years and he hated to see her going through all of this on her own.

"Why are you just staring at me like that? I sounded crazy in the car huh?" she said taking a bite out of her dinner roll.

"No I don't think you crazy at all. I can't imagine what you going through sis. Let me ask you something though?"

"What's up?"

"In the car you said that you miss Kalil. Don't you two stay together – what you mean you miss him?" Chanae took a sip of her drink before responding. She was a little embarrassed that she let herself slip up and tell how she was really feeling inside.

"Yes we still stay together but lately Kalil is barely home during the day. It's like we started growing apart after Khalid got taken from us. We forgot about the love that was there way before we created him and the one I am carrying now." Chanae started staring off into space as she thought about how and where they started and where their relationship was now.

"I figured you and Kalil was going through something because he had been kicking it at our house with Nassir a lot lately. I just didn't know it was this serious though." Zahyir was now second guessing talking to her about what he had been dealing with lately since she was obviously dealing with her own issues.

"Hold up Kalil been at your house all this

time?" Chanae was confused. She felt bad that she'd been accusing him of cheating but they still haven't figured out where the panties and note came from.

"Yeah, where you think he has been?"

Chanae didn't answer she was too stuck on who could have written the mystery letter that threatened to tear her family apart.

"Sis you okay?"

"Yeah I'm fine…" she finally replied focusing back on her brother. "Now enough about me, let's get to why you really called me up." She smiled at him letting him know she saw right through his excuse about he missed spending time with her.

Zahyir returned her smile.

"So I can't just want to spend time with my big sister?"

"Spill it Zahyir Williams." Chanae said picking

her fork up.

"Kamira might be pregnant." Chanae dropped her fork and looked as if she was about have a heart attack. If it wasn't one thing it was always another.

Chapter 36

Zahyir had been sitting at the table stone faced listening to Chanae chew him a new one. He didn't even think she took time to take a breather - she was too busy ranting and raving about him using protection.

"Boy, I know you hear me! Don't just sit over there like you couldn't care less about what I am saying to you!" Chanae leaned back in her seat waiting for him to respond.

"I was just waiting until you were done talking that's all. You seem like you had a lot to say I didn't want to interrupt." He said with sarcasm dripping from every word.

Chanae grabbed her purse and stood to her feet.

"Let's go."

"What? We haven't even finished eating yet." The look she gave him made him hop up out his chair as if it was on fire. When they made it to the car and got in, Zahyir started the car but didn't pull off.

"Where are we going back to the hotel where I picked you up at?

"No we're going to go pick up Kamira and head over to the hospital. She's going to get a *real* pregnancy test done by a doctor. Let's hope for the both of you that this is a false pregnancy. Neither of you are ready for the responsibility of taking care of a child." She gave him a worried look. If the test came back positive she knew her brother and Kamira would have some important decisions to make.

Zahyir looked at her and knew everything she was saying was true. He didn't respond to what she said he just pulled off and headed to the highway. *"Kamira is going to kill me for this."* He thought to himself. She didn't want them to tell anyone yet but he had to talk to someone and his sister was the one person he knew wouldn't judge them.

Thirty minutes later, they were in Jennings pulling up in front of Kamira's house. Zahyir turned the car off and sat there causing Chanae to look over at him like he lost his mind or something.

"So you going to go and get her or would you like me to knock on the door? You know I have no problem walking up those steps and saying, *'Hey, is Kamira home? I would like to take her to get a pregnancy test done. You know how these kids are these days; they act like they don't know what the hell protection is when they fucking… "*

"Okay I am getting out the car! Just stop talking about it!" Zahyir shouted interrupting her in the middle of her rant. He slammed the door getting out the car signaling to Chanae that he had an attitude but she couldn't care less.

She lowered the window so that he could hear her. "Oh no, trust I am just getting started little brother. Just go get her so we can go and get this over with Mr. No Protection!" Chanae yelled out the window. Zahyir could have died when he saw the people walking down the street look over at him.

"I should have kept this to my damn self." He mumbled.

"Did you say something?" she yelled out to him. He looked back at her then went to knock on the door.

A few moments later someone came to the door that made Zahyir wish he had of called before coming over.

"Hey Zahyir I haven't seen you in a while. Still looking good I see." She flirted but he frowned.

"Where is Kamira? I need to talk to her right quick." He said looking behind her trying hard to avoid looking directly at her.

"Why you have to be so rude every time we see each other? I mean we are really going to be seeing a lot more of one another now that you got my girl pregnant. I am going to be here every step of the way to support her so you should try to be nicer." The look on Zahyir's face when she said those words were priceless. He didn't know if he was more pissed off at Kamira for telling her about the pregnancy or the fact that Symone thought she was coming anywhere near a child of his.

"Are you Kamira's sister?" a voice said from behind Zahyir. Turning around, he saw the voice belonged to Chanae.

"No I'm her friend Symone. Remember I was at your baby shower awhile back.." She said with all smiles. Her smile faded with the next words out of Chanae's mouth.

"Oh well you're a non-factor at the moment where is Kamira?" Chanae had no time to play around with these kids all day; she had business of her own to take care of.

"Hey Chanae, Zahyir what are you doing here?" Kamira said walking up behind Symone with Tara behind her. She looked at Zahyir and could tell he was pissed about something.

"Hey Kamira are your parents at home?" Chanae asked seeing that this task was going to be more difficult than she thought.

"No they're not here. We were just hanging out since there was no school today." She replied still waiting for Zahyir to say something. She was confused but she hoped Symone didn't tell him that she told her and Tara about the pregnancy.

"So it's just you three here?" she replied with a head nod.

"Okay well here's the deal because I don't have all day: I need you to come take a ride with me and Zahyir. You can have your friends wait here for you or they could wait at home until you get back. This won't take long at all maybe an hour at the most." Chanae said not really trying to come off rude but she was on borrowed time.

"We need to go to the hospital to get a proper test done by a doctor so that we can be 100% positive that you are pregnant. There isn't any sense in beating around the bush sis she already told them. I'll be in the car when you decide what you going to do." Zahyir walked off the porch and got in the car slamming the door behind him.

Kamira stood there shocked and hurt. She looked from the car to Symone who was now mouthing the words 'I'm sorry'. "I'll grab my coat. You guys should head home and I will call you when I get back." Kamira said turning around to get her things while Tara and Symone did the same. Since they stayed down the street from one another it was nothing for them to walk home from her house.

Kamira got into the car with Chanae and Zahyir and immediately began staring out the window trying to make sense of it all. She didn't understand how he could be mad at her for telling her friends when he told his sister. Now she was the one pissed off. *"How dare he be mad at me for doing the same shit he did? I can't wait until we are alone I am going to curse his ass out!"* she thought to herself giving him the death stare from the back seat.

❤ ❤ ❤

Zahyir and Kamira had been waiting in the room for the doctor to come back in for ten minutes now. They hadn't spoken two words to one another the whole time they had been there. Kamira decided to be the first one to break the silence between them.

"Where did Chanae go?" she asked sitting on top of the bed swinging her feet back and forth due to being nervous.

"She said she had to take care of something else while she was here." He replied dryly causing Kamira to roll her eyes and jump off of the bed. She stood over him with her arms folded.

278

"What?" he asked looking up from his phone.

"What is your problem Zahyir that's what?"

"You really want to do this right now?" he asked with a raised eyebrow.

"Stop answering my questions with a question. Yes I want to do this right now. I'm tired of you giving me the cold shoulder like I did something to your ass."

"Okay cool." He stood up in front of her. Now she had to look up to look in his eyes but she didn't care she just wanted to know what the hell was wrong with him.

"Let me see; where I should start at, oh I know how about you running your mouth and telling Tara and Symone *our* business." Kamira took a step back and stared at him for a minute before responding.

"You mean the same business that you ran and told your sister? How are you getting mad at me for the

279

same thing you did Zahyir?"

"I told my sister because I needed advice on what to do about this. I needed someone I could trust that wouldn't judge me or you. Can you honestly stand here and say the same about them? Tara, yeah I can see you telling her but Symone though? Hell no!" Zahyir shouted more than he intended too.

"I don't know what it is you have against Symone but she is one of my best friends of course I am going to tell her stuff like this. I was scared and needed someone to talk to about this too. You can't be mad at me for that Zahyir." Kamira was on the verge of breaking down. She always felt she had to choose between being with him and being friends with Symone.

"You right. I understand that this can't be easy for you but Symone ain't who you think she is. You so stuck on defending her all the time, how about you just sit back and pay attention to her. You may be a friend to her but she damn sure ain't a friend to you." Before any more words could be exchanged there was a knock at the door. Chanae walked into the room followed by the doctor. She looked from Kamira's to Zahyir's face and could tell that she and the doctor had walked in on a heated discussion between the two. She decided she would worry about that later seeing as she just got some crazy news of her own today. Now she just prayed that the two teenagers wouldn't be walking out of the doctors' office preparing to become new parents also.

Chapter 37

The car ride back to Kamira's house was a quiet one. No one spoke a word since they had all left the doctor's office. Kamira was in the back twirling her thumbs around in deep thought about the situation she was in. Zahyir tried to focus all his attention on the road but every so often he would look back at Kamira. His head was swimming with what if questions. Chanae on the other hand looked back and forth between Zahyir and Kamira. She couldn't take the silence any longer.

"I'm glad the test came back negative. You two really aren't ready to be parents. I would have thought that you two would be a little more excited that you wouldn't become teen parents though. Being parents is a great responsibility because you are responsible for another life. You have to be able to put their needs and wants before your own. They are the reason you will fight to see another day just to watch them grow up. Teens becoming parents is happening every day and most if not all of those kids are not ready for that kind of responsibility they can barely take care of themselves. Adding a child to the mix will not only be hard for the teens but also their parents who most likely will be forced to help take care of the baby. All I ask is that you two be careful. There is so much going around these days pregnancy isn't the only thing you would have to worry about if you are not careful and using protection." She continued to look between the two and when no one spoke she kept talking.

"Do you two understand what I am saying?"

"Yes." they both responded.

Chanae turned around in her seat a little where she could get a better view of Kamira who was seated behind the driver's seat.

"Kamira are you okay? I know I haven't asked that while we were there or hell before we even got to the clinic but I am definitely here if you need someone to talk too. Even if that talk is bashing a certain person we know." She said nodding over towards Zahyir which caused Kamira to smile for the first time since she got in the car with them.

"What? I'm your brother you would talk about me behind my back?" Zahyir asked trying to sound hurt.

"No of course not." She replied. He shook his head in approval.

"Good sis."

"You're my brother silly I would never talk behind your back. I will say it all in your face that way you know it's real." Chanae and Kamira bust out laughing while Zahyir cut his eyes at her.

"Whatever punk!"

"You know I love you baby boy!" she reached over and grabbed his face kissing him on the cheek.

"Ewww, you going to make me crash." Zahyir complained.

"Boy please we were at a red light." Chanae looked back at Kamira and winked. She knew they were going through something in their relationship so she tried lightening up the mood in the car. Plus it helped get her mind off of her own situation.

They pulled up at Kamira's house in no time. She said bye to Chanae before getting out and walking to her front door. Zahyir got out the car and ran up the steps before she opened the front door.

He put his hands in his pants pockets and looked at her.

"I know you mad at me about what I said and even though I meant it I want to say sorry for yelling at you. I know you probably confused about the whole thing but all I ask is that you pay close attention to the people around you. They all not there to wish you well, some might just be there waiting for your downfall." He looked back at the car before turning back around to face her. "Anyway, I know we still need to talk about this whole situation so I will call you when I get home alright?"

"Okay." was all that she could say because she honestly didn't know what to think about any of the things he just said to her.

"I love you, Kamira." He said kissing her on the cheek and turning to head back to the car.

"I love you too, Zahyir." He turned and smiled at her. He waited until she got all the way in the house and shut the door before getting in the car and pulling off. He knew that he and Kamira were going to have to work hard to repair their relationship after this but he was willing to put in the work. Zahyir was glad he had his sister here to help him through all this. He was a little curious about what she had to take care of at the hospital. He noticed that when she came back to the room she looked a little worried and confused about something.

Looking over at her in the passenger seat with her head leaned against the window he could tell she was tired. This pregnancy was a lot different from when she was pregnant with Khalid. To him, she was a lot less bitchy. He laughed at that thought which caused her to look over at him funny.

"Thanks for everything sis I really appreciate you being here for me and Kamira. Even with the bitchy mood swings you been having all day." He laughed when Chanae reached over and punched him in the arm.

"Don't make me hurt you little punk! Anyway you know I got you and I am always a phone call away." She smiled at him as they enjoyed the rest of the ride back to the hotel in silence. Chanae was thinking of how she was going to break the news to Kalil about what the doctor had told her as she willed herself not to break down and cry.

❧ ❧ ❧

As soon as Chanae made it back to the hotel she showered and ordered herself some room service since she never got to finish her food at the restaurant. Once she finished in the shower she threw on a fluffy white bathrobe and sat in the middle of the bed waiting for her food. She thought about calling Kalil again but she changed her mind. When she called him earlier at the hospital he didn't answer his phone but instead sent her a text stating that he would call her when he finished doing whatever it is he was doing.

At first she had an attitude because she felt the same amount of time it took him to text her, he could have answered the phone and told her that. That was until she remembered that he was probably just talking to his employees at the restaurant. Plus she remembered that Nassir was with him so she knew he was safe.

While flipping through channels she heard someone from the other side of the door trying to get into the room. Before she could move from the bed she saw Kalil walk in with a frustrated look plastered on his face. She released the breath she didn't know she was even holding in.

"I didn't expect to see you back so soon. I thought you and Zahyir would be out doing some sister and brother bonding type of thing." Kalil said walking over to the mini bar that was in the left corner of the suite.

Fixing himself a drink he threw it back before fixing another one and taking a seat on the chaise next to the bed. Chanae stared at him debating with herself on whether to throw the remote that sat in her hand at his head or not.

"You know if you would have answered your phone when I called I would have told you that I was coming back to the hotel early." She said bouncing the remote in her hand.

"You could have told me that in a text. If it

wasn't life or death I don't see what you fussing about."
He said taking the drink in his hand to the head. He
didn't mean to come off rude but the stress from what
he recently found out had him on edge.

Kalil caught her movement just in time and he
moved over to the side a little but before he had time to
completely get out of the way he was hit in the shoulder
with the remote control that was lying in Chanae's
hands just moments earlier.

"What the hell is your problem!" he yelled
standing to his feet.

"You are my damn problem! What the hell do I
look like to you huh? I am not one of your little side
bitches. Don't send me to voicemail then send me no
damn text!" Chanae was now off the bed and making
her way over to Kalil.

"First of all, I don't have any side bitches! If I

am not at home with you, I'm at Nassir and Zariya's house trying to figure this shit out! Therefore I don't have time to cheat on you. Oh and you really want to know what you look like to me?" He said bringing the tone in his voice down a little.

Chanae was now standing in his face with her hands on her wide hips. They were so close her pregnant belly was poking him at the bottom of his stomach. "What?" she asked waiting for him to say something slick so she could slap the hell out of him.

"You look like a damn crazy ass pregnant woman who just lost her damn mind. That's what you look like now I advise yo..." Chanae reached up to slap him but was too slow he grabbed her by her hand just in time before it reached his face.

"You know better than that. Pregnant or not, don't put your hands on me because you damn sure wouldn't want me putting mines on you." He said as they stared each other down for a good minute or two. The next thing Kalil knew Chanae burst into tears falling into his arms. As he held her in his arms it hit him and he realized that she wasn't mad at him, she was mad at their situation. They were fighting all the time and every day they were calling the case workers that are on their son's case trying to see what is going on with getting their child back. Not to mention they had another baby on the way and they were still trying to figure out who is out to get Chanae and why Mo would try kidnapping Za'kiya and not their son Khalid. For Chanae nothing was adding up and she was beyond frustrated. All she wanted to do was get her family back together, marry the man she loved, and live happily ever after. Now with everything going on around her she was having second thoughts about the life she dreamed of sharing with Kalil.

Pulling out of his arms she looked up at him with a tear stained face. He gently wiped the tears from her eyes and kissed her on the forehead. "The baby." She whispered softly.

Kalil took his hand and rubbed it in circular motions on her belly. "What about the baby?" he looked her deeply in the eyes waiting for her to continue what she was trying to say.

"When I went to the clinic with Zahyir and Kamira…"

He stopped rubbing her belly for a second but kept his hand on her stomach.

"What did Zahyir and Kamira need to go to the clinic for? Please don't tell me she pregnant?" he asked with a questionable look on his face.

"No she is not pregnant."

"Okay so what are you talking about then?"

"While I was there I went and got my check up and…" Chanae didn't know how to tell him what the doctor had told her today.

"And what?" Kalil asked anxiously waiting for her to just come out and say what she beating around the bush to say.

"Do twins run in your family?" she asked with a slight smile.

"My father was a twin but what does that have to do with anything…wait are you saying what I think you saying?" he looked at her to confirm what he is thinking.

Chanae's smile grew bigger as she placed her hand on top of Kalil's and started rubbing her stomach. "We are going to be parents of a set of twins." She looked him in the eyes with her face still holding a smile. She was nervous because he hadn't said another word; he just continued to stare at her while rubbing her stomach. Two minutes passed before Kalil grinned at Chanae. He grabbed her face with both of his hands and kissed her as if his life depended on it. It took a minute before Chanae started to kiss him back.

Kalil released her lips and looked down at her.

"I knew the first day I laid eyes on you that you would become the woman that I'm meant to share forever with. That you would be the woman to give me something to live for other than myself. I swear with every fiber of my being to the blood that flows through my veins I love you and our kids. I would never do anything that would risk me losing you. Any of you." With those words Kalil was letting Chanae know that he would rather die than lose her. He would never risk that by cheating with someone who wasn't worth the loss of his family.

Chanae stood on the tip of her toes until her lips met his again. She kissed him as a way to show him that she believed him. "We can get through this as long as we are together." Kalil smiled and whispered over and over 'I love you' into her ear. They spent the rest of the day together in bed making love and in between their love sessions they made some plans to get their family back together as one.

Chapter 38

Javon pulled up to the restaurant that Andra suggested they have dinner at. He shook his head when he realized that the restaurant she recommended was none other than Kalil's. He was about to get out of the car when he saw Andra walking over towards him. He slid his hand under his shirt where he nine rested when she knocked on his window.

Lowering the window down a little, Andra looked at him funny but quickly brushed his awkwardness off.

"There is a slight change in plans tonight; the restaurant is closed down for whatever reason. No one is saying why though. So where would you like to go instead?" she asked leaning on the car with one hand giving him a great view of her cleavage.

"How about we try that new seafood restaurant they just built out in St. Charles?" Javon suggested looking at her breast through the crack in the window.

"Okay that's fine. I know where that's at I will meet you there." she said looking at him suspiciously as she backed away from his car and made her way back to her own car.

"This is going to be easier than I thought." She said getting into her car and pulling out of the lot.

"Ha, this shit is going to be a walk in the park." Javon stated to himself pulling off behind her.

It took them fifteen minutes to get to the seafood

restaurant. Once they were inside and seated Andra

tried her hand with Javon but he soon nipped all that in

the bud with the few words that left his lips.

"I know what you did last night at the motel."

He said picking his water up and taking a sip.

"What are you talking about?" she asked trying

to play dumb.

"Come on, let's not sit here playing dumb. I

know what you did to ole boy at the motel. You know

the one you left in that room stinking on the floor with

his brains blown out?" He sat his water back down on

the table making eye contact with Andra.

"So what do you want? Are you going to go to

the police and tell them that I am the murderer?" Andra

played calm but inside she was steaming mad. She

wished like hell she would have brought her gun into

the restaurant with her.

"I thought about doing that but then I realized that maybe we can help each other out." He grinned at her making Andra want to knock that grin clean off his face.

"What could we possibly help each other with?"

"You could help me get something or better yet *someone* who belongs to me back." Andra leaned forward in her seat he really had her full attention now.

"You want me to help you kidnap someone; is that what you're asking of me?"

"That is exactly what I am asking of you." Javon sat back in his seat and waited for her reaction to his request or more so demand. She really didn't have a choice in his book.

"What do I get out of all of this? How will you be helping me?"

"Let's just say if you help me do this no one will

ever know that you are the one who killed the man in the motel room last night and spend the rest of your pretty little life in prison. The same man who was a manager at the restaurant you picked for us to go to tonight for dinner." Javon chuckled at her face when she noticed he done his homework.

"Let me guess you chose to go there to see what the people are saying about his murder huh?" she wanted so bad to reach across the table and knock that smirk off his face. He had her in a hard spot and at this time there wasn't much she could do about it but go along with whatever he had planned.

"How do I know when I am done helping you that you won't run to the police and turn me in?" Andra mind was running rapidly with a million thoughts per minute. She was thinking of a way to get out of the predicament she now found herself in.

"You don't know so at this time you will just have to trust me." Javon stood to his feet to leave. Andra looked up at him with a confused look written all over her face.

"Where are you going? We have to finish discussing this."

"Naw we done talking for now I will call you with the details of whom, what, and when. Make sure you answer your phone when I call little mama." With that he made his way out of the restaurant with a satisfied look on his face.

❧ ❧ ❧

Andra found herself back to sitting outside of the Marriot Hotel that she had last seen Kalil and Chanae walk into the night before. She was so lost in her own thoughts she didn't realize her phone had been ringing until it rang for the third time. Reaching over to grab her purse from the passenger seat she made sure to keep her eyes on the entrance of the hotel just in case she saw Kalil leave out.

Digging through her purse she grabbed her phone but before she could answer it the caller hung up. Right when she was about to search the call log to see who it was calling her phone rang again.

"Hello?" she answered on the first ring without even looking at the screen.

"I have been calling you for days. What the hell have you been doing?" Andra could tell from the voice that it was her silent partner and from the tone they took, she knew that they were not happy about her dodging their phone calls.

"I'm sorry about that I had to take care of some things. I *did* want to talk to you about the new plan I have." Andra said biting on her finger nails.

"New plan? What new plan? We didn't say

anything about changing nothing. You are starting to get a little out of hand with things. There is no way I am going to let you or anybody else ruin what I have planned for that bitch who is part of the reason my friend is no longer here. I advise you to calm your ass down on what you out here doing before they start putting shit together and the arrow starts pointing at you." Andra took the phone from her ear and looked at it strangely. She found herself getting pissed at what was just said. She was the one doing all the grunt work, putting her life and freedom on the line. Yes, she enjoyed doing most of it but that did not give anyone the right to downplay her role in this whole thing.

"Okay, let's get something straight because I honestly think you may be a little confused about things. I am the one who's doing all the work while you sit back with your feet up and do nothing but dish out orders. Enough is enough I am tired of people thinking because they have something over me that they can use me and have me doing their bidding. So like I said there is a new plan and you can either get with it or stay the hell out of my way. So what is it going to be?" Andra had finally stood up to the person on the other end for the first time ever and she felt great about doing so.

"Hahahahaha!" the caller laughed out loud uncontrollably into the phone Andra had to move it away from her ear a few inches.

Andra was getting heated by the minute feeling as if she was being taken for a joke. "What is so damn funny?"

"You are what's so damn funny! Now it is my turn to give you a reminder because apparently you must have forgotten who the hell I am!" the caller shouted into the phone.

"I know exactly who you are!" Andra resorted.

"Naw you don't so let's refresh your memory. Do you remember when we first met back in high school?"

She scrunched her face up at the phone.

"I am not about to go down memory lane with you. I am in the middle of taking care of something." She looked up at the entrance of the hotel to be sure she didn't miss Kalil or Chanae walking out of it.

"Hahaha I think it is too funny and cute how you think that you have a choice. You forgot who was there when all those kids used to pick on you and whoop your ass damn near every day at school. How about when I had to stand up for you because you were too afraid to do it yourself? Oh let's not forget when you had that little crush on that one guy who was captain of the basketball team. Um what was his name…?"

"Shut up."

"Ooh was it John…Joe…Jason…I know it started with a J." she continued totally ignoring Andra.

"SHUT UP!" Andra shouted gripping the phone with her right hand and the steering wheel with her left. She was holding on to them so tight her knuckles were starting to turn white.

"Oh I know it was Jacob…Jacob Banks. Remember when you told him that you had the biggest crush on him and would love for him to go to homecoming with you?" the laughter on the phone was making Andra's blood boil.

"Shut the hell up you don't know what you are talking about!"

"Oh I don't? So that wasn't you who not only killed him but his on again off again girlfriend all because he rejected you? Haha his exact words were 'I would..."

"I would never date a sloppy looking girl like you who probably never heard of a comb and a brush." Andra interjected while staring off into space as silent tears ran freely down her face. Growing up Andra was a little too big for her 5'2 height. Her mother never taught her how to be a girl because she always wanted a boy so her hair was a little on the nappy side. That was until she met Sandra and her best friend, Leah. They showed Andra how to show her feminine side and gave her a full makeover. That gave Andra the courage to approach the guy she had had the biggest crush on since middle school.

When he rejected her something inside her snapped. That day she hid in the backseat of his car and waited for him. He didn't go straight home that day instead he picked up his girlfriend and drove to the riverfront where people always went to hang out. Once she saw him and his girlfriend in the front seat making out after getting back together again, she emerged from the backseat and attacked them with a huge butcher knife she stole from the cooking class at school earlier that day. Andra stabbed them both over thirty five times each. Stabbing the girlfriend deeper and rougher than the guy as if it was her fault the guy rejected her. Sandra was the person she ran to and told what she had done. She helped her get rid of the clothes and murder weapon and promised never to tell a soul.

She was brought back out of her thoughts with the sound of the caller's voice in her ear.

"Andra are you over there having a flashback of what you did that day?" the teasing in their voice made Andra snap out of the trance she didn't know she was in.

"Sandra what do you want from me?" Andra asked feeling defeated.

"I want you to help me get justice for the murder of my best friend. You owe this to Leah. She was always nice to you and helped you stand up for yourself. I want Chanae dead and her fiancé too." Sandra spat with every word laced with hatred.

Andra's head snapped up at the mention of Kalil. She was all for getting rid of Chanae but Kalil was hers for the taking. There was no way she is going to kill him. That was however if he didn't reject her love for him then his blood would be on her hands as well. *"No it won't come to that though. With Chanae out the way he will fall in love with me and forget all about that bitch."* She mumbled to herself while shaking her head roughly.

"Andra, did you hear what I said?" Sandra shouted into the phone capturing her attention once again.

"Why do you want Kalil dead?"

"Because I believe if she wasn't trying to get him to love her then she would still be alive. Plus I have a feeling that he has something to do with her murder. We still haven't found her baby yet you know. There is no trace of her; it's as if she never existed. I know he played a part in her murder I just know it and Chanae has to die for what she did to my friend while she was pregnant."

Andra sat back in her seat and listened to everything Sandra said. She couldn't help but compare what she was doing to what Leah had done or better yet tried to do. In her eyes it was different because she was going to succeed. In the end Kalil will be her man and

312

Chanae will be long gone. Anybody who doesn't like it or try to get in her way will come face to face with their creator.

She was now on a new mission of making sure she came off on top in the end. She preferred that be on top of Kalil on a private island somewhere where they couldn't be disturbed. What they both failed to realize though is that Chanae wouldn't be going out without a fight.

Chapter 39

The Following day....

Chanae awoke to the ringing of her cell phone. When she looked over to the side of the bed that Kalil was on she noticed that it was now empty. She reached for her phone on the nightstand and answered it without looking at the screen to see who was calling.

"Hello?" she answered in a sleepy voice.

"Hello, may I speak with Chanae Walker or Kalil Barber please?" the caller asked as soon as someone picked up the phone.

Chanae sat all the way up in bed and looked at the phone. She didn't know the number so she placed it back to her ear before speaking again.

"This is Chanae Walker; who may I ask is calling?"

"Oh hi Miss Walker this is one of the social workers on your case about your son Khalid Barber. We tried to get in contact with Mr. Kalil Barber but we couldn't get an answer." Chanae's ears perked up at the mention of her son's name. She heard a vibrating sound and looked over to where the noise was coming from. When she moved the covers back she saw Kalil's cell phone. *"He must have forgotten it when he left to go wherever the hell he went."* She thought to herself.

"Hello Miss Walker are you still there?" the social worker asked.

"Oh yes I'm sorry I'm here so you were calling

about my son's case?"

"Yes I would love to meet somewhere with you and Mr. Barber to discuss everything about the case and what we have discovered. Would this afternoon say around one be too soon for you?"

"No that would be just fine." Chanae said nervous yet excited about what they would have to discuss with her and Kalil.

"Great we can meet at Forest Park over by the playground area."

"Okay good we will be there thank you." They ended the call. Chanae got out of bed walking into the bathroom to take care of her morning duties.

When she got out of the shower she saw Kalil sitting at the table in deep thought.

"I ordered us some room service; you need to eat something." He said now looking Chanae over from head to toe with lust in his eyes.

"Where did you go this morning? I woke up and you were gone I didn't even feel or hear you leave out." She walked over to her suitcase and found something comfortable to wear. She settled for a beige sweater, some blue jeans, and a pair of brown cowgirl boots.

"I had to take care of some business concerning the restaurant and the manager. The police wanted to ask me a few questions so I went to take care of that. Where are you about to go?" he asked once he realized that she was now fully clothed.

"Is everything okay with the restaurant, what did the police want with you?" She asked completely ignoring his question.

"They wanted to know if I noticed anything strange or different about him lately. Your ass ain't slick either Chanae I know you heard me ask you where you going?"

"Well actually it's where WE are going. I got a call from the social worker about Khalid they want to meet with us today at one to discuss everything about the case." Kalil smiled at the thought of possibly getting their son back. He thought for sure he was going to have to pull a kidnapping move to get him back.

"Okay then you need to get over here and put something in your stomach so that we can be heading out soon its already going on twelve."

"I'm not really hungry though; I'm excited that we could be getting our baby back." She said sitting on his lap and kissing him on the cheek.

"You still need to eat though Chanae didn't you just tell me that we having twins?"

"Yes but bae…"

"But bae nothing feed my queen and my babies

woman." Chanae rolled her eyes while picking up the fork and knife to cut her French toast with. Kalil smiled as he watched her eat he couldn't wait to have his family back together. Right after he takes care of some unfinished business he planned on taking his family on vacation and marrying his queen.

By twelve thirty, Kalil and Chanae were at the park sitting on the bench feeding the ducks while anxiously waiting for the social worker to arrive. Kalil had called his mother to see if they had called her about Khalid and she told him no. That threw him off a little because if they were thinking about giving them their son back he was sure they had to call the guardian of the child to discuss things with them. He didn't tell Chanae because he didn't want her to get upset but he knew if the social worker came talking some bullshit that is exactly what is going to happen.

At exactly one o'clock they both turned when they heard leaves crackling under someone's feet. They noticed the male social worker that was at the hospital walking towards them. Chanae looked around to see if she spotted the woman social worker but she didn't.

"How are you today Miss Walker and Mr. Barber?" he asked once he was standing directly in front of them. Chanae and Kalil stood to their feet and shook the man's hand.

"We would be doing a lot better if we had our son with us." Kalil said taking his seat back on the bench next to Chanae. The man sat on the other side of her.

"Well that is what we are here to discuss. Now after a thorough investigation we find that the drug that was found in you and your son's system had to be placed there through the water you ingested."

"What? How did it get into the water?" Chanae asked. She been drinking that brand of water for years and never had something like this happen.

"We don't know but what we do know is when we went through your trash and the things we collected from your house the water is the only place we found the drug. The caps were still on some of the water that contained traces of the drug in it." He explained to them.

"Okay so what does any of this means to us getting our son back then?" Chanae asked scared that he may say something about them never getting Khalid back. If that is the case then she and Kalil are going to go head and move forward with their plan they discussed last night.

"Well since the other connection to the drug you have is that it was also in your system as well we really can't hold you accountable for this. We have already contacted the water company and got their brand removed off shelves." He stood to his feet preparing to leave. Kalil was about to say something until the man spoke again.

"Mr. Barber and Miss Walker I am happy to give you the great news that you will be receiving back full custody of your son Khalid Barber." A smile spread across Kalil and Chanae's at the news. They smiles got bigger when the heard the sound of their son's voice calling out to them.

"Mommy, daddy!" he shouted running full speed towards them. When Kalil looked up he saw his mother standing next to the female social worker smiling at her son.

Khalid ran up to his parents and Kalil picked him up burying him in a tight hug. Chanae joined them and Kalil wrapped his arms around his family as tight as he could as if they were going to fly away.

"Daddy you and mommy are squeezing me!" they all laughed at him. Chanae kissed him all over his face she was so excited to have her baby back.

From afar in a parked dark blue fusion someone was watching their little family moment. That person was also unaware that someone was watching them as well. Their time on earth was now being spent on borrowed time. They started their car up and pulled off into traffic as the driver parked three cars down from them did the same.

"When will these muthafuckas learn that you can't destroy what plans God has already set in motion?" the driver following the blue Fusion asked out loud.

"They will never learn; the hatred they have in their heart is too overpowering. If they did by chance just so happen to realize it by then it would already be too late. The hatred would have already cost them their lives." The passenger said sitting back in the seat and watching the person in the Fusion maneuver their way through the busy streets of St. Louis.

Chapter 40

Three weeks later…

Kalil and Chanae were getting back into the groove of things after getting settled in their new home. They moved closer to Nassir and Zariya out in Chesterfield. Their new five bedroom home took them a whole week to fully decorate and furnish. Chanae loved every minute of it though. Today they were getting ready for their first house warming with family and friends. Khalid was running around the house in his Spiderman boxers with a cape on screaming he was a super hero. Chanae looked at him run back and forth while shaking her head.

"Kalil can you please get your son and make him put his clothes on; our guests will be here in thirty minutes! This fool running around damn near naked." She shouted up the steps.

"Baby, what you think the red shirt or the black one?" Kalil appeared at the top of the staircase holding up the two shirts on the side of him with nothing but his boxers and a pair of socks on.

"You can't be serious right now?" she narrowed her eyebrows.

"What, you don't like neither one?" he asked her waving the shirts up and down.

"I'm Superman!" Khalid yelled coming to a halt next to his father with his chest sticking out and his fist balled up at his sides.

"This don't make no damn sense; I swear I am

about to be on the next season of Snapped if you two don't put some damn clothes on." She snapped walking away from the stairs still talking about how she was going to stage her alibi.

"What's wrong with her?" Kalil asked his little prince. Khalid shrugged his shoulders and ran down the hall to his room screaming at the top of his lungs that he could fly.

Fifteen minutes later, Kalil came down the stairs with himself and Khalid fully dressed. They walked into the kitchen to see what Chanae was up to.

Chanae had her back to the door with her attention on stove. She felt a pair of strong arms wrap around her waist. Kalil kissed her up and down her neck as he rubbed her huge stomach.

"Bae, stop I am trying to check the collard greens." She giggled when she felt his tongue touch her earlobe.

"It smells good in here baby but try not to stand on your feet too long you know how they swell up on you when you on them too long." He said smacking her on the ass and walking over to the table where Khalid was trying to reach for a cookie.

"Well if they swell up then you can give me one of your famous foot massages." She said with a smile.

"What I get in return?" he asked with a sneaky smirk.

"Why you have to receive something in return? How come you can't just give me what I want with no questions asked and go on about your business?" Chanae turned around and chuckled. She knew he was about to say some slick shit in response to her comment.

"You know damn well ain't nothing in this

world fre…" his statement was interrupted by the doorbell. Khalid took off running to the door with Kalil not to far behind.

"We will finish this conversation later." He said walking out the kitchen.

"Yeah whatever just go get the door and put a smile on your face while you at it Mr. Butler." She joked.

Kalil looked through the peep hole and saw that it was Nassir and his family at the door. Opening it up for them, Za'kiya came running inside.

"Za'kiya, stop running I am not going to tell you no more." Zariya said walking in giving Kalil a hug.

"Uncle Kalil, did my Te-Te Chanae have my baby yet?" she asked walking into the kitchen like she lived there.

"No she's still pregnant and I didn't know you

were the father." he laughed giving Nassir a pound.

"I'm not the father but it's still my baby though how many times we have to go through this?" she walked into the kitchen leaving him standing there cracking up at her statement.

"Man, what are you two going to do with her?"

"You mean what he going to do with her? I ain't doing nothing; *he* created that monster. I just can't wait until she gets to the age where she wants a boyfriend." Zariya laughed her way into the kitchen because she could hear Nassir and Kalil talking shit about Za'kiya not dating until she was sixty-years old.

"Hey girl it smells good in here. What you in here cooking up for tonight?" Zariya asked walking over to where Chanae was placing some dinner rolls into the oven.

"Let's see, I made some fried chicken, baked

bbq chicken, homemade macaroni and cheese, collard greens, candied yams, cornbread, and some potato salad for you folks who eat that mess. Oh and dinner rolls for people who may not want cornbread."

"Well damn you been throwing down up in here I see."

"Well you know I try my best." Chanae joked as she took a seat at the table her feet were killing her but she didn't want Kalil to know that. Not yet anyway she still needed to finish setting the table before the rest of the guest arrived.

Zariya saw the look of pain written all over Chanae's face she knew it all too well.

"Sis, what else needs to be done? I can do it for you so that you can rest your feet some. I know you've probably been on them since you woke up this morning."

"I have to set the table in the dining room but I can do it sis that's not a problem."

"Nope. I will set the table and have these men out there place the food out. You did enough work by making this huge meal, it is the least we can do." Zariya insisted. She started making her way to the dining room but stopped when Chanae kept fussing about doing it.

"Zar, really I can do it. You are my guest; you shouldn't have to lift a finger." She rose up out of her seat.

"Chanae, if you don't sit back down I will tell Kalil you in here trying to work on sore feet and stressing his baby out." She threatened.

Chanae knew by the look in her eyes she was dead serious so she sat back down and rolled her eyes.

"Don't be threatening me heifer I will get my niecey pooh on you." She joked sticking her tongue out at her. Right when she said that Za'kiya came walking over to her.

"Te-Te Chanae is mommy messing with you?" she asked like she was going to do something about it if she was.

"Naw baby she know I will get you on her if she messed with me."

"Oh okay well let me know because I will put her in time out with no dessert." She said before walking back out the kitchen to go play with her juicy cheeks. Chanae couldn't stop from laughing she knew if Zariya heard that she would kick her little butt.

Twenty minutes later, all their guests had finally arrived at Kalil and Chanae's house. They guys were in Kalil's man cave down in the basement while all the women were in the kitchen sipping on some wine. Chanae stood to her feet and walked to the basement door to announce to the guys that it was time to come and eat.

"Hey bae it's time to eat so can you all come on we hungry up here." She knew they were up to something because they'd been down there on hush mode. Chanae knew that usually when they are all together they were making all kinds of noises.

Zahyir and Qadir were the first to come up the stairs. They both kissed her on her cheeks before walking towards the dining room. Nassir, Charles, Demarco, Kalyah's boo Markel, and Kalil all followed suit. Chanae laughed at them all kissing her on the cheeks and then she remembered that she was wearing a 'Kiss the Chef' apron.

Everyone gathered around the table and joined hands as Kalil blessed the food.

"Amen." They all said in unison when he

finished.

"Before we get started, Chanae and I have some news we would like to share with you all." Chanae stood up next to Kalil holding his hands.

"You got a new puppy!" Za'kiya shouted causing everybody to laugh.

"No we don't have a puppy, baby girl." Kalil chuckled.

"Aw maaaaan nobody wants to get a puppy for me to play with." She said with mean look gracing her face.

"Nassir, please get your little monster." Zariya whispered nudging him with elbow. Demarco had a busy NJ in his arms who was trying to reach for the silverware that was sitting in front of him.

Nassir gave Za'kiya one look of disapproval and she straightened her face up in a hot second.

"Okay as we were saying we have some good news to share. We're having twins!" Chanae was cheesing hard she was excited to see her babies faces.

"Oh my god I'm going to be Te-Te of a set of twins!" Kalyah jumped up and ran up to Chanae hugging her.

Everyone congratulated them on their great news. "Do you know what you are having?" Zariya asked.

"Yes we are having girls." Chanae took her seat as Kalil did the same.

"Oh snap I can't wait to hit the mall up for some new baby shopping for my niecey poohs!"

"Wait so I get two babies?" Za'kiya said smiling while rubbing her hands together.

"No Kiya you only get one and I get one." Kamyra corrected her.

"Oh okay, so me and Kamyra both get a baby. When are you going to give us our babies Te-Te Chanae?" Zariya smacked her hands over her eyes. She looked up at Chanae and Kalil staring at her like they was waiting on her to break the news to the girls.

"Oh don't look over here at me that is all Nassir's doing right there." she said pointing to her husband who was looking at Za'kiya like she had lost her mind. All he kept hearing was her saying 'her baby' and he shook his head as if he was trying to get the thought out of his head.

Kalil started cracking up at the faces his boy was making.

"We have some more news; we finally set a date for the wedding. Next month, we will be getting married on the island of Tahiti. The wedding planner is setting everything up." Everyone was excited for them.

Altar'd

Everyone except the person across town pacing the hotel floor talking to himself...

Chapter 41

The pacing back and forth he was doing was starting to wear thin on the cheap motel carpet. It was now showing the dent of his foot trail. His face was fixated in a mean mug as he continued to stare at the picture that was sent to his phone over thirty minutes ago.

"I can't believe this bitch went and got pregnant by this nigga again!" he shouted at the top of his lungs as he looked at the picture of Chanae with her belly looking as if it is the same size as a bowling ball.

"How the fuck am I going to explain that shit to my daughter? She is going to need *all* of her attention when we go back home." Von said thinking out loud. His mind at this point was so far gone that he should be evaluated on his sanity. He needed a mother for his little girl and he wanted Chanae to be that for her. He didn't think nor did he care that he would be taking another child's mother away from them by doing so.

Von pulled a picture of his daughter out of his back pocket. He stared at the picture rubbing it with his thumb before kissing it.

"Daddy is going to bring your mommy home to you if that is the last thing I do. I promise you that princess." He kissed the picture again before returning it back to his back pocket.

He stopped pacing the floor and started bouncing his head up and down as if he was agreeing with himself about something. "Yup I'm going to give my little girl the mother she deserves even if that means I have to kill to do so." Grabbing his jacket off the chair he made his way out the door.

Von got into his rental car throwing his cell phone on the passenger seat but before he could start the ignition his phone made a buzzing noise signaling that he had an incoming phone call. Picking the phone up he looked at the name on the screen right before answering it.

"You must really think this is some kind of a game and I am playing with you, huh?" He said into the phone.

"I take it that you didn't like the picture of your ex bitch living happily ever after without your no good ass huh!" the person laughed in Von's ear so loud he had to hold the phone away from his ear a few inches.

He looked at the phone again to be sure that he was correct on who he assumed was on the phone. He saw that the number was right but the voice didn't match his assumptions.

"Who the hell is this?" he asked getting irritated with the caller.

"Oh you don't remember me huh Javon aka Von the man whore. You know I never could figure out why my friend even messed around with you. Then again, liquor always did fuck up her better judgment."

"I'm about to hang up on your ass because I see you don't know who the fuck you talking to." He was just about to end the call when the caller's next words stopped him dead in his tracks.

"Oh but aren't you the least bit curious on how I am answering Andra's phone? What about: how I know about what you have planned? Oooh, or here is a good question: don't you want to know why or how I sent you the picture of Chanae?"

"Who the fuck is this playing on my phone?" He asked again this time even louder than before.

"Von, I never could understand at first why women would flock to you. Then I realized that you a weak nigga and they must feel that they can use you for money."

"Bitch I will ki…"

"Aww, did I upset you Vonnie? Leah told me the night that you two fucked that you was a part of the flash team." The caller laughed so hard they were bent over holding their stomach.

Von could feel his temperature starting to rise. Gripping the phone tight in his left hand, he spoke through clenched teeth.

"Let me let you in on something you stupid

bitch; I am *not* to be fucked with right now. Okay so you know what my plans are so the fuck what! What are you going to do; go tell them niggas I'm coming for them and MY bitch? Too late, I already sent that message weeks ago. No one and I do mean NO ONE is going to stop me from getting what the fuck belongs to me!" He finally snapped. Spit dripped from his mouth with every word he spoke. The caller was smiling from ear to ear at the hatred in his voice when speaking of Kalil and Chanae.

"Are you done?" when Von didn't say anything the caller continued. "First off, I didn't say anything about telling them what you were up to. I called to send you a warning." Von took the phone from his ear and looked at it as if something foul was coming out of it.

"What the fuck you mean a warning? Look Sandra I'm telling you now, do not find yourself in the same residential spot as your girl Leah." When she didn't respond he grinned and kept talking.

"Oh you thought I wouldn't figure out who you were huh? That bitch Leah only had one friend, come on ma I did my research on her ass right before I killed her." Sandra eyes grew bigger at the confession Von just gave. All this time she thought Kalil and Chanae were the ones responsible for her best friend's death.

"You son of a bitch! You're the one who killed my friend? You killed Leah…" Sandra stopped abruptly when something came to mind.

"Where is her baby? Did you kill an innocent child too?" this phone call did a whole 360 on Sandra. She was calling to let Von know that if he got in her way of getting rid of Chanae and Kalil then he would be meeting the Creator right along with them. Now she was confused on what her next move should be. Leah may have been after them but they were not the ones who killed her. Von was the culprit. Her mind was swarming with thoughts on how to handle the situation.

"Sandra, is you still there?" he chuckled a little knowing that he got to her.

"Now to answer your last question why would I kill my own daughter? She looks just like me so I knew she was mines. Leah had to go because she was more focused on money and trying to get a nigga that didn't want shit to do with her whether than taking care of her baby."

"You are the father of her baby?" out of everything he just said to her that was the only thing she focused her attention on. Leah never really told her who exactly the father of her child was. Sandra was now thinking of a way to kill Von and get Leah's daughter back. She knew now that she was going to have to play nice in order for it all to work out in her favor. She would deal with Andra's unloyal ass later. Sandra knew by now she was wondering what happened to her cell phone.

"Yes that is my little girl. The best thing Leah's hoe ass ever did in her entire life was give birth to my little princess. Now I know you must be thinking why would I be telling you all this without assuming you wouldn't go straight to the police?"

"That may have crossed my mind. Why are you telling me all of this knowing Leah was one of the only people I had left on this earth and you took her away? So what makes you think I won't go right over to the precinct and tell them everything you just told me?" It was now Sandra's turn to pace back and forth.

"Well I would probably say it is due to the fact that I have evidence that you were a willing participant in a shooting a while back. A case that is still open at the moment." He sat back in his seat in smiled. He was not expecting this call at all. True enough at first he was pissed about someone coming at him the way she did but once he realized who it was he knew that he would be able to use her to do his bidding.

"What the hell are you talking about?" she stopped pacing and prayed like hell Von was just bluffing trying to get underneath her skin.

"Come on now, Sandra do not play dumb with me. You know exactly what the hell I am talking about. The shooting that took place outside of Chanae and Kalil's house. Does any of that ring any bells for you?"

"What kind of evidence you THINK you have on me?" She began to bite her fingernails, a nasty habit she picked up from Leah a long time ago.

"Oh I don't think I KNOW! The gun you used

in the shooting was placed at Andra's house where you thought no one would ever look."

"My fingerprints are wiped clean from the weapon so you have nothing."

"Yeah at first I thought so too until I saw the footage of you in a blue Fusion shooting at them. I bet you didn't know your girl Andra had cameras watching their house huh? I later saw you in that same car when I had followed you from the park. I think you know what day that was so I don't have to remind you. See what you fail to realize Sandra is that I am not that same Von that left a few years ago. Trust me when I say I came back prepared to get what is mines. You can either get with it or get buried right alongside of your friend I'm sure she is lonely in hell and would love the company." Von hung up the phone in her face pulling off of the motel lot.

"I'm going to have to kill her I can't afford for some bitter bitch to fuck up my plans. When I am done with her I will handle Andra too. Damn you can never find some good help around this muthafucka. Damn shame." He said out loud to himself as he headed to his next destination to send someone off to the burning depths of hell.

Chapter 42

Sandra sat on the floor of the Canfield apartment she had been staying in for a few months now. Her head was buried in her hands as she tried to think of a way to get herself out of the jam that she now found herself in. When Leah was murdered and her daughter came up missing the only thing that consumed her mind was revenge. She wanted someone to pay for taking the only family she had left away. She was all alone and hurting. All she wanted was for someone to suffer the same way she was suffering every day. Sandra had thought for sure that Chanae and Kalil were the reason her friend was dead. In some sick twisted way even though she knew now that Von was the murderer she still wanted Chanae and Kalil dead. Leah was on a mission to take Chanae's spot in Kalil's life and become his woman. Sandra could remember as if it was yesterday the whole restaurant scene when they first saw Kalil and Chanae together.

"What the hell you mean we ain't allowed in here? I know the damn owner and he wouldn't say no shit like that, so what I want you to do is take your ass back there and get him!!!" Leah had yelled to the manager of the restaurant.

"Ma'am I'm going to have to ask you again to leave that was the order given," the manager said. *Sandra could see that he was trying so hard to stay professional and not curse them out for being so rude to him and disturbing the whole restaurant.*

"And I muthafuckin' said we ain't going no damn where until we speak to the owner!" Leah yelled again as she folded her arms across her chest with Sandra doing the same.

"Look ma'am if you don't leave I'll be forced to call the police and...."

Interrupting the manager, Sandra remembered being the first to spot them sitting in the back so she yelled out, "wait girl ain't that him over there sitting with some bitch?"

"Where?"

"Over there girl." she said pointing to the table that Kalil and Chanae was sitting at. They both looked and started heading towards the table with the manager following behind them trying to stop them.

"Ma'am you can't just walk in here and over to a customer's table," the manager said continuing to *follow behind them trying to get them to stop but it was too late they made it to the table.*

"So this is why you can't answer any of my damn phone calls or texts huh?" Leah had said tapping her foot waiting for him to answer her.

"Kalil, who are they?" Chanae asked nodding her head towards Leah and Sandra.

"Some chick I used to mess with that is a non factor now and I'm guessing her friend." he answered with an annoyed look written all over his face.

"Okay cool no worries then." she said as she leaned back in her chair as if she was waiting to see what happened next. Sandra had figured that Chanae wanted to see how Kalil would handle himself in that type of situation.

"Why haven't you been answering any of my calls or texts Kalil?" Leah asked him again like he

didn't hear her the first time.

"Let's get something straight real quick Leah, you ain't my woman, you never was and never will be and you knew this before we started fucking. We haven't spoken in two months and the last time we did talk I told you that what we were doing was over, seeing as the dude that was at your crib that night was doing you just fine." her eyes got big as saucers at that statement, she didn't know Kalil overheard her on the phone she had dialed his number by accident while fucking some guy she met earlier that day.

"So don't come up here in my restaurant starting up some bullshit." giving her a look that said fuck with me if you want too. But Leah didn't take the hint and kept on running off at the mouth. She couldn't let Sandra see her punk out seeing as she did all that talking in the car on the way to the restaurant.

# Altar'd

"I wasn't your woman but you stayed in my bed.

So you sitting here with whoever the hell she is really

don't mean shit to me because sooner or later you'll be

right back in MY bed!" Leah shouted drawing an even

bigger audience.

Laughing right there in her face Chanae looked

at Kalil with a look that said the shows over get rid of

this thirsty bitch.

"What the hell you laughing at; he will be

dumping you soon and in my bed by night fall." she

boasted which only made Chanae laugh even harder

while thinking the thirst is definitely real. But all that

did was piss Leah off even more than she already was

from seeing Kalil with another chick in the first place.

"Don't hold your breath for it Leah, now I'm

only going to say this once so listen up and hear me

clearly. There will never be anything between us; all we

were to each other was a fuck which is what we BOTH agreed on. So you and your friend have 10 seconds to get the hell out of my restaurant and don't ever disrespect my woman like that again. This is your first and last warning Leah and you know I don't give those out easily" If looks could kill Leah and Sandra would have been dead on the spot.

Sandra remembered her and Leah making a quick dash out of his place of business. After that she knew her friend was obsessed with Kalil because she really started plotting on how she was going to get him. Leah thought her plan was foolproof.

Something clicked in Sandra's head about what Kalil had said that day at the restaurant. He had broken her friend's heart with his words. *"I'm still going to get rid of them both that would be a great gift to my girl may she rest in peace."* Sandra got up off of the floor and walked towards the front door picking up her keys off the table as she walked by.

"I need to get that bitch Andra too with her snake ass." She opened the door to leave but before she could do so a fist came smashing into her face breaking her nose and splitting her lip on impact.

"I told you that I followed you before so why would you think that I wouldn't know where you live and come pay you a little visit?" Von said slamming the door behind him and locking it. When he turned around to face Sandra she was trying to get up off of the floor while holding her nose to stop the blood from leaking. He walked right up to her and kicked her in the stomach, sending her flying over on her back in pain.

"Ahhhhhhhhhhhhhhhhhhh! Please I will do anything you want." She pleaded with him.

"It's too late for that I don't need you for

anything. Don't worry though; your girl Andra will be joining you soon. You both can each get a spot right next to that bitch Leah." He walked up to her and stomped her in the face causing more blood to spill out on to her living room floor.

"Please, I'm begging you not to kill me." Sandra cried out.

"I find that funny as hell seeing as you was planning on killing other people. Where was this feeling sorry shit then? Hell you probably was planning on killing me too. Good thing I beat you to the punch though." With that Von pulled out his gun and shot her twice. Once in the center of her forehead and once in the chest. He then wiped down the doorknob and anything else he may have touched before making a quick exit.

❤ ❤ ❤

Andra was searching her house from top to bottom looking for her cell phone. She had been looking for it for two hours now and still came up empty handed. She searched her car and everything and still nothing at all.

"Where the hell did I put that phone? This is crazy, I know I had it earlier today so where could it be." She said talking to herself. She plopped down on the couch racking her brain trying to figure out where she had her phone last.

"Of course! I left it in Sandra's car. It has to be there because I know I had it before we met up to discuss business. I remember getting upset and making a quick exit." Andra remembered. She picked up her purse and walked out the door.

Fifteen minutes later she was pulling up on Sandra's street. She noticed that her apartment building was swarmed with police and an ambulance vehicle. She saw the EMTs bringing someone out on a stretcher. She saw that they were in a body bag letting her know that a murder had taken place in the apartment building.

Andra grabbed her purse and started looking for her phone to call Sandra to see if she knew what was happening in her building. She smacked herself on the forehead when she realized that is why she was there in the first place to get her cell phone. She parked the car on the side street and got out. Walking over to where a crowd of people were standing around she asked them if they knew what happened.

"Hey, what happened over here?" she asked to a group of men.

"That chick from 23B got murdered." One guy said.

"Yeah somebody beat the fuck out of her and

then shot her ass twice. My sister said she saw her lying on her living room floor dead. She was on her way out and saw the door wide open. Somebody did her ass in." another guy said. Andra was barely listening as she walked swiftly back to her car and got in.

"I can't believe someone killed Sandra." She said to herself as she pulled off. She knew they were talking about Sandra being the woman who was murdered because 23B was her apartment.

"Who could have killed her?" she asked thinking to herself while driving back home to think of what she will do now. She still had to figure out a way to get her cell phone from out of Sandra's car if she didn't take it out already. Andra didn't want anything to come back pointing in her direction but she knew her cell phone held some incriminating evidence that would not only get her locked away but Von too.

"I have to get to that phone before someone else does." She pulled up to her house but sat in the car for a moment in a daze. The fact that Sandra was dead was now hitting her hard. Yes she thought of killing her herself but she never thought for a second Sandra had other enemies out there somewhere. She had a feeling this would become another unsolved murder just like Leah's case.

Chapter 43

A few days later Chanae, Zariya, and Kalyah were at the St. Louis Mills Mall getting pictures taken of the kids. Kalil and Nassir had to take care of some business but they had insisted that Zahyir and Qadir go with them to the mall. At first the boys protested having to be walking around a busy mall on a Saturday with a group of females and some kids. Once Kalil stressed to them how important it was for them to go and watch over them the boys agreed as if they really had a choice in the matter anyway.

"You two could at least pretend that you want to

be here." Zariya said to Qadir and Zahyir while pushing NJ in the stroller.

"Come on Zar you know we love ya'll but walking around the mall with whiny kids is not something we pictured doing on this Saturday afternoon." Qadir complained.

Za'kiya stopped dead in her tracks when she heard him say that.

"Hold up, who you calling whiny? I'm not whiny and neither is my Kamyra and my juicy cheeks. Now my NJ he cries a little but that is because he is a baby. You better stop talking about us before I tell my Tara on you." She said rolling her eyes at him before turning back around and continued walking.

Qadir looked at Zariya who was trying hard to suppress the laughter she so badly wanted to release.

"Short stuff ain't nobody scare of Tara you

better go on somewhere with that." He said waving her off.

"I bet if Tara was here right now you would be saying something totally different." Kalyah laughed at him.

"Hey guys I think Nassir said that the studio was this way." Chanae said pointing towards the south of the mall.

"See we lost; why couldn't you just wait until Nassir was able to do the pictures himself?" Zahyir scoffed.

"Because Nassir is busy and we need to get the Fall pictures out the way because soon it will be time for the winter pictures." She said pushing him in the direction she just pointed to.

"Yeah plus Nassir wanted to see if the new guy he just hired can handle himself under pressure. We all know that Chanae is picky as hell and will drive someone crazy." Zariya half joked.

"Oh whatever heifer!" Right when they found the studio Chanae's phone rang. By the ring tone she had set, she could tell that it was Kalil calling her. She smiled answering the phone as she had flashbacks of last night events. Kalil had literally fucked her to sleep and she couldn't wait to get home so that her man can give her a repeat of last night.

"Hello."

"Aw man, now when we get here you want to get on the phone and have a conversation?" she cut her eyes at her brother letting him know he was two seconds away from getting slapped. He rolled his eyes and walked into the photo studio with everyone else but Zariya following behind him. She was bent over fixing NJ in the stroller.

"Hey baby, who was that Zahyir?" Kalil asked.

"Yes him and Qadir been complaining since we got here."

"That's because they had plans today but this is more important so those two niggas will be alright. Now how you feeling today sexy?" He could hear Chanae giggle on the phone and knew that she was on the other end blushing.

"I'm doing good thanks to you, sexy chocolate." Zariya looked over at Chanae and bust out laughing. Chanae gave her the middle finger which only resulted in her laughing even more.

"You know I have a surprise for you today?" he told her knowing that would make her even happier.

"Oooh what is it?"

"If I told you then it wouldn't be a surprise now would it nosey woman."

"Bae just tell me and I will act surprised for you later."

"Nope I'm not telling you anything. Oh yeah, before I forget while you at the mall why don't you pick up some new teddies from Victoria Secret though?" He grinned.

"Nope I'm not picking up anything since you don't want to tell me what the surprise is you got for me."

"Fine then. I prefer you butt ass naked anyway lil sexy." Chanae laughed at his silliness.

"I'm not messing with you Mr. Barber."

"Well see about that sexy lady especially since you said that a few weeks before we get married there will be no sex. You know I have to get all mines in now then." Kalil turned when he heard someone unlocking the door.

"Baby, let me call you back I have to do something. Make sure you take a few pictures too while you there. I love you."

"Okay I love you too bae." They ended the call with Zariya staring at Chanae with a wide grin on her face.

"What?" Chanae asked cheesing hard.

"If your ass was not already pregnant, Kalil would damn sure have your ass knocked up in no time."

"Girl that's my baby I love him so much I just hate the hoes that try to come in between what we have. These hoes are doing the most to get Kalil's attention." She sighed.

"They just see all the love and affection he's giving you that is all." Zariya said as they started walking into the studio.

"They need to find their own damn man to give

them all the love and affection they looking for because Kalil Taheir Makai Barber is all mines." Chanae said with a serious face.

"I am so glad Nassir only had one crazy ex bitch and the rest of these bitches know to back the fuck up off my man because Mrs. Williams don't have a problem putting her foot up in a hoe's ass about mines. Girl, you better start setting these tricks straight when it comes to your man."

"Oh don't worry they keep testing me and I'm going to tuck those hoes into their early graves real nicely. Since they keep asking to meet the man of their dreams I'm going to help their ass out. I know Jesus is just waiting for them at the pearly gates and that is the man of everyone woman's dreams." Zariya smiled at Chanae when she saw how violent she sounded when it came to Kalil.

"That's right sis; protect what belongs to you because if you don't it will only give the next chick room to slide right into your spot."

"That is not going to happen." Chanae said with confidence.

The ladies joined everyone else so that they can get started with the photo shoot. Unbeknownst to them across town Kalil was preparing to help rid their lives of one of the main problem sources that they been having for months now.

Andra walked through her door exhausted. She had just put in 12 hours straight at work and her feet were killing her. Even though she was tired, she still had plans of going to camp out at Kalil's sister house to see if she could maybe spot him or Chanae there. After they had moved she lost all contact with them and since she killed her tech guy she didn't have an inside man anymore. She walked through the living room and turned the light on but kept walking towards the kitchen. Once inside the kitchen she turned that light on as well and opened the refrigerator to grab a bottle of water. Closing the door she damn near jumped out of her skin at the figure sitting at her kitchen table.

"Ahhhhhhhh!" she screamed at the top of her lungs and ran towards the front door but was stopped by the barrel of a gun staring her dead in the face. Her eyes got big as the realization set in at who the person was that was holding the gun.

"You can stop all that damn screaming; ain't this what you always wanted?" he said as he lowered the gun down to his waist.

"Wha-what are you doing in my house?" she asked with a shaky voice.

"Man, we need to get this shit over with our family is waiting for us." Nassir said coming from behind her. He was the figure she saw standing in her kitchen before she took off running.

"Damn Andra I thought for sure you would be happy to see me. I mean you had cameras watching my house. You poisoned and tried to kill my fiancé and my son." Kalil never ever laid his hands on a female but after all the shit she caused his family he was going to enjoy killing her ass.

"I didn't mean for your son to get hurt I swear to you. Please don't hurt me." She cried. She wish like hell she would have kept her gun on her.

"Bitch please you can save those fake ass tears because no one in here gives a fuck about you crying. You didn't give a fuck when you sent that bitch to kidnap and kill my daughter did you?" Nassir walked up to her and smacked the shit out of her with the gun he held in his hand. Andra's mouth started to bleed instantly as a few of her teeth went flying across the floor.

Kalil anger matched his boy's but like Nassir said they had to get back to their families. He wanted to make her suffer for what she did. Snatching her up off of the floor by her throat he drug her over to a chair that Nassir had brought in from the kitchen.

"We're going to see how much pain you handle sense you love dishing it out. We figured out everything thanks to your little secret lover. I bet you didn't know he kept records and evidence of everything he did for you and everything that you did." Kalil laughed at her shock expression she shown at the mention of her secret lover. He tied her up to the chair and placed a dirty sock that he got from a bum off of the street into her mouth before taping it shut.

Nassir stood off to the side glaring at her. All he could think about is her set his baby girl up to be kidnapped and murdered. He walked over to the side of the couch and picked something up from off of the floor.

Andra noticed his sudden movements and started to panic. "Mhmmm!" she mumbled under the tape but all they heard was muffled sounds.

Nassir walked up to her with a cigar cutter in his hand. He grabbed Andra's hand and started chopping each of her fingers off one by one.

"I bet your ass is now thinking twice about ever sending someone to touch my daughter you crazy sadistic bitch." He spat as he watched the blood squirt from her numbs where fingers used to be.

It was now Kalil's turn; he walked up to Andra

holding a spoon in one hand and a lighter in the other. He placed the lighter under the spoon and begun to heat it up. Once he felt it was hot enough without warning Kalil dug the spoon into Andra's eye scooping out her left eyeball.

"Mmmhhhummm ahhhhmmm." She cried out.

"I bet all those times you watched me and my family inside our home you now wish that you hadn't." Nassir looked at his watch and tapped it looking over at Kalil. Kalil shook his head in understanding.

He untied Andra and watched as she fell to the floor as blood continued to spray out everywhere. Kalil knew that they had to hurry up they had their family waiting for them at the photo shoot. They both nodded at the unheard agreement.

Nassir and Kalil both raised their weapons up at the same time. Andra started to plead for her life as she now sat on her knees in a praying stance.

"May you rest in hell with the rest of the muthafuckas who tried to fuck up what was already ordained by God himself." Nassir professed before he and Kalil emptied their entire clips into Andra's body.

They stared at her for a second before cleaning and wiping down everything they touched even though they were wearing gloves the entire time. *"You can never be too sure."* Is what Kalil said before they entered the house.

"Good thing we got silencers on these guns because I'm pretty sure we would have woke the whole neighborhood with that noise." Nassir said as he and Kalil hopped in their ride and drove forty-five minutes out before stopping at a bridge and tossing their weapons in the water. They drove a little farther before ditching the car they were in and getting into Kalil's

Range Rover.

"Now all I need to do is find out where that nigga Von is hiding out. I been looking everywhere for this nigga and he keep slipping away. I bet his as is right in plain sight and I just keep missing him." Kalil was angry that he had been looking high and low for Von and continued to come up empty handed.

"Man trust we will find his ass. There is no way out of all the shit he put you and the family through that we going to let him get away this time." Nassir assured his boy.

"You right man we just have to think like a weak ass snake like him and I know we will find him." They drove out to Nassir house to change before driving out to the mall where everybody was at still taking pictures. Even Qadir and Zahyir started to enjoy themselves and took a few pictures with the kids.

Chapter 44

"Wake up baby, it's time to go." He said kissing her neck then her lips.

A moan escaped Chanae's lips.

"Baby I'm too tired to get up; you wore me out last night." She chuckled but still hadn't opened her eyes.

"Baby, you have to get up or we're going to be late. I thought you would be excited to become my wife. All those nights we used to talk about our wedding day and having a house full of babies running around." He laughed kissing her on the neck again before standing to his feet.

Chanae smiled and opened hers eyes. She got up out the bed and walked over to him and kissed him on his bare back since he was turned with his back to her.

"Baby I love you so much. I am grateful for the day you came into my life." She expressed while kissing his shoulder.

"If you love me so much then why did you turn around and fuck the next nigga huh?" Chanae frowned at his question as she took a few steps back. She noticed the sudden change in his voice. She stood in shock as she finally paid close attention to his body frame. She turned to run out of the bedroom but he had anticipated her running away and he grabbed her by the arm yanking her towards him.

"Bitch I loved and gave you anything you

wanted; why would you go and fuck that nigga? My enemy at that huh you fucking slut." He slapped her across the face and watched as her face begun to swell up.

"Then you turn around and go get knocked up by this nigga again. Now you say that you want to marry him." Chanae watched the color of Von's eyes change.

"I don't love you I love Kalil he is the man that I am meant to be with not you!" Chanae shouted at him. Von punched her in the face. She fell to the floor trying to protect her stomach. He noticed what she was trying to do and kicked her with all the strength he had in him dead in the stomach.

Chanae cried out in pain as blood started to gush from between her legs. It was pouring out at rapid speed she couldn't stop it.

"You already had his baby once you really think I'm about to let you walk down the aisle to this nigga and give birth to more of his kids? Naw I'll rather see you buried six feet than living happily ever after with my enemy!" he shouted at her at he continued to punch and kick her all over her body.

Chanae shot straight up in the bed breathing hard with sweat seeping from her pores. Kalil was just getting out of the shower and making his way into the room when he noticed that she looked to be hyperventilating. He rushed over to her and began cradling her in his arms.

"Baby what's wrong; did you have a bad dream again or something?"

Chanae didn't say anything she just cried in his arms while he held her.

"Chanae baby I need you to tell me what's

wrong. How else am I supposed to help you if you don't tell me?" Chanae pulled herself away from Kalil a little looking up into his eyes.

"I'm starting to have the dreams again."

"The dreams with…"

"Von." She said finishing his sentence.

"Baby you don't have to worry about him he is not going to hurt you."

"How can you be so sure Kalil? He is still out there somewhere."

"He won't be for much longer Chanae. He's going to slip up and show his face and that is when he will pay for all the pain he has caused you and our family."

"I hope you're right bae."

"Look, we need some time away from all the drama and unnecessary bullshit. What do you say to us pushing the date of the wedding up some and taking that vacation time now?" he suggested.

"You want to get married sooner?"

"Yes. Plus baby I would love to be married before our princesses get here. So what do you say to becoming Mrs. Chanae Barber sooner rather than later?"

She smiled at him then kissed his juicy lips.

"I say okay let's do it bae!"

Kalil kissed her again. "I will set everything up and call everybody and let them know what the deal is."

"Okay great." Kalil got up to start making calls but Chanae pulled him back down towards him.

"Baby, I meant okay we should go ahead and push the date up but when I said let's do it I meant just that bae *'let's do it'*." Kalil laughed at her demand.

"You didn't get enough last night baby?" he

asked pulling the covers off of her revealing her naked body.

"If you want to push the date up you should be trying to get all that you can right now."

"Why is that sexy?" he said kissing her neck.

"Because I meant what I said when I said there will be no sex before the wedding. It was supposed to be weeks but since you pushed the date up we will have to go with days." Kalil stopped at her thighs and looked up at her.

"So you were serious about that?" he asked with a raised eyebrow.

"Yes I am." That was all Kalil needed to hear before he went diving tongue first into her sweet spot.

He listened to the different noises that escaped Chanae's mouth. As he went deeper and licked harder she tried to close her legs. He held each of her thighs with a good grip so that she couldn't move. He felt her body tense up and knew that her creamy nectar wasn't too far away. His licks became faster and harder sending her body into shock as she begun to pour down on to his tongue. Kalil lapped up every single drop not stopping until she stopped dripping.

Kalil then stood up and took off the basketball shorts and boxers he had on. He joined her back on the bed.

"Turn over and get on your knees for me baby." He demanded in a raspy yet sexy voice. Chanae did what she was told turning over and getting on her knees with her elbows resting on two pillows.

He positioned himself behind her entering her inch by inch until he was completely inside of her. He started off with slow strokes while holding on to her waist. She was so wet he was sliding in and out of her with ease.

"Oooh shit baby that's my spot!" she cried out in pure ecstasy. Kalil begun to pick up speed as his strokes started to become a little faster and harder. Chanae had tears coming down her face she was loving every second of their love making.

"Baby I'm about to cummmm..." Kalil could feel her warm cream coating his dick as he continue to stroke in and out of her for another fifteen minutes before he came deep inside of her.

Chanae was spent and now all she wanted to do was shower and try to go back to sleep but Kalil had other plans. He gently turned her over on her back and sliding right back inside her. They continued to make love for two more hours before he decided to let her get some rest. As soon as he busted with seemed like his tenth nut Chanae was already halfway passed out snoring lightly.

Kalil chuckled to himself as he cuddled beside her. *"Now that's how you make her ass tap out."* He thought to himself as he drifted off to sleep right along with her.

Chapter 45

It had been three hours since everyone got off the plane in Tahiti and retreated to their suites. Of course Chanae had one to herself as did Kalil. They both were nervous and excited about what was to go down three days from today. Khalid was in the suite with his father and he had just awoken from a nap. He now sat up in the bed watching his dad sleep. He smiled and giggled as he watched his dad's chest heave up and down while listening to him make funny noises from his mouth. He crawled over to where he was passed out on the bed and decided to play with his phone that was lying on his chest. Kalil had fallen asleep talking to Chanae on the phone. He was trying hard to get her to go back on her rule of no sex for a week before the wedding but no matter how hard he tried she wouldn't budge.

Khalid gently grabbed the phone and swiped his finger across the screen to unlock it to get to the main screen; something he watched his father do numerous times before. Once there he started pushing numbers until the phone started ringing. He put it to his ear and waited for someone to speak on the other end.

"What's up man? Don't tell me you over there in that room getting cold feet already?" the person who answered the phone joked.

Khalid frowned up his face and looked at his feet.

"My feet not cold I have socks on." He said

laughing.

The person on the phone took the phone from their ear and looked at it before returning it. "Khalid?"

"Yes uncle. I'm Khalid, where my Kiya at?" He crossed his feet and leaned back on the pillow holding the phone to his ear.

"Boy where is your daddy at?" Nassir asked.

"My daddy right here he tired so he had to take a nap. I think he got a grass machine in his mouth." Khalid looked over at Kalil and giggled again.

"A grass machine? You mean a lawn mower?" Nassir couldn't help but laugh.

"Who needs a lawn mower?" Zariya asked while NJ's changing diaper.

Nassir took the phone from his ear and looked over at her. "This Khalid, he said Kalil sleep and he think he has a lawn mower in his mouth." She looked at him funny and bust out laughing.

"He over there scaring my baby with his damn snoring. Tell that nigga wake his ass up it's almost time for dinner. He must really be loud if the baby said a damn lawn mower." Zariya and Nassir were laughing so hard he hasn't even noticed Khalid calling him.

"I'm sorry little man what's up?"

"I said where is my Kiya at?" he said as if he was tired of repeating himself. Nassir chuckled before responding.

"She in the room with your aunt Kalyah and Kamyra. Wake your daddy up I need to talk to him." He ordered.

"Okay." Khalid leaned forward and got on his knees next to Kalil. He leaned down in face to where they were face to face. He then took his free hand and started playing with Kalil eyelids trying to open them.

"Daddy wake up!" he screamed in his face holding his left eyelid open. Kalil's eyelids fluttered opened and he smiled at his son who smiled back at him.

"Unh daddy my uncle on the phone for you."

"Oh yeah? Did he call or was you playing on my phone again?" he leaned up on the bed with his back against the headboard pulling Khalid with him.

"I called my Kiya but she wasn't there." Kalil shook his head and started tickling him then reached for the phone that was still in his hand.

"What's up man?" he asked once the phone was to his ear.

"You finally woke your ass up and stopped sounding like a damn lawn mower huh?" Nassir couldn't help but take a jab at him on that note.

"Man I don't sound like no damn lawn mower."

"Yes you do daddy you got one in your mouth." Khalid stated sounding dead serious and he was. Kalil looked at him and cracked up putting him in a gently head lock.

"Shut up little punk you snore too."

"No I don't daddy you do mommy say you need to go to doctor to get that checked out." He laughed and started jumping on the bed. When Kalil put his ear back to the phone he could hear Nassir cracking up on the other end.

"What the hell you over there laughing at?" he chuckled.

"You nigga! For real though you and my nephew ready; it's almost time to head down to the restaurant?"

"We about to shower right quick and then we will be there."

"Aight see you then and don't be over there getting cold feet either because you know Chanae will hunt your ass down and fuck you up!" Nassir laughed as he ended the call.

Kalil looked at the phone and shook his head. "You ready to shower and go eat little prince?"

"Yes daddy I'm hungry and I want to see my mommy." Khalid said as he stopped jumping in the bed.

"Aight let's go little man." Kalil scooped his son up in his arms and headed towards the bathroom that was located right across from the bed. They showered and got dressed making their way out of the door to go meet up with the most important people in their lives.

❤ ❤ ❤

Everyone was seated at the huge table in the restaurant waiting for Chanae and Zariya to arrive.

Zariya had gone to help Chanae with something and told Nassir that they would be down in a minute. That minute then turned into twenty. The kids were getting fussy and restless and the adults were all starving.

"Man where the hell is these big head ass girls at; a nigga hungry." Demarco complained.

"Nigga don't be talking about my damn wife when your girl head over there looking like it's too big for her body." Everybody at the table broke out into laughter.

"I know you didn't go there nigga I will kick your ass up in here." LeRae said rolling her eyes at Nassir.

"Hold up hold up Te-Te don't be threatening my daddy like that. You going to get in big trouble; we don't play those kinds of games." Za'kiya said with her arms folded across her chest. She was mugging LeRae like she wanted to fight her for saying something out of line to her daddy.

"You know what type of games I like to play? It's called ass whooping games don't make me get a belt and whoop you for what would probably be your first whooping ever. Little badass." Za'kiya gave her an '*I wish you would*' look and put her hands on her hip.

"Oh, hold up don't be threatening my baby with an ass whooping for standing up for her daddy; that's how the Williams roll over here we stick together."

"What are you in here talking about?" Zariya said as her and Chanae made it over to the table and sat down.

Chanae sat between Kalil and Zahyir at the table. Kalil helped her into her seat before giving her a kiss on the lips. She looked around at her family and smiled. This is what she always wanted a family that loved each other no matter what even through the fights and disagreements they still stood beside each other through it all.

"Baby, what took you two so long to get down here?" Kalil asked her as he watched her watch everyone else around the table with a smile on her face.

"For starters, I had to go pee every five minutes thanks to your little princesses being on my bladder. Then I was having a little trouble finding something to wear. I just wasn't feeling comfortable in anything." She explained then chuckled when Khalid threw a dinner roll at Qadir's head because he put his arm around Tara.

"Alright Kalil and Chanae this little nigga going to come up missing out here if he keep it up." Qadir joked.

"Get your arm away from my girlfriend!"

Khalid yelled mean mugging him. Everyone at the table broke out into laughter at the seriousness in his face and voice.

"Wait, I thought I was your girlfriend?" Kamira asked pretending to be sad.

"You are my girlfriend too. You both are my girlfriends." He said grinning at her.

"Un huh, Kalil what you over there teaching my baby? Talking about he got two girlfriends with his little ass." Zariya and everybody else couldn't stop laughing.

"Wait, mommy that is not your baby you have your own baby that's my baby. We talked about this already and all the time." Za'kiya said shaking her head.

"Oh lawd girl hush you always talking about somebody your baby." Nassir shook his head at his queen and princess. He chuckled because he knew they were about to start a whole debate on babies.

"Daddy, tell mommy that is *my* baby and she got her own." Za'kiya whined

"Girl bye that is *your* daddy not mines so he can't tell me anything." After that everybody started clowning on who ran things in the relationships: the men or the women. Of course the men let the women think they did just so they could get them some tonight. Well everybody but Kalil that was; he was still trying to get Chanae to go back on her rule of no sex before the wedding.

"You know we can sneak off to one of our suites and no one would even notice we were gone." He leaned over and whispered in her ear causing her to giggle like a little school girl.

"Oh really and what would we be doing in the

room once we got there?" she looked him in the eyes and saw the lust burning in them.

"We can connect as one and let our bodies do all the talking." He was ready to take her to the room and have his way with her. Once he saw Chanae shake her had no he knew he saw a cold shower in his near future.

"Bae trust me once we say 'I do' and go on our honeymoon the wait will be worth it." She kissed his cheek and tried hard to keep from laughing at the face he was making.

Everyone enjoyed dinner together as always. They all went back to their rooms to get some much needed sleep. The next day after they did the rehearsal and checked on everything for the wedding they decided to enjoy their stay in Tahiti. They went as a group sightseeing and engaging in different activities. It was the day before the wedding and everyone was excited to see Kalil and Chanae become one and share the rest of their lives together as husband and wife.

Chapter 46

The men and women decided to split up and head over to their respective bachelor and bachelorette parties hosted by Nassir and Zariya. Zariya and Kalil's moms decided to watch the kids for them. Kalil wasn't happy about the idea of a party at all but Zariya and Kalyah shut his protests down quick and sent him on his way. He wasn't feeling some stripper dancing all up on his pregnant fiancé. He walked up to Chanae and pulled her to the side. She was grinning a little too hard for his taste so he wanted to nip some shit in the bud right quick.

"Look, don't be letting them talk you into letting no nigga swing his dick all up on you. I am not playing I will come and fuck everybody up in there up Chanae." He warned.

She laughed in his face which pissed him off even more. She didn't mean to but he was so handsome to her when he was upset and jealous. The look on his face though caused her to stop laughing. "Oh that's funny? Okay just remember this for every nigga you let dance up on you there will be two chicks that do the same with me." With that he walked away mad as hell, leaving Chanae standing there now with a frown stuck on her face.

"Girl don't pay his ass any damn mind he just talking shit. He won't even know what is going on at the party. Plus no one said anything about strippers anyway." Zariya tried to reassure her.

"Exactly, don't trip off of him let's just go have some fun before you become Mrs. Kalil Barber." Kalyah said agreeing with Zariya and trying to cheer Chanae up.

"Plus I had plans of crashing they shit anyway once we were done having our fun." Zariya said nonchantly with a shrug. All the women looked at her like she was crazy.

"What? Girls, let me put you up on game. If they have strippers up in there tonight which I know they will those hoes come with a mission. Some not all but the ones that do they come to make that money by any means necessary. So of course they plan to shake they ass all up in our men's faces and their ultimate plan is to come up on some serious bread. Which means in other words they don't mind sleeping with a nigga to get a few more hundred dollar bills in their pockets. Now I trust my husband but I don't know these hoes to trust them so with that being said I will be crashing that muthafucka. The only ass my man getting tonight is mines." She looked around at everyone to see if they understood what she was saying. They all smiled and nodded their heads.

"All you tricks is crazy." Chanae said laughing.

"Oh hush your pregnant ass is going to be leading the pack." LeRae laughed.

"Hell yeah I didn't say I wasn't going to be amongst the people who crashed they little hoe bash. I'm just stating facts that you heifers are crazy that is all." They laughed and headed up to their suit where the bachelorette party was being held.

Two hours later and the bachelorette party was in full effect. There were male strippers dressed as fire men, police officers and the UPS delivery man. He definitely had a special delivery for the ladies and they enjoyed every bit of it. Chanae face was red from blushing so much in once night. Her face then turned serious when she read the clock that said eleven-thirty. After she finished receiving her second lap dance from each stripper she threw the rest of her one dollar bills in the air.

"Okay ladies I don't know about you all but I'm about to wobble my ass over to the men's suite and crash that shit before any of those strippers get any ideas." She stood to her feet and made her way to the door with Zariya, Kalyah, LeRae (who was strapped just in case she had to pistol whip somebody), Kamira, and Tara following right behind her. The rest of the guest stayed behind to continue enjoying the male strippers' company.

Once they made it down the hall where the guys' suite was they could hear the music loud and clear. Chanae noticed a big man posted up outside of the door like a statue. As soon as the women stepped in front of him he put his hand out to signal them to stop.

"Sorry ladies, no women allowed in there unless you plan to shake some ass and undress for some cash." He stated rude as ever.

"Un un move out the way Chanae because I just know this muthafucka did not just say some foul shit like that to us like we some damn groupies trying to make a come up." Zariya spat stepping in front of the big ass linebacker looking guard. She couldn't believe Nassir hired a guard to keep them out of the bachelor party.

"Look ladies, no disrespect but you all are going to have to take your money hungry asses elsewhere if your plan ain't to shake some ass tonight." He dismissed them with a wave of his hand not knowing that they were indeed the bridal party.

"Watch out I got this Zar." Chanae pushed her to the side and got right up in his face.

"If Kalil finds out that you are the reason he missed out on the birth of his daughters I pray for your family ever finding the pieces to your body to make sure you receive a proper burial." She sneered at him.

"You don't look like you in labor to me and how do I know that you are even his fiancé? Look lady go pull that bullshit on someone else because you two seconds away from getting the shit smacked out of you. Real talk!" he spat back. Chanae smiled at him and stepped to the side. The movement was so quick he never even saw it coming. Next thing he knew he was on the ground with a loaded pistol staring him in the face.

"Now I am only going to say this once and once only. If you do not move out of our way I will let her empty that whole clip in your disrespectful ass mouth. Oh and another thing if I was you I will stay as far away from the guys as possible because they will be informed of everything you just said to us. Especially that smacking the shit out of me part - Kalil is going to have a field day whooping your ass about that one." They watched as he scattered to his feet and made a quick exit down the hall to the elevators.

"Are you ladies ready to crash this party or what?"

"Hell yeah!" they all shouted as Zariya twisted the doorknob to the suite to find that the door was unlocked already. "Let's go."

When they walked into the suite they saw a

room full of naked women and horny looking men shouting for the strippers to take it off and twerk that ass. They were so busy trying to see some ass they didn't even notice Chanae and her crew walk in. The girls all split up to go search for their men who they noticed weren't in the room with the rest of the men.

Chanae walked over to one of the closed doors that she assumed was one of the bedrooms. She put her ear to the door to see if she could hear what is going on, on the other side of the door when she couldn't make anything out she cracked the door open just a little. Her eyes bulged out at the sight before her. She could see a man blowing some chicks back out doggy style. Neither of them heard the door open, their sex noises and the music playing drowned out the sound. Chanae felt like a pervert standing there staring at them but she couldn't seem to tear her eyes away from the sex scene before her. She blamed it on herself for coming up with that no sex rule before they said their 'I do's'. She was kicking herself in the ass for that one.

Chanae damn near jumped out her skin when she felt a hand touch her on the shoulder. She turned around holding her chest and came face to face with Kalil who was wearing a wide grin on his face. She frowned at him letting him know that she didn't like what he just pulled.

"You scared the hell out of me Kalil what are you trying to do make me go into early labor?" she snapped.

"That is what your ass gets you not supposed to be in here anyway." He reached behind her and pulled the door closed. Grabbing her hand he led her off onto the balcony sliding the doors closed behind them.

"What are you doing in here Chanae?" he

smirked because he knew exactly why she was there. He spotted her and her girls when they walked through the door.

"You can wipe that smirk off your face and explain what all that slick stuff you was talking earlier?" she put her hands on her hips.

"That wasn't me talking slick I meant everything I said." He stared her in the eyes.

"Did you let them nasty girls out there dance on you?"

"Did you let them niggas dance on you?" Kalil asked with a raised eyebrow.

Chanae turned her head avoiding eye contact with him. Kalil shook his head reached out turning and lifting her head up to look him in the eyes. "I take that as a yes." He chuckled a little.

"It was just a little..." he stopped her with a

finger to the lips.

"I don't need or want a run down on it because I already know. Don't ask me how because I'm not going to tell you. Let's just get something straight though that was a once in a lifetime thing. We won't discuss it, just know that you got a pass with that shit."

Chanae looked at him as if to challenge what he just said but the look he shot her changed her mind instantly. She wasn't for strippers dancing on her like that anyway but she couldn't get pass the thought of a stripper bitch dancing on her man though. "You must have enjoyed yourself some of those strippers in there that's why you trying to leave it at that huh?"

"Don't I always mean my word?"

"Yes but what does that have to do with this?"

"I told you for every one you have dance on you I will have two."

415

"You had six naked bitches dancing all up on you!" she yelled in his face.

Kalil stepped back and ran his hand over his chin.

"So you let three niggas shake they shit in your face?" Chanae looked at him with a frown when she realized that she fell right into his trap. He got her to confess without even asking her the question.

"Nobody shook nothing in my face. Yes I received lap dances but that was it. Can you say the same?" she asked in an accusatory way.

"If you got something you want to ask then do that then don't beat around the bush." He said growing agitated.

"Did you do something else with one of these strippers? I noticed you weren't in the room with the rest of the men." It was Kalil's turn to laugh in her face.

He couldn't believe she was asking if he fucked a stripper out of all people.

"You know what, Chanae maybe we ain't ready for this step. You can't even trust that I won't fuck a stripper right down the hall from where you were. Damn, you think I'm that trifling? When did we get to the point again where you feel you can't trust me?"

"Kalil I just ask…" Chanae tried speaking but he stopped her she could feel her chest tighten with each word he spoke.

"No need to speak; you already said enough. I never cheated on you and I never plan on cheating on you. One thing I am tired of you doing though is accusing me of something the last nigga did to you. It's been how long now and you still got me paying for the mistakes he made?"

Chanae felt like she had a lump in her throat. She could

feel the tears on the edge of her eyes tempting to fall. She opened her mouth and tried to speak but nothing would come out.

Kalil felt himself getting pissed with all the shit she put him through because of her ex. He shook his head as he ran his hand over his face and looked at her.

"I can't do this shit no more Chanae. If you can't trust that I would never in this lifetime or any other hurt you then this will never work. I love you and I'm thankful for the children that you blessed me with. But I will not continue to be accused of shit I didn't do. I can't." with that Kalil kissed her on the forehead opened the sliding doors and walked away.

Chanae broke down as she watched the love of her life walk away from her and the life they shared together. She couldn't fathom a life without Kalil and she didn't want to.

Chapter 47

It was the day of the wedding and Chanae was under the covers in her suite crying her eyes out. She had been crying nonstop since Kalil walked out of the suite last night. She had been calling his phone all night only to be met with his voicemail every time. Zariya and Kalyah had been with her the whole night trying to get her to calm down. In the men's suite at the bachelor party when they saw her crying and screaming after Kalil they knew something must have went wrong. When they made it over to her she cried even harder. They couldn't make out a word she was saying. It wasn't until they got her back to her own suite that she was able to tell them what happened. Kalyah tried to soothe her by saying that Kalil was just upset and wasn't talking straight and that everything would be okay. Chanae wanted to believe her but the look in his eyes was telling her otherwise.

Chanae could hear the curtains in her room being pulled back. She then heard footsteps and movements coming towards her. She felt the covers being pulled away from her body.

"Get up Chanae it is your wedding day and we have a full day ahead of us. Not to mention it is going on nine o'clock already." Zariya demanded.

She opened her eyes and peered over at Zariya with a frown. "No just leave me alone Zar. You know there is not going to be a wedding today. Kalil walked out on me last night remember?" She reached down and pulled the covers back over her head.

Zariya pulled the covers all the way off of her and tossed them on to the floor out of her reach.

"Chanae get your ass up out of this bed. You have a wedding to get to today. You know damn well Kalil would not leave you hanging like that."

"Zar, you didn't see his eyes he really means it this time." She whined balling herself up in a fetal position.

"Now Chanae you know damn well I taught you better than that!" Chanae sat straight up in the bed at the sound of voice that bounced off the walls. Sonja walked over to her and sat on the bed beside her.

"Ma, he don't love me anymore I lost him forever this time." She cried leaning on her shoulder.

Zariya wanted to wash all her pain away. She felt in her heart that Kalil would never leave his family.

She sent Nassir off last night to look for him. He said that he hadn't gotten in contact with Kalil and no one knew where he was.

"This can't be the end for them they are so perfect together." She thought to herself. She began cleaning up and getting Chanae's things ready for her big day. She knew Kalil wouldn't leave Chanae at the altar; he worked too hard for the life they share together.

"Chanae, let me tell you something. That man loves the ground you walk on. I don't believe that he would just walk away from you and everything you two have built together. Now I know from experience that every relationship goes through its ups and downs. The real challenge and proof of true love is how you stick it out as one and overcome it together not battling with one another." She lift Chanae's head up so that they were looking eye to eye.

"Baby, in your heart without a doubt do you love Kalil?"

"Yes." She answered without a second thought.

"Do you think that he would ever intentionally hurt you?"

"No." Chanae realized where Sonja was going with her questioning.

"Okay, now here is the most important question. Do you trust Kalil with everything in you and believe without a doubt that he loves you with all his heart?"

"Yes I do." Chanae realized that she had hurt Kalil by questioning his love for her. She knew that a relationship was built on love and trust; you can't have one without the other if the relationship is ever going to work.

"Now you know what you have to do?" She asked Chanae as she stood to leave.

"Yes ma'am but what if he doesn't show up?" she feared that Kalil is really fed up with her bullshit and won't show up to meet her at the altar.

"Faith baby it is all about faith. You have to believe it in your heart that he will be standing at the end of the aisle waiting to make you his wife." Sonja walked to the door and turned to face her daughters.

"I love you two and I am very proud at the women you have become. Now let me go get my grandbabies ready so that we can watch my second baby girl work that aisle." She winked at Chanae and smiled.

They watched her leave and looked at each other. "Well what are we doing, sis?" Zariya asked her.

Chanae smiled and got up off the bed.

"We're going to get ready and dolled up sis I have a wedding today." Zariya smiled inside happy to see that she cheered up now.

"You still haven't heard from Kalil?" Zahyir asked fixing his collar. The men were in their dressing room inside of the hall where the wedding was to take place outside on the beach.

"No but I know my boy and he loves Chanae. He wouldn't leave her at the altar." Nassir said getting NJ dressed.

"I hope so because if he do that will surly break my sister's heart. She been through so much within the last two years, hell the last few months it ain't even funny." Everyone in the room agreed with that.

"I can't believe the women brought they ass to the bachelor party last night." Demarco stated trying to lighten the mood up in the room.

"Right man, Tara came up in there flipping out

on a dude talking about I should have went to my suite when I saw it was going to be strippers there." Qadir said with a frown. The men laughed because their women came and showed out last night when they saw all those naked women in the room.

"Shit, your crazy ass cousin threatened to shoot a nigga shit off if I had got a lap dance from any of them." Demarco shook his head at his crazy ass girl but that was his baby though.

"Hahaha maaaaan I can't believe she made them strippers line up against the wall and asked them if they gave you a lap dance. I was cracking the hell up." Zahyir said doubling over in laughter.

"Man shut up you wasn't doing too much laughing when Kamira threatened to do the same damn thing to your ass." Zahyir went on hush mode at that statement and everybody broke out laughing at him.

"Let me go try Kalil again here Qadir hold my little man right quick." Nassir said kissing his son's cheek and handing him over to his uncle.

"Come here little dude." Nassir walked out of the room to get some privacy.

Ringing...

"Yeah man?" he answered with a frustrated tone.

"What the hell you mean yeah man? Kalil where are you at? Your ass do remember that you have a damn wedding today right?" Nassir was looking at the phone just knowing this can't be his boy on the phone acting like shit is gravy.

"Man Nassir I don't know about this shit. I mean I love the hell out of Chanae. I love that woman more than I love myself. But she doesn't trust me and I can't marry somebody that don't believe in me. She basically saying that she don't believe in the love I have for her." Kalil felt like he was losing a part of his heart with every word he spoke.

"You have to remember man that she pregnant and emotional. Her hormones are all over the damn place you can't take that shit she said to heart. You know Chanae loves you just as much as you love her." Nassir was trying to talk some sense into him because he can tell that Kalil wasn't feeling shit that Chanae said to him.

"I don't know I would get it if she said the shit once but man this ain't the first time. I am not about to be with someone who don't fucking trust me. I would give my damn life for that girl and all she do is accuse me of shit I don't do. Nassir I...I don't know what to do at this point man." Kalil was trying to be tough about it but he wanted to break down at the thought of not spending the rest of his life with Chanae.

"If you think the love Chanae has for you ain't real then I say don't show up, just be there for your kids. Now if you know deep down you just fucked up on what she said but KNOW that she loves your stank ass draws...."

"Man you a damn fool." Kalil laughed.

Nassir continued. "If you know she loves your stanky ass draws and would do anything to make sure you happy. Then you need to get your ass here ASAP and marry the woman of your dreams and mother of your children. The choice is yours though; if your heart ain't in it then do what you have to do." Kalil held on to the phone still unsure of what he should do.

"Aight man. I have to go figure out what I'm going to do." He said into the phone.

"Aight man WE will be where the wedding is

taking place. If we don't see you there then we know what is up." Nassir ended the call praying that his boy made the right choice.

Kalil grabbed two pieces of paper. On one sheet he wrote a goodbye letter to Chanae. On the other sheet of paper he wrote a new set of wedding vows. When he was finished writing he sat there and stared at the letters for a while. He got up and packed his clothes before walking out of the hotel suit door on his way to his next destination. He never thought he would ever have to make a decision on leaving or marrying Chanae. In his heart the answer would have always been marry her. Now after everything that they have been through and the obstacles that they overcame, her words to him had him second guessing things. Trust meant everything to him and if the woman he planned to marry couldn't trust him then there was absolutely no hope for them and their future together.

Kalil sat in the back of the taxi cab after telling the driver where he wanted to go. He leaned his head back and closed his eyes. He thought long and hard on what he had to do as he finally came to a decision. Wiping his hand over his face he sighed deeply keeping his eyes closed.

Chapter 48

Chanae stood in front of the full length mirror
inside of her dressing room and smiled at her reflection.
Her makeup was flawlessly done and she looked
absolutely gorgeous. Her hair was in a curled bun with
a curly wrap in the front. The bun was held together by
diamond accents. The wedding dress she was wearing
was white with silver embellishments all over the top
portion. The organza bottom flowed down to her feet in
a wavy pattern. She rubbed her huge belly and thought
about the life her and Kalil have together. *"He is going
to show I know he is."* She said to herself with

confidence.

She turned at the sound of someone knocking on the door. "Come in." she turned back around to face the mirror. She watched through the mirror as Zariya's father and Charles walked into the room.

"Look at our baby girl. Ain't she just as beautiful as the day she was born?" he asked Looking over at Charles.

"Yes she is all grown up now. I can't believe she's getting married and have a growing family of her own now." Charles responded.

"Has Kalil made it yet?" Chanae asked causing them both to look at each other not saying a word.

She turned around to face them. Once she saw the looks on their faces she swallowed hard.

"That's okay I am sure he will be here soon he's probably just running a little late that's all. No worries, right?"

"Of course sweetheart today is not the day you need to be worrying about anything other than looking beautiful." Charles stated with a smile.

"Okay daddy." She turned back around and looked at herself in the mirror. Charles walked up to her and placed something around her neck. She looked at the beautiful piece of jewelry he had placed on her neck that went perfect with her dress.

"Daddy it is so...so..." Chanae felt her eyes watering and she got upset with herself because she didn't want to mess up her makeup.

"It's okay baby girl don't cry. This necklace belonged to your mother. I gave it to her the first day I ever told her that I loved her. It just so happens that today is the anniversary of that day. I thought that she would love for you to wear it on your wedding day to have a piece of her with you.

"Oh thank you so much daddy I love it and I love you too." Charles smiled at his daughter as he wrapped her up in a tight hug.

"I'm glad that I will have you two walk me down the aisle to my future husband. That means the world to me." Both men gave her a hug and a kiss on the cheek.

"I sure hope you two ain't in here messing up my baby's makeup." Sonja said with her hands on her hips. Zariya walked in behind her mother shaking her head and laughing. She had been throwing orders at everybody today.

"Oh woman ain't nobody messing up nothing." Her husband said walking up to her and kissing her on the cheek before making his way out the door behind Charles who was already halfway out the door. He smacked his wife on the butt as he walked pass.

"Ew daddy I didn't need to see all of that!"
Zariya shouted.

"Close your eyes then youngin." He yelled over
his shoulder before shutting the door behind him. Sonja
giggled like a little school girl.

"Look at you acting like a little high school girl
over there giggling and stuff." Zariya teased her
mother.

"Oh hush child you're going to be doing the
same thing when you get this age and see how much
you and your husband are still very much in love."

"I want that." Chanae blurted out. They both
turned to look at her at the same time.

Sonja walked up to her and smiled giving her a
warm motherly hug.

"And you will have that and so much more baby

you just wait and see." Chanae smiled at the thought of her and Kalil many years later still deeply and happily in love with one another.

"You working that dress sis pregnant and all you are a hot mamma." Zariya said and they all laughed. The door opened again and in walked the two prettiest flower girls they have ever seen.

"Granny, you like me and Kamyra's dresses?" Za'kiya said as her and Kamyra spun around in a circle so that everybody can get a good view of their dresses.

"Oh baby I love your two dresses." She replied.

"They not as pretty as my Te-Te Chanae's dress but we look good too." They laughed at her little comment knowing she meant every word she said.

"Aw thank you niecey pooh and you do look good; you two young ladies are working those dresses." Chanae smiled at them causing both girls to blush.

"I know right Te-Te." Za'kiya said shaking her head.

"I like your hair Te-Te Chanae." Kamyra complimented.

"Aw thank you sweetie. I love your hair too." The stylist did a great job on their hair. "She really got my vision for them." She said looking at both of them and admiring how cute they were.

"Yeah at first I didn't think she would get how we wanted the curls but she aced it." Zariya said also looking the girls over. They were dressed in pretty little white fluffy dresses with light sliver flower patterns covering them that matched Chanae's dress. Their hair were in two small ponytails on each side of their head in the front with swirly curls hanging in the back of their head and out of the two ponytails. Both girls had hair that reached the middle of their backs so their hair was really bouncing with every move they made.

"Okay ladies we should start getting ready to make our move out the door and to the beach where the entire wedding party is waiting for you to become Mrs. Kalil Barber." Sonja said ushering everyone out of the room so that they could go and take their places. *"I sure hope Kalil is waiting for me at the end of the aisle when I make it there."* Chanae thought to herself as she followed them out the door.

Chapter 49

"Excuse me have any of you seen the groom around here anywhere? We are set to start in five minutes and I haven't spotted him yet." The wedding planner asked walking up to where Nassir and the guys were standing. At the sound of her voice they all turned around to face her just as she made it over to them.

"No we haven't seen him but I know he will make it here in time for his wedding." Nassir assured her. He was so confident that his boy would make the right choice which would explain why he stayed calm and collected compared to everyone else who was panicking.

"Well he was supposed to be here hours ago with the rest of the wedding party. I sure hope I don't have a runaway groom on my hands." She said walking away in a haste to go check on the bride. *"This will be so damn embarrassing if he doesn't show up. All I know is I still better get paid either way or I will go from professional to ratchet on they ass in two point five seconds."* She thought to herself.

"Aye I can't stand that chick she rude as hell." Zahyir expressed scrunching his face up at her backside.

"Me either I know Kalil used to say he was close to cursing her ass out about four times during the planning process but Chanae stopped him." They all laughed as they heard her announce that it was time for everyone to take their places. Now people were really starting to get worried because Kalil still hadn't arrived yet.

"Papa, where is my daddy at?" Khalid asked Charles looking up at him with a frown on his face as he pat him on the leg. He could sense from everyone else's mood that something wasn't right. They were all on edge about something and he wanted to know why his daddy wasn't around.

Charles looked down at his grandson then at everyone else because now they were also staring at him wondering what he would tell Khalid. He scooped him up in his arms and looked at him for a second before answering his question.

"Little man your dad is probably just running a little late I'm sure he will be here soon." Charles hoped like hell that was true or him and Kalil will be having a long talk whenever they do run into each other again.

"Okay papa but daddy better hurry up mommy coming and she don't like when daddy is late for stuff." The guys laughed as they heard the wedding planner shooting orders at people again to take their places.

"Okay gentlemen lets go it's time to start the ceremony. Can any of you get in touch with the groom or should I be letting everyone know that the wedding is off?" She asked with her hands on her hips.

"Did the bride or groom tell you that the wedding was off?" She turned around to the voice she heard come from behind her. There stood Kalyah with her arms folded across her chest.

"No they didn't I..."

"Well then the wedding is still a go so you should be going to make sure everything is perfect like you're getting paid to do." Kalyah dismissed her with a wave of her hand. The wedding planner debated on whether to comeback at her with a snappy comment but she decided not to after sizing Kalyah up. She settled for rolling her eyes before walking away.

"Okay so no one heard from Kalil?" Everybody shook their head no. Kalyah walked away pissed at the thought of her brother running away from marrying Chanae after all the love he claimed to have for her. *"Something isn't right my brother would never do something like not showing up to his own wedding."* She mumbled to herself.

"Kalyah did you see your brother when you went out there?" Chanae asked as soon as she stepped into the bridal waiting area.

Kalyah couldn't fix her lips to tell Chanae that he wasn't out there so she shook her head no instead. She watched as Chanae plopped down in a chair with a sad look plastered on her face.

"He really left me at the altar." She came to the realization talking more to herself than anyone else.

"I'm sorry call me an old romantic but I don't and won't believe that Kalil would leave you at the altar. He loves you too much and the love you two share is something that I used to hope and pray that one day me and my husband would share." Zariya said shaking her head.

"What? Zar, what you and Nassir have is real true love." Chanae said looking at her confused.

"Yeah of course we do I know that silly. I was referring to before we got married and before we became inseparable. You and Kalil had that love at first sight thing going on whether you want to believe it or not. That night we all met he made it his business not to leave that hospital before knowing that you were okay.

The man didn't know you from Adam but he stayed. The connection between the two of you was something you don't just see every day Chanae." Chanae looked at her and thought about what she just said. Right when she was about to respond Zariya interrupted her.

"Look, we are going to go out there and do what we came all the way to the beautiful island of Tahiti to do. Have a damn wedding. If you get out there and see that Kalil isn't there then turn right back around and don't look back I will take it from there. But Chanae you have to have faith in you guys love for one another." With that Zariya walked over to Chanae and kissed her on the forehead then got all the ladies ready to go out and take their places with their mates.

There was a path that led from the hall to the sandy white beach where the wedding ceremony will be taking place. The guests were all seated in their chairs as they waited for it to start. Two minutes later they heard the soft melody of Monica seeping through the speakers as 'For You I Will' played. The first couple up to walk down the aisle is Qadir and Tara. Qadir just like all the rest of the men in the wedding party wore a white suite with a peach colored vest and tie. Since peach and white was the colors Chanae chose for her big day Tara just like the rest of the women dresses were peach as well. The only differences are they wore different style dresses because Chanae wanted the dress to fit each woman's style. Tara dress was a short wrap around with one over the shoulder strap. It came down to her knees to show that it was both elegant and sexy. Her hair as down in spiral curls that came to the middle of her back.

Next up to walk down was Zahyir and Kamira who wore the same length dress as Tara but hers was an off the shoulder strapless dress. Her hair was in the short Italian bob she loved to wear with a simple curl to it. Her whole look was simple yet very classy. After they took their place it was then Demarco and LeRae turn to walk down. LeRae wore a long dress with her shoulders out with both straps tied around the back of her neck. The dress clung to the upper part of her body while hanging loosely at the bottom.

Kalyah dress matched LeRae's dress expect hers didn't have any shoulders to it at all it was strapless. So her top portion matched Kamira's dress. Kalyah walked down the aisle with her boyfriend Markel they met at Zariya and Nassir's wedding and been close ever since.

Now it was the best man and maid of honor turn to walk down the aisle. Zariya noticed that Kalil still haven't showed up yet. She looked over at Nassir and as if he read her mind he gently squeezed her hand while whispering 'everything that is meant to be will be baby'. She smiled at him and he smiled back as he led her down the sandy beach. She could feel the sand on her feet as they made it to the end he kissed her cheek then took his place. They all watched as Khalid walked down the beach holding on to the pillow that had the rings lying on top of it. He looked around at all the people as if he was looking for someone. They knew exactly who that someone was. He walked up to Nassir and held the pillow out for him to take. The guest giggled Nassir leaned down and picked him up with his right arm.

Everyone then turned their attention to Za'kiya and Kamyra making their way down. Every few steps they both would stop and strike a different pose for the cameras.

"Make sure you get our good sides okay?"

Za'kiya said to one of the cameramen. Zariya shook her head looked over at Nassir and placed a hand over her eyes. She tried hard to hold in her laughter. "My baby is something else." She said to herself.

When they reached everyone else they went over to where the band was. Za'kiya stopped looked around and then turned to her daddy. "Daddy where is my uncle Kalil at?" All of the guests turned to him because she asked the question they were all thinking at the time.

Chapter 50

Before he could answer Zariya stepped in.

"Za'kiya, you and Kamyra go get where you supposed to be right now." Both girls did as they were told.

Picking up the microphones that were set out for them Kamyra and Za'kiya waited for their cue. As soon as they got the signal from the wedding planner the band started playing and the girls began to sing. As Chanae stepped onto the sand holding on to the arms of both of her fathers as the girls sung the song 'Wedding Vows by Jamie Foxx'. The song was actually the one

Altar'd

Kalil felt that they should sing because in his heart he knew those same lyrics to the song mirrored his thoughts and feelings for Chanae on their wedding day.

"Well it's been 5 years

Can't hold back my tears

Cause I'm just so happy I'm marrying an angel today

oooo

As I take your hand

I pledge to be your man

I vow to love to hold to cherish

And never disrespect the love we share

I'll be honest I cannot lie

There'll be real good days

There'll be some bad times

I'll be standing right beside you my sweet baby

With the love of mine

Altar'd

And you take this ring

And I place it on your sweet and lovely hand

We will show our kids

They will tell their kids

What mom and daddy did

On the day I married my angel

I love you my angel..."

Chanae finally got the courage to look out at her guests and the bridal party. Her heart broke into a million pieces when she didn't see Kalil waiting on her at the end of the aisle. She stopped and started to turn around and run back inside.

"Hold up baby girl not so fast look pass everybody and everything else and have faith and believe." Charles whispered to her. She looked at him confused not understanding what he was really telling her. He then nodded his head towards the walkway down the aisle. Once she turned around and looked past everyone else on the other side walking towards them from the opposite side was Kalil dressed in his all white suit.

Chanae smiled big as she grabbed hold of their arms once more and let them lead her to her future. It was as if her and Kalil were both walking down an aisle to meet each other at the altar. The whole wedding party finally released the breath that they didn't know they were holding in.

Kalil was the first to make it to where everyone was standing. He came up from around the reverend and took his place next to Nassir.

"I knew you would make the right choice." Nassir whispered to his boy. Khalid popped Kalil in the back of his head and laughed which caused everyone else to laugh to.

He stepped forward when Chanae made it down. He lifted his hand out for her to take. She looked him in the eyes and then down at his outstretched hand. They stood there like that for three minutes but to Kalil it seemed like forever. Chanae finally put her hand in his and let him lead her in front of the reverend.

"We are all gathered here today to watch as two souls become one. As the beating of two separate heartbeats merge together and beat as one beautiful melody. We will witness the union of Chanae Walker and Kalil Barber becoming Husband and wife. They both decided to write their own vows. Chanae, go ahead." The reverend nodded his head for her to begin.

"Kalil..." She looked up at him trying to fight the tears back from falling.

"Don't cry mommy!" Khalid yelled out from Nassir's arms. Chanae chuckled a little before continuing.

"Kalil, my King I love you more than any amount of words can ever express. You came into my life during a time when I didn't even know what the true meaning of love was. You taught me something that I will take with me forever. I still have the very first note you ever wrote me the day we met. Who would have thought that what you put in that note would someday be our reality? You said that you were my future and I wouldn't have wanted it any other way. I love you and TRUST you with my life, my heart, and my soul." Chanae looked into Kalil's eyes and mouthed the words 'I'm sorry'.

"Kalil, now it is your turn to read your vows." The reverend said. Kalil nodded to him and pulled the paper with his vows written on it out of his pocket.

"Chanae, my beautiful Queen you are part of

456

the reason I fight to live. Each day I wake up to you I thank god for the gift he made just for me. My heart doesn't beat properly if I don't see your smile in the morning or the look you make when you don't get your way. The day you came into my life you changed it for the better. You truly have no idea what your presence that day meant for me. You gave me a handsome prince and soon two little princesses. I pray that I would never have to suffer a day without you in my life. That is how much I love and cherish you. I'm honored to be chosen as the man you plan to spend the rest of your life with. I wouldn't have that any other way." He smirked at her and she blushed.

"Through marriage, Kalil and Chanae make a commitment together to face their disappointments, embrace their dreams, realize their hopes, and accept each other's failures. They will promise one another to aspire to these ideals throughout their lives together through mutual understanding, openness, and sensitivity to each other. Can we please have the rings now?" the reverend asked.

"No these are my mommy and daddy rings you get your own." Khalid frown his face up at the reverend. Nassir placed Chanae's ring in Kalil's hand while Zariya gave Chanae Kalil's. Khalid folded his arms across his chest. Nassir had to whisper into his ear for him to chill out.

"Do you, Chanae take Kalil to be your husband to live together after God's ordinance in the holy estate of matrimony? Will you love him, comfort him, honor and keep him, in sickness and in health, for richer, for poorer, for better, for worse, in sadness and in joy, to cherish and continually bestow upon him your heart's deepest devotion, forsaking all others, keep yourself only unto him as long as you both shall live?" Chanae placed the ring onto Kalil's finger.

"I do."

"Do you Kalil take Chanae to be your wife to live together after God's ordinance in the holy estate of matrimony? Will you love her, comfort her, honor and keep her, in sickness and in health, for richer, for poorer, for better, for worse, in sadness and in joy, to cherish and continually bestow upon her your heart's deepest devotion, forsaking all others, keep yourself only unto her as long as you both shall live?" Kalil slid the ring onto Chanae's finger and smiled at her.

"I do."

You have pronounced yourselves husband and wife but remember to always be each other's best friend. What therefore God has joined together let no man put asunder. And so, by the power vested in me by the State of Missouri and Almighty God, I now pronounce you man and wife and may your days be good and long upon the earth. You may now kiss the bride."

Everyone jumped up from their seats and clapped as Kalil tilted Chanae back and kissed her long and hard. When they finally came up for air everyone was cheering for Mr. and Mrs. Kalil Barber.

Chapter 51

Kalil and Chanae stayed a week in Tahiti after the wedding before heading back home. Chanae missed Khalid and so did Kalil. After all that stuff that went down with the custody and the case workers they hated being away from him for too long. Christmas would be soon rolling around in a few weeks and everyone was excited. Chanae noticed that Kalil had been on edge a lot lately so tonight she planned on finding out what is bothering him.

Chanae moved around the house at a slow pace due to her pregnancy. She couldn't wait to give birth to her daughters. She and Kalil decided to try something different with this pregnancy. They wanted to do a water birth either at the hospital or the house. Chanae was still indecisive on which one she wanted to do but she knew she had to decide soon since she was now eight and a half months.

Chanae was sitting in the living room folding clothes and watching TV while Khalid played on the floor with his toy trucks and cars. Kalil had run out to the restaurant to check up on his employees.

"Mommy my brain hurt." Khalid whined walking up to her and patting her on the leg. He was just starting to come down with a bad cold so he had been fussing on and off a lot lately.

Chanae placed the shirt she was folding down next to her and pulled Khalid closer to her. "Your brain hurt?"

"Yes mommy it hurts bad." He said nodding his head up and down. He started coughing uncontrollably.

"You mean you have a headache? Your head hurts?" Chanae asked getting up off the couch and leading him by the hand to the bathroom. She gave him some children's Tylenol.

"Mommy I'm so tired." He complained rubbing his eyes.

Chanae took him up to his room to put him down for a nap. He got in the bed and stared up at her with sleepy eyes. She hated when her baby got sick. There were plenty of times when he was running around jumping on furniture that she wished he was calmer but the only time that seemed to be is when he sick.

"You want mommy to lay with you until you

fall asleep?"

"Yes." He said softly. She got on the other side of him and laid down wrapping her arms around him.

"Mommy your belly too big." Chanae laughed then scooted back a little in the bed to give him more room.

"That's because your sisters are in my belly."

"They need to come out so your belly can go back small mommy."

"Yeah baby they do come on so you can take your nap by the time you wake up daddy should be home." They cuddled in his Spiderman bed together until he fell asleep. Chanae got up to call Kalil to see when he would be coming home.

"What's up baby?" he answered on the first ring.

"Hey baby when will you be coming home?"

she asked walking in their bedroom to put the clothes away she folded earlier.

"I should be there in about an hour maybe sooner. What are you and my prince and princesses doing?"

"Well our prince is down for a nap he still not feeling well. Oh and that reminds me I need you to stop by Walgreens and pick up some more cough medicine for him." She said hanging some shirts in the closet.

"Okay I will pick some up when I leave here. What about my princesses what they doing." Chanae laughed into the phone causing Kalil to chuckle.

"Your little princesses are doing a lot of kicking and moving around. Other than that they are fine. Now my question is you asked about the prince and the princesses but not once did you ask about your queen. Now why is that Mr. Barber?" Kalil smiled.

"Now you know I was getting to that I would never forget to ask how my queen was doing."

"Un huh whatever say you ain't slick. Okay let me let you get back to doing what you were doing so you can hurry up and come home."

"Alright baby I will be there soon I love you Mrs. Barber."

"I love you too Mr. Barber." She hung up the phone and went back to putting the clothes away she had just folded.

After she finished hanging up the clothes she already had upstairs and then went back downstairs to finish folding clothes down there. When she finished with that she went to throw a new load in the washer.

Kalil had just hung up the phone with Chanae and pulled into the restaurant lot. He got out the car about to walk through the door when his cell phone rang again.

"Hello?"

"Aye Kalil what's up this Zahyir?"

"Aw what's up Zah, what you need?" he asked pacing outside of the restaurant door.

"I was calling because I wanted to check on Khalid. I remember Chanae saying he was sick."

"Yeah my little man been coughing and running a fever on and off for a few days now."

"Dang I was trying to call the house and Chanae's phone but no one is answering."

"She probably don't have the phone on her while she taking care of our little man but aye I need you to do me a favor though."

"Okay what's up?" Zahyir said getting into his car; he was just leaving Kamira's house.

"I need you to go Walgreens and pick up some Children's cough medicine for Khalid and take it to Chanae for me. I told her I would pick some up but that won't be for another hour or so after I leave here. I would feel better if he had it now just in case he may need it."

"Alright man no problem I'm heading out that way now. Is it anything else they need from the store?"

"Naw that's it do you still have your key to the house?" Kalil asked waving at an employee that just walked out of the restaurant.

"Yeah I got it."

"Aight good thanks Zah."

"Man no thanks needed you know I would do anything for my nephew and sister. I'll call you when I make it to the house to let you know he got the medicine."

"Alright." Hanging up the phone Kalil walked into his place of business feeling relieved that his son will have the medicine he needed sooner rather than later.

Chanae had just finished loading the dryer and putting another load of clothes in the washer when she heard a door closing from upstairs. Walking out of the laundry room she made her way to Khalid's room to check on him. When she walked past the front door on her way up the stairs she noticed that the door was cracked open a little.

"I know this was locked before I went downstairs." She thought out loud looking around before closing it shut and locking it. She took two steps towards the stairs when she heard faint voices coming from upstairs.

"Kalil must have come back early or something." Taking the steps one at a time when she made it to the top she stopped for a second.

"Damn we need an elevator those steps are going to kill me." she walked down the hall to her son's room. When Chanae pushed the door open she saw Khalid sitting straight up in his bed. When he noticed her he smiled making her smile back at him.

"Hey little man you awake already. Who were you talking to?" Chanae started walking over to his bed as he reached his hand out and pointed his finger. At that exact time she heard the door slam shut. The door was so loud it caused Chanae to jump and turn around towards the noise. When she did the person she now saw standing in front of the door with a grin on his face damn near made her jump out of her skin clutching her chest.

Chapter 52

"You looked scared as hell." He laughed.

"That was not funny you scared the hell out of me Zahyir. What you trying to do get your nieces here early?" she snapped rolling her eyes at him.

"I'm sorry sissy please forgive me." He gave off his saddest puppy dog face.

"I can't stand your ass sometimes I swear. What are you doing here anyway?" She sat down on Khalid's bed and he crawled over to her laying his head down on her lap.

"Oh yeah I almost forgot Kalil asked me to bring my little dude some more medicine." He said holding up the Walgreens bag in his hand.

"Aw okay thanks Kalil must have figured he needed it now and didn't want him to wait on him for it." Zahyir handed her the bag.

"Yeah that's what he said that he would rather him have it sooner rather than later when he may need it now." Walking over to his nephew he rubbed is head.

"Man I ain't ever seen him this quiet before this cold must really be kicking his ass."

"Yeah it is but if it gets worse I'm taking my baby to see the doctor."

"I feel you sis well let me get going do you two need anything before I go?" he said preparing to leave.

"No we good thanks again little brother."

"I thought we talked about that little stuff I told you I am a grown ass man."

Chanae cracked up laughing when he said that.

"I'm sorry but every time you say that I think of Kevin Hart saying I'm a grown man hahaha." She couldn't stop herself from laughing. Zahyir just stood by the door staring at her.

"I can't take neither one of ya'll LITTLE asses saying that grown shit." She smacked her leg while trying to stop laughing.

"You know what I'm out of here call me if you need me little bighead ass girl." With that he left out the room.

"Oh and don't forget to shut and lock the door this time!" she yelled after him.

"Uncle Zah crazy ain't he baby." Khalid shook his head yes.

Chanae and Khalid sat like that for fifteen minutes until he fell back to sleep. She put him back under the covers and left out the room leaving the door cracked a little bit. She went into her and Kalil's room to lie down and try to get a nap in while Khalid is taking one.

Around four o'clock in the afternoon Chanae shot up in her bed at the sound of Khalid crying. She pulled the blanket off of her and got up out the bed. Making her way down the hall to his room she could her him getting louder and louder the closer she got to the room. Opening the door all the way she walked in and over to him. He was sitting in the middle of his bed again but this time his face was covered in tears. He was crying so hard it seemed as if he could hardly breathe.

"Aw mommy's prince what's the matter did you have a bad dream?" she asked him sitting down on the bed cradling him in her arms. Khalid started pointing towards his room door. When Chanae followed his finger she almost passed out.

"You don't look to happy to see me baby. I missed you, haven't you missed me at all?" Chanae watched Von push the door close and walk closer to her and her son.

"Stay the hell away from us! Kalil will be here any minute!" she shouted at him while holding on to Khalid tight as if trying to shield him from harm.

"You really think I give a fuck if that nigga is on his way or not? You must have forgotten who the fuck I was or something. Don't worry though I am about to remind you today exactly who the fuck I am." Chanae tried to get up off the bed when she saw him moving towards them but she was too slow. Von walked up on her while she held her son in her arms and smacked her so hard across the face her bottom lip split on impact.

"Ahhhhhhhh!" she screamed. Khalid started crying even more when he saw that. He had fallen out of Chanae's arms. Luckily they were on the bed or he would have hit the floor.

Von snatched Chanae up by the throat. She started scratching at his hands trying to get him off of her. He then reached his hand back and smacked her again causing Khalid to cry out louder than before.

"See what you making me do? This was not my plan all I wanted to do was come here and get you so that we can go home to our daughter. I never wanted to hurt you Chanae but you made me do it. It's like you know which buttons to push to make me want to knock the fuck out of you." She continued trying to pry his hands from around her neck but he had a tight grip.

Khalid hopped up on the bed and started swinging on Von for him to let Chanae go.

"Leave my mommy alone let her go!" He yelled pounding away at Von's arms.

Von swung his arm back at him knocking him off the bed and into the nightstand on the side of his bed. Khalid hit his head before hitting the floor with a loud thump.

That's all it took for Chanae to truly snap. She started punching Von in the face and anywhere else her hands landed. She was fueled by hatred not for what he did to her but what he just did to her baby. She was like a mama bear protecting her cub and there was nothing that was going to stop her if she felt that harm of any kind has come to it.

"Calm your ass down Chanae!" he screamed

letting her go to try and protect his face. Her hits were harder than he expected them to be.

"Fuck you nigga don't you ever put your fucking hands on my child!" she lost it she was swinging with all her might. She looked over on the nightstand and grabbed the lamp sitting on it. She swung it as hard as she could at him. The lamp connected to the side of his head making a cracking sound.

Chanae watched Von fall back onto the floor. She stepped over him and rushed over to her baby. Dropping to her knees she dropped the lamp next to her and picked her baby up in her arms.

"Khalid baby wake up for mommy. Get up for mommy baby please get up for mommy!" she cried rocking him back and forth in her arms. He wasn't moving and Chanae was crying hard while holding him.

"Little prince please wake up for me please! God please don't take my baby from me he's just a baby. It's not his time I promise I will take better care of him just please god don't take my baby." She prayed and cried. She was in complete shock until she snapped out of it and realized that she needed to call the police. She laid her son down and went to get up off of her knees. When she stood to her feet and turned around she was met with a fist to the face sending her into complete darkness.

"Finally you decided to come back around." Von said to a tied up and gagged Chanae. She was still in Khalid's bedroom but now she was tied to a chair with some scarfs he had found in the master bedroom. She looked over at Khalid who was now lying on his bed but he still wasn't moving. Tears begun to roll down her face nonstop as she thought about her baby laying there looking lifeless.

Von followed her eyes over to her son. He sat down on the bed next time him.

"Oh don't worry he's still breathing. He might need to see a doctor but he should be fine. That is if he gets some help in time." He said turning to face her. "He look just like that nigga. How could you go and get pregnant not once but twice by that nigga? You were my fucking girl Chanae how could you fucking betray me by fucking my enemy? Huh?" he walked up to her and snatched the tape off of her mouth.

"I didn't betray you Von what about all the times you betrayed my love and trust? I don't love you I never will ever again. Kalil is the man god placed on this earth just for me as he did me for him. You can pull all the stunts in the world but that would never make me want you." Von was seething and Chanae could tell. He begun to pace the floor in front of her.

"You talk so highly of him like he perfect that punk ass bitch has flaws too!" he spat.

"I never said he didn't but I know that no matter what he does, it still won't make me want your weak small dick ass!" she glared at him.

"I wasn't hearing you say shit about this dick when I was digging your back out."

Chanae laughed at his stupidity. "Please don't flatter yourself because of you I learned to fake a good orgasm. I never knew what one felt like until me and my husband first made love. Hell I didn't know anything about deep stroking until he had my legs in there air hitting my g spot. Shit with you I didn't even think I had a damn g spot you wasn't hitting anything. Hahaha hell my walls couldn't even get any action and you know how tight I am. That says a lot pencil dick." Chanae laughed because she knew from his facial expression that she is getting under his skin.

Von was about to say something until he felt and heard Khalid move and moan out in pain. That drew both him and Chanae's attention. A smiled spread across Von's face as an idea came to mind. Chanae watched as he got up and walked out of the room. She looked confused and scared for her son and unborn daughters. It was at that minute she realized that her sweat pants were wet. A sharp pain that felt like a knife was stabbing her shot through her lower back and stomach.

"Damn my water just broke." She said through clenched teeth. She squeezed her legs together when she felt a contraction coming.

"Oh god Kalil where are you?" she closed her

eyes to try and block out the pain she was having.

Von walked back into the room holding a huge butcher knife and a wide sinister grin.

Chapter 53

"You know Chanae, whether you believe it or not I did love you. Then you turned around and disrespected me by marrying this fool." Von stated calmly walking towards her holding the knife handle in his right hand while swirling the tip on his index finger.

"Oh my bad Von I didn't know that all the cheating and punches to my face was acts of love. Save that shit for someone who gives a fuck my husband will be here soon and you will be just like the rest of those fuckers who tried to come between us. DEAD!" Chanae was trying to keep him talking for as long as she could until Kalil came home. Chanae was trying to loosen the scarfs off of her hands at the same time she was finding it hard to breathe from the contractions.

"You really think I give a fuck and I'm scared of him huh?" He asked walking up to her and backhanding her.

Chanae head snapped back. When she turned back to face him she had a disgusted look on her face. She spit the blood that was starting to fill the inside of her mouth out in Von's face.

"I'm not that same weak girl that I used to be when we were together. I'm now the bitch who would if given the chance take that knife and send it straight through your cold ass heart." She could feel another contraction coming.

"Aw yeah? Hahaha let's see how you feel

watching me drive this muthafucka through your son's heart bitch!" he turned on his heels towards Khalid.

"Noooo don't you touch him you stupid son of a bitch!" Chanae screamed out struggling to free her hands from the scarfs.

Von laughed as he stood over Khalid with the knife dangling inches away from his chest.

"Any last words before I kill your little bastard?" the sinister laugh he gave made Chanae's stomach turn.

She didn't say anything just moaned out in pain. Von got ready to stab Khalid when he abruptly turned back around to face Chanae.

"On second thought I don't want to deal with blood getting on me." He looked down at his bloody shirt at the blood that came from the gash on the side of his head and back up at her. "Well not anymore blood that is." Sitting the knife down on the dresser he proceeded to snatch the pillow from underneath Khalid's head.

He smiled back at Chanae before placing the pillow over his face. "Noooo STOOOOOOP!" She cried out helplessly.

Von was so occupied with trying to kill a three year old that he didn't pay attention to his surroundings. Out of nowhere he was knocked to the ground by force.

Chanae watched as Von and her brother tussled with each other on the floor. Zahyir had just come back because he forgot to give Khalid the stuffed tiger he picked up for him earlier at the store. To his surprise when he walked back through the door he heard screams coming from upstairs. Screams that belonged to his sister; at first he thought she was in labor or something so he rushed up the steps. He was shocked to see Von standing over his nephew with a pillow over his face.

While they fought Chanae was busy trying to free herself. Zahyir was starting to get the upper hand on Von punching him in the face.

While Zahyir sent blow to blow at him he tried hard to block them. Von felt himself losing and when his back was against the wall he had no problem fighting dirty. He grabbed Zahyir's arm and sink his teeth into it until he drew blood. Zahyir reached for his arm and Von took full advantage by punching him in the jaw and pushed him off of him. He quickly got to his feet running for the knife on the dresser. When he reached it he turned to catch to straight jabs to the chin.

Stumbling back a few feet Von tried to catch his balance. Zahyir rushed at him and was met with a knife to the abdomen. Chanae screamed as she watched her brother fall to the floor holding his blood seeping stomach.

"Ahhhhhhhhhh! I hate you I hate you!" Von turned as attention to her.

"You know what bitch you hate me so much you can fucking go to hell right along with your brother and your son will soon follow." He walked over to her still gripping the bloody knife in his hand. The blood was dripping from the knife leading a path of blood as his trail.

"I'm going to cut that fucking baby out of you and leave it as a gift for that nigga you treasure so much. Then, while he is mourning his little beloved family, I'm going to catch his ass slipping and kill him too – that way you fuckers can all be together in hell because there is no way you're going to be with him while I'm still walking this earth." Right when he was about to drive the knife into her pregnant belly, Zahyir knocked into him with his shoulder knocking him to the floor and the knife out his hand. He was losing blood at rapid speed which made his strength weaken by the second but looking over at his sister who was silently crying and confined to the chair, Zahyir forced himself off the ground. If he died, he wanted to die protecting his sister and her children.

"Come on. Get up bitch!" Zahyir egged Von on and grimaced in pain as he tried to steady himself. Von tasted the thick blood that coated his tongue and spat a huge glob of it onto the carpet before getting up. The sadistic look in his eyes showed that he had murder on the brain and at the moment, Zahyir was his target. Von charged full force towards Zahyir like a professional linebacker but Zahyir had already contemplated that's what he would do and as Von neared him he sidestepped and tripped him causing Von to fall to the floor face first. As soon as he hit the ground Zahyir climbed on top of him and began raining blows all over the back of his head and back. Chanae watched on in anticipation as her brother literally struggled to fight to death for her.

With her hands still behind her back, she had finally located the knot Von had tied in the silk scarves that confined her wrists and she began tugging at them to pull them apart. Several minutes later she had finally freed her wrists and quietly knelt down beside her to pick up the bloody knife.

Von lay completely still on the floor allowing Zahyir to pummel his back. He knew he was losing blood at rapid speed and sooner rather than later he'd slow down and that's exactly when he'd strike. Once Zahyir's breaths became labored and his punches slowed, Von threw him off his back and watched as he slid across the room and hit the dresser. His eyes were hungry for blood and he would not stop his rampage until his thirst was quenched. Walking over to where Zahyir had slumped to the floor, Von placed his foot over his gushing wound and pressed his weight down on it causing blood to seep out faster.

"Get away from him you bastard!" Chanae cried out as she saw her brother had no more fight left in him. Von turned and walked over to her. He was sick of her mouth and he was ready to end her life. Just as inches stood between them, Chanae jumped up and drove the bloody knife directly into his heart and began twisting it with every fiber of her being. Von couldn't believe she had stabbed him.

"You bitch!" he exclaimed as his hands fell over hers trying to grab the knife. The last thing he saw was the look of fear mixed with satisfaction in Chanae's eyes as he dropped to his knees and fell forward onto the carpet beside her feet. Chanae knew what she did had killed him and as he bled out, she rushed over to her brother trying to wake him up.

"Zah! Zah, come on baby brother please don't die on me. I just found you. Ahhhhhhhh!" she cried as another contraction hit making the pain unbearable. She managed to get Zahyir's phone to call 911 and let them know not only does her son has trauma to the head, her brother has been stabbed, there was a dead body on the floor and she was currently in labor.

Kalil pulled up to his house with a dozen pink and red roses and some chocolate turtles for Chanae since they were her favorite. He grabbed some gummy bears and juice for his little prince as well. Walking up to the door he was about to unlock it with his key when he noticed it was already open. Pushing the door opened all the way Kalil immediately dropped what was in his hands and drew his gun. He was slowly making his way further into the house when he heard Chanae screaming for help. He dashed up the stairs taking two to three steps at a time following the sound of her voice.

When he reached Khalid's room he stood in shock at the scene before him. Quickly coming out of his mini daze he ran into the room to his son whom he saw lying on the bed with blood coming from a gash on his head.

"What the fuck happened Chanae?" he went to pick his son up when the next words out of her mouth stopped all movement.

"Von broke in the house and tried to kill us. He

hurt my baby and my brother." She cried.

Kalil turned to face her as he looked on the floor for the first time. When he saw his son in the bed bleeding he didn't see anything else. "Did you call the police?" he asked getting his phone out.

"Yes baby I need help Zah….Ahhhhhhhh god this shit hurts!" she screamed with pain dripping from her voice.

Kalil rushed over to her with his blood boiling. He couldn't believe that nigga pulled some shit like this. Kalil knew if Von wasn't already dead he would have sent a bullet straight through his head.

"Baby, what's wrong is something wrong with the babies?" Kalil asked that just as he heard the paramedics yelling for someone. He rushed out in the hall to get them.

"Up here! My family needs medical attention

NOW!" he shouted over the banister. They quickly went racing up the stairs into the room where the scene was a bloody mess. As soon as they stepped foot in the room they got the work on Khalid and Zahyir.

Kalil watch them work but soon his attention was drawn over to Chanae again when she screamed out for help. "Baby, what's wrong talk to me?"

"Bae I'm in active labor! Oh god I can feel the head coming out!" Kalil didn't have time to panic like he wanted to he yelled for someone to help his wife.

"This night is the damn twilight zone." He said himself as he watched them carry Chanae out the room.

Chapter 54

The paramedics set Chanae up in the master bedroom. They knew they were not going to make it to the hospital in time so now Chanae didn't have a choice in the matter she was giving birth to her babies at home. Kalil called Nassir and Charles to get to the hospital with Zahyir and Khalid. They called him when they made it there. Zariya and Kalyah came to support Chanae and Kalil during the home birth.

"Baby it hurts so bad!" Chanae yelled to Kalil who was right by her side. He felt torn because he wanted to be here to watch his daughters be born but he also wanted to be at the hospital with their son. Nassir assured him that he and Charles would look after him. They also called Sonja and Karla to come to the hospital to be with Khalid.

"Baby, you got this; you been through so much I know you can handle this. Chanae, I'm counting on you to bring our babies into the world." He coached.

"Okay I got this. Khalid baby, what about our prince is he okay?"

"Yes he going to be just fine." He told her hoping it was the truth.

"The head is coming out now!" one of the paramedics said to the other.

"Ma'am on the count of three I'm going to need you to push as hard as you can okay?" Chanae nodding her head yes.

"One…two….three."

"Ahhhhhhhhhhhhhhhhhh oh my godddddddd!"

she pushed with all her might. She was pushing so hard

her face was turning red.

"Okay stop." The medic ordered.

Within seconds they were pulling a baby girl out

wiping her down.

"Waaaaaaaaaaaaaah!" Kalil and Chanae heard

one of the loudest cries coming from their first little

princess. They watched the doctors clean her off and

then hand her over to Kalil.

"Baby, look at our beautiful princess; Tyesha

Mya Barber." He beamed with pride rubbing his nose

against her cheek.

"She is beautiful baby she looks just like you."

Chanae said right before another contraction hit her

letting her know it was time to push again.

"Okay Mrs. Barber, give us another great big

push." She did as she was told and within ten seconds of pushing another Barber baby girl was brought into the world.

"Waaaaaaaaaaaaaaaaa waaaaaaaaaaa!" They cleaned her up and handed her over to Kalil as well.

"Aww bae look at her, she is beautiful." Chanae smiled at her babies.

"They both are beautiful sis looking just like Kalil." Zariya said snapping pictures already with her phone.

"What's her name?" Kalyah asked as she played with their little fingers.

"Her name is Myesha Tya Barber. Our little princesses…" Chanae was stopped with what she was about to say with another sharp pain shooting through her body.

"Oh noooo something isn't right!" she yelled.

"I thought the afterbirth wasn't really painful?" Kalil asked thinking that is what's wrong with his wife.

"I see another head!" one of the paramedics yelled out getting back into position to deliver another baby.

"A WHAT???" Kalil and Chanae shouted at them at the exact same time.

"Come one Mrs. Barber we need another big push."

"I'm not pushing shit ain't no more babies in there you crazy people are seeing shit now. Un un no way was I carrying around three babies and the doctor didn't catch it. You can forget about me pu...." Her ranting was interrupted by the pain she was feeling. She found herself giving them another great big push.

For one whole minute there was complete silence in the room and until they all heard something that shocked them all.

"Waaaaaaaaaaaaaaaaaaaa!" it was the cry of a baby that they never knew they were expecting. Kalil handed his two princesses off to Zariya and Kalyah as he watched a paramedic walk over to him to hand over his mystery child.

"Congratulations you two are proud parents of a set of triplets." He said handing Kalil the baby.

Kalil looked over at Chanae and smiled. She returned that smile as she watched him with the baby.

"So bae is it another girl?" she asked curious.

"No baby it's a boy. You just gave birth to two girls and a boy."

"Wow that's crazy you guys didn't know. How did the doctor miss that?" Kalyah asked while holding baby Myesha in her arms.

"Well it is possible. Some doctors call it the

502

invisible baby. They might not have seen him because he was hiding directly behind one of the other babies. Their heartbeats had to have been beating in sync with one another. That is very rare but it does happen and today that is exactly what happened." One of the paramedics explained to them.

"We need to get her and the babies to the hospital to make sure they are perfectly fine." One of the other paramedics said preparing to transport Chanae and the triplets to the hospital.

After getting herself and the babies checked out Chanae insisted that someone bring her Khalid and tell her what was going on with her brother.

"Baby as soon as we know something we will tell you. Nassir said that Zahyir is in surgery now. Khalid is getting moved over here into your room; I took care of all that so can you please calm down and stop stressing yourself out?" He kissing her on the forehead while holding their second son in his arms.

"Baby we never gave him a name. What are we going to call him?" she asked looking at her handsome little man. It was crazy how all of their kids looked like Kalil and only held a few of her features. Other than that it looked as if he literally pushed them out himself.

"This little prince will be named Kalil Taheir Makai Barber Jr." he stated happy as hell.

"Aww you finally got your junior."

"Yeah, I have my wife and now four beautiful kids. I couldn't ask for a better life than the one I'm living right now."

"Awww baby." He leaned over and kissed her gently on the lips trying not to hurt her where it was split at.

The detectives wasted no time questioning Chanae about what went down at her house. After she explained everything and they put everything into perspective they declared it a closed case. They had concluded that Von tried to kill her and her family but luckily her brother showed up when he did or Khalid, Chanae, and their triplets would not be here.

"Kalil I'm scared. What if he doesn't make it? I just found out I had a brother a few years ago I can't lose him. Not now, not like this." She cried into her hands.

Kalil placed his Jr. in his bed next to his sisters. He then hugged Chanae tightly letting her know that everything would be fine if she just had a little faith.

"Baby Zahyir is a strong person and he did what he felt he had to in order to protect you and our four babies. One in which he didn't know about. So imagine how surprised he's going to be, hearing he is now the uncle of four."

"Nope six you know he counts Za'kiya and Kamyra as his nieces too."

"Yeah that's true so you need to calm down and have faith that it will all work out okay?"

"What would I do without you?" she asked with a smile.

"You would probably be the old lady on the block with about fifty cats, three dogs, and a parakeet." He joked causing her to laugh. That's all he'd been waiting for; for her to give him a big hearty laugh. After all she had been through today alone, he was happy to see her smiling. That was a very traumatic thing she went through in the last twelve hours. He just wanted to make sure she was good after all that and her smile and laugh confirmed to me that she is.

"Whatever punk, I hope you know that you are not getting any more kids out of me. Four is more than enough you have your two boys and two girls you even now player and my baby making bank is closed. There will be no more deposits I'm closed for business." She looked at him with a raised eyebrow waiting to hear what smart comeback he has to come at her with.

"Whatever you say, Mrs. Barber."

"Kalil, don't start no shit." She glared at him.

"I just said whatever you say; I'm agreeing with you baby."

"Ummm huh." She threw him the side eye.

Qadir came busting through the room door startling her a little bit. He was out of breath as if he had been running a marathon.

"Boy, what's wrong with you why are you breathing like that?" she asked him giving him a funny look.

"It's Zahyir." Were the only words he got before Chanae started having different thoughts running through her mind about her brother not making it? The look on Qadir's face caused her to break down right then and there.

"I can't lose him after just finding out about him that's not fair." She cried so hard she started hyperventilating. It got so bad doctors had to come into the room and sedate her.

Chapter 55

A few hours later…

Chanae was starting to stir in her sleep. The sweat pouring out from her pores coated her entire face. She squeezed her eyes shut tight before popping them wide open seconds later. Darting her eyes around the room she was trying to remember where she was. When she saw that she was in the hospital visions of her night started to come back to her piece by piece. She put her hands over her stomach trying to feel for her pregnant belly. She started to scream when she realized that it was flat.

509

"Calm down baby don't you remember you had the babies already? You at the hospital now." she heard Kalil tell her. She looked around and spotted him leaning over their babies' beds. She sighed heavily releasing the breath she didn't even realize she was even holding in.

"Let me see them baby." she asked him holding her arms out to receive them.

"Sure, I might as well let you hold them one last time before I take them away from you… Just like you took me away from my daughter." He turned around to face her and that's when she saw a bloody Von with blood dripping from his head and a knife sticking out of his chest.

"Ahhhhhhhhh!" she screamed at the top of her lungs.

"You see what you did to me bitch! All I wanted

was for us to be a family and this is what you do!" he shouted coming closer toward her still holding one of her babies in his arms.

"Chanae….Chanae wake up baby….Chanae get up you scaring the babies." She jumped up out of her sleep feverishly shaking her head from side to side while looking around the room.

"It's okay baby it was just a dream." Kalil said trying to get her to relax.

Chanae could hear faint cries in the room. She looked next to the guest chair and saw her three babies in their bassinets. When she looked over on the other side of them she saw her little Prince Khalid sleeping on the other bed. Looking up at Kalil she smiled seeing her family all together.

"I told you baby everything will be okay."

"Yes you did baby." Chanae's smile quickly

turned to a frown when she thought of her brother.

"Zahyir…"

"Baby, he fought to protect you and our children. For that I will forever be indebted to him. I need you to be strong not just for yourself but for those four over there too. He would want you to be strong for them that is the reason he fought so hard baby." Kalil caressed the side of her face with the back of his hand. A single tear slid down Chanae's face he wiped it away.

Before either of them could say anything else there was a knock at the door that drew both of their attention.

"Wow, you were supposed to be making me a grandfather of three and ended up giving me four." Charles smiled walking all the way in the room over towards his daughter.

"Hey, daddy I'm sorry…" he stopped her with a

finger to his lips.

"How are you feeling baby girl?" he asked her.

"Daddy, I'm tired of being asked that question. How do people think I am supposed to feel? I feel like shit! Because of me ever being involved with Von my family has been through hell and back seven times over. I almost lost all my babies and my own life. Not to mention my brother that I just really started to get to know is now dead because of me!" Chanae cried into her hands.

"Wait what? Who told you that Zahyir was dead?" Kalil and Charles said at the same exact time.

Chanae looked over at Kalil confused. He was standing there when Qadir came running into the room with the devastating news. "Kalil, you were right there when Qadir brought us the news. Why are you acting as if you don't know what I'm talking about now?"

"Chanae baby Qadir didn't say that Zahyir was dead he said that Zahyir came out of surgery okay and should make a full recovery." He explained.

"What?" she looked from him and her father to confirm that they are telling her the truth. Not that they would lie about something as important as this but she still needed to confirm it.

"Baby before you gave him a chance to explain you started flipping out and crying uncontrollably so the doctor had to sedate you. Chanae, your brother is very much alive."

"Really? I want to see him. I have to see him!"

"Actually that is another reason why I am here other than checking up on you and my grandbabies. Zahyir demands that he see you for himself. He doesn't believe any of us when we tell him that you and the babies are fine. He says he has to see for himself that you all are okay or he's not accepting that."

"Kalil, get me a wheelchair I'm going to see my brother."

"No wait Chanae I was just going to say you call him and maybe he will calm down. You have to remember you've just been through a horrible ordeal too. You were beaten and gave birth to three babies." Charles said with concern.

"Daddy, just like he needs proof that I am okay I need it too. I have to see him." She looked over at Kalil for him to understand her reasoning for wanting to see her brother.

"I'll go get a wheelchair. Charles will you stay here with the kids please?"

"You don't have to ask me that of course I will."

Kalil went to grab a wheelchair for Chanae and they made their way up to Zahyir's room. When they made it outside the door Chanae looked up at Kalil and he smiled back at her. Pushing the door open he rolled her into the room causing all eyes to be locked on them.

"Look at you; I can't tell one bit that you just pushed out three babies." Nassir said walking up to Chanae and kissing her on the cheek before hugging her.

"I will definitely take that compliment." She laughed never taking her eyes off of her brother.

Kalil rolled her up next to the bed. She grabbed ahold of Zahyir's hand as they stared at each other like no one else was in the room.

"How about we give them some time alone?" Zariya suggested. They all left Chanae and Zahyir alone to talk. Kamira kissed Zahyir on the lips before leaving out the room closing the door behind her.

"You scared me little brother."

He smiled at her.

"There you go with that little crap I keep telling you that I am a grown ass man."

"Hahaha, yeah whatever you say Zah you not *that* grown. You still watch cartoons." That comment made them both laugh.

"Ohhhh shit!" he groaned in pain while holding onto his stomach.

"What's wrong are you okay? Should I get the doctor? I'm going to call for help." She said getting ready to turn around and head for the door.

"No sis that ain't necessary I'm fine. As long as I know that you and my nephew and nieces are okay I'm good."

"Nephews." She corrected him.

"What?" he asked with a raised eyebrow.

"I gave birth to two girls and a boy. So you have

two nephews now."

"Oh word?"

"Word." They cracked up laughing, Zahyir not as hard as before.

"I'm so sorry Zah. All of this is my fault; if I had never got involved with Von none of this would have happened. You wouldn't be laid up in the hospital with a stab wound." Chanae felt the tears about to pour out again as she try hard to fight them from releasing.

"Chanae don't do that okay. Please don't."

"Do what?"

"Blame yourself for the actions of someone else. Especially not a weak ass nigga like Von. What he did is not your fault - that's his guilt to take to hell with him. Okay?"

"Okay."

"Now, how are you though? Real shit too, don't

give me that weak shit either Chanae it's not every day you have to body a nigga because he was trying to cause you and your family harm."

"I know that I am going to have nightmares about what happened last night for a while. Kalil suggested that I talk to a professional about what happened."

"What do you think about that?" he asked cautiously.

"I think I'm going to do it. I know it will help me get over this." She said looking down at her hands holding on to his.

"That's good, sis." Before they could say another word the door came open and in walked Za'kiya.

"Oh my Zahyir, are you okay?"

"Yes I'm fine short stuff." He chuckled.

"Good now umm, Zahyir don't think because you at the doctor's office you don't still have to play with me at home. You missed our play date today." She stated with a frown.

"Za'kiya, I told you to wait until Chanae came out before coming in here." Zariya said walking into the room a few seconds after her.

"But mommy I needed to talk to my Zahyir. Oh and my Te-Te Chanae too... Te-Te when will I be able to take my babies home with me?"

"Girl, bring your butt on here." Zariya grabbed her hand and led her out of the room. When the door closed shut Chanae and Zahyir stared at each other for a full minute before busting out laughing.

"I'm glad you came into my life sis."

"I'm glad that we found each other thanks to Kalil."

"Yeah we blessed huh?"

"Very blessed, little brother, very blessed." They continued to spend a little bit more time together before Zahyir meds kicked in. Chanae kissed her brother forehead and went back upstairs to her babies. Their bond will forever be cherished by them both. No one will ever be able to break what was destined to be.

Chapter 56

A few weeks later...

It was now Christmas day and everybody was excited to be together for the holidays. The family couldn't decide who house they would have Christmas dinner at so they all agreed to do it at Kalil's restaurant. They brought all the gifts to the restaurant and decided to open them there. They let the kids open their gifts at the house when they woke up that morning.

"Do you all need any help with the food or anything? Kalyah asked her mother and Sonja as she walked into the restaurant.

"No baby we got it. Go ahead on over there and have a seat." Sonja replied.

"Are you sure?"

"Yes we got it." She responded putting a platter of food on the table.

"Okay." She walked over to where Zariya and Chanae were sitting.

"Hey ladies!"

"Hey boo, where is my baby Kamyra?" Zariya asked her.

"Girl, she saw Za'kiya, Kamira, and Tara and straight dissed me for them." She said with a laugh.

"Hahaha aww don't feel bad honey, Za'kiya dissed me for them and her Zahyir and Qadir too."

"It's like they say screw us as soon as they see them."

"Yup." Zariya giggled.

"Hold the hell up, Zar you see what I see?" Chanae asked her nodding her head over at Kalyah.

"What?" Kalyah asked innocently.

"It ain't no damn what heifer what is that blinding my damn eye sight?" Zariya joked.

"Oh you mean this!" Kalyah held her left hand up.

"Are you saying what I think you saying?" Chanae asked excitedly.

"Yessss!!! My baby asked me to marry him this morning and I said hell yeah! I swear I haven't been this happy in forever!" she screamed jumping up and down. Zariya and Chanae both hopped up from their seats running up to her and giving her a hug.

Across the room Nassir, Demarco, and Markel stood staring at them as if they were crazy.

"Damn, what you trying to do get me cursed the fuck out on Christmas day?" Demarco asked looking at Markel like he had six heads and seven arms.

"What'd I do? I just finally decided to take that big step. I love the hell out of Kalyah and Kamyra. I just want them to be happy man that's all." Markel confessed.

"I'm glad to hear that man because those two mean the world to Kalil and I personally want nothing more than to see them happy. And I noticed that since you came into their lives they've been nothing but that so I'm glad to have you part of the family and I'm sure Kalil feels the same." Nassir said.

"Thanks, man that's means a lot."

"All you muthafuckas trying to make it hard for me and shit." Demarco complained.

"Boy, I know one thing you better watch your

mouth. This is Jesus' day and you will not talk that way on His day." Sonja disciplined. Everybody laughed a Demarco's expense.

"Ohhhh, you said a bad word you know what that means." Kamyra said holding out her right hand while pointing to it with her left.

"Aw hell, you worse than Za'kiya damn." He said digging in his pocket for some money.

"Ohhh you cursed again you might as well double that." she said as serious as a heart attack.

"You heard my baby; pay up playa!" Kalyah said walking over to them.

"Plus, you are being loud knowing my baby cousins over there sleeping so I'm going to need another ten spot for that too. You know Granny said when inside we have to use our inside voices." Demarco looked around at everyone because he can't believe what he just heard.

"Well uncle Marky?" she said with her hand out.

"I can't believe I'm getting played by a damn six year old and you all just standing there." he said handing over thirty dollars.

"Um you a little short uncle Marky." Kamyra said licking her finger before counting out the money.

"Look you ain't getting no more money so you might as well go hustle somebody else. You have been around Za'kiya too long." He said dead ass serious.

"Fine cheap meanie." She whispered.

"Uncle Nassir where is Za'kiya at?" she asked now turning to him while stuffing her money in her little purse she got for Christmas.

"She went to the store with her uncle Kalil and cousin Khalid. The moms needed some ice or something." He answered.

"Yeah I know my baby is driving him crazy too." Zariya laughed walking up with NJ on her hip.

❧ ❧ ❧

"Uncle Kalil, can we talk?" Za'kiya asked as he helped her out of the car.

"Yeah, what's up baby girl? You know you can talk to me about anything." He said pressing the locks on the key ring to lock the door before grabbing her hand and walking into the store.

"Well I was just wondering when you were going to give me my babies. You and Te-Te Chanae had them long enough don't you think?" she asked as they made their way over to the freezer section.

"What? Baby girl you know that you can't have them for your own but they will always be your cousin." He tried explaining to her but the look on her face said she wasn't going for it and he was going to have to come way better than that.

"Uncle Kalil I want them to come live with me I promise to take very good care of them." She pleaded.

Kalil grabbed two big bags of ice and headed cover to the counter to pay for them.

"Za'kiya you're too young to take care of three babies or any babies for that matter." He paid for his purchases and lead ushered them out of the store but Khalid wanted some candy.

"Daddy I want this." He said holding up a bag of Cherry Clans.

"Naw little man you haven't even eaten yet. You can get some later on our way home alright?"

"Okay daddy." She aid taking Za'kiya hand while she holds on to Kalil's with her other hand.

"What if you come and see them on the

weekends?" Za'kiya said still at it.

"Za'kiya…"

"My daddy give me what I want; why won't you? Don't you love me uncle Kalil?" she asked as he put them both in the car and buckled their seatbelts.

"I do love you but they can't live with you baby girl. How about you ask your parents once we get back okay?"

"Okay uncle Kalil." She agreed.

By time they arrived back at the restaurant all of the food was ready they were just waiting for them to arrive. Once everyone got seated around the huge dining table they joined hands and said grace. About ten minutes after they started eating Chanae told them that she had an announcement to make.

"Oh Te-Te is it that you finally letting me and Za'kiya have our babies?" Kamyra asked.

"Lord, not you too." Kalil said while shaking his head.

"Uhhh, no baby.... Anyway after talking it over with Kalil I have decided to write a book about our life." She announced happily.

"Oh my god that is great Chanae I am so proud of you sis. Not a lot of people can go through what you been through and openly share it with the world." Zariya congratulated her sister and friend.

"That's not all; I got a three book deal with Simon and Schuster to publish my work." She smiled and Kalil couldn't help but smile seeing his baby happy about something she really wanted to do.

He whispered in her ear how much he loved her and how proud he is of her.

"Thank you baby." She kissed him on the lips.

Everyone congratulated her on her new venture

and wished her much success.

"So does this mean my babies finally get to come live with me or what?" Za'kiya asked in an even tone causing the entire room to erupt in laughter.

"When you're married and in your own house then of course you can have babies of your OWN live with you. Keep in mind that by the time you start dating, you will be about sixty-five." Nassir stated seriously. Everyone around the table laughed as Nassir and Za'kiya started having a back and forth debate.

Chanae looked over at her babies who were lying beside her in their bassinets that they brought with them from the house. She then looked over at Khalid who was laughing and playing with his uncle Zahyir after stealing a dinner roll off of his plate.

"We created some beautiful babies if I must say so myself." Kalil said to her with a grin.

"Yes we did but remember you ain't getting anymore from me Mr. Barber."

"If you say so, Mrs. Barber. I have something for you though." He said sliding an envelope over to her.

"What is this?"

"You will never know if you don't open it beautiful."

Chanae opened up the envelope smiling big at the contents. "Baby, you got us two plane tickets to Bora Bora?"

"What you think about us in a few months taking a much needed trip there?"

"I would love that. I need some alone time to get to know my husband all over again."

"Good. You are my world you know that?"

"Yup; without me you would be an old lonely

man in a house full of smelly dogs." The laughed and talk as if they were the only two there. Their lives have been chaotic from their first introduction but through it all they came off on top. Even with their lives being altered they still share the same love they did when they first met an unbreakable bond that even near death experiences couldn't break.

Epilogue

The only sounds that could be heard were the waves bashing against the sides of the boat. The moonlight glistened over their bodies as they engaged in their third round of love making since climbing aboard the yacht. Every kiss, lick, and stroke sent chills throughout both of their bodies. They were in Heaven and thankful to be in each other's arms. He thrust his pelvis against hers one more time before they both exploded sending them over the edge with eternal bliss.

"I swear every time I make love to you it seems as if it is the first time all over again." Kalil said kissing her soft lips as they lay on the floor on the front of the yacht under the night sky.

"That is a good thing seeing as how I pushed not one or two but four of your big headed ass babies out." Chanae joked.

"Aye! Don't be talking about my babies, woman!" they both broke out with laughter as Kalil lay on his back pulling Chanae close to him. Silence engulfed them as they looked at the stars. They both were thinking back on their lives before they had become one leading up until now.

"You know we been through a lot of shit since the day we met. I knew once I laid eyes on you that I had to have you though. I was willing to do anything to get you. You had me shook though I'll say that." he admitted looking up at the sky in deep thought.

Chanae raised her head up a little on his

shoulder so that she was looking directly at him.

"What do you mean I had you shook?" she asked with a confused frown on her face.

"Well you see I knew that one day you would be my wife. The obstacles that kept getting in our way are what had me shook. I thought for sure you would leave and never look back but you didn't. I thank God for you everyday Chanae because without you, there would be no me. I don't know if you know this or not but you saved me in a way." He looked into her eyes and smiled.

She smiled back but was a little curious to what he meant so she asked him to clarify his statement.

"I don't understand bae; how did I save you? When we met that night at the club and when the shooting started you actually saved me. If you wouldn't have pushed me down in time I probably would have been riddled with bullets."

"No what I mean is that the night at the club I was battling with the thought of getting back in the game. I was trying to figure out a way to tell Nassir. He's my partner and best friend - we ran the streets together and got in and out before it was too late. I was just starting to feel like I was wasting my life away. All I was doing was clubbing and dealing with chicks that shouldn't have had a minute of my time. That all came to a stop when I laid eyes on you at the club that night. You saved me from the streets and the loose women that meant me no good." Chanae saw the stressful look on his face as if he was battling with his words. He sighed deeply before continuing.

"Chanae. you were my gift from God. He sent you to me that day to save me from myself. I am grateful and thankful to call you my wife, my best friend, the love of my life, and the mother of my children. I love you for never giving up on me, on us. Baby, with everything in me I love the day you came into my life and changed it for the better."

A single tear slid down his cheek as Chanae wiped the ones that escaped from her own eyes.

"Kalil Barber, I love you so much and I couldn't have asked God for a better husband than the one he blessed me with. Not only that you are a great father to our children. You weren't the only one battling with the thought of giving in that night I was too. I was tired of being treated like shit instead of the queen I should have been treated like. I never knew what it felt like to be worship as someone's woman. Well that was until I met the love of my life." she smiled at him while looking into his eyes.

"Who Tree from that fictional novel you read

like a million times? Chanae, are you trying to tell me that you been cheating on me with a dude from a book?" he joked and chuckled.

"He's from Hood Symphony and bae I didn't know how to tell you that I was in love with another man. I'm so sorry." She cracked up laughing with Kalil face went from a smirk to a frown.

"Chanae, please don't make me kick your ass and then burn all of your books. That includes your little secret stash you got hidden in the girl's nursery too. I bet you won't be claiming to love no more of those damn fake ass niggas from those books under my watch no more." He laughed when she looked shocked and surprised.

"Yeah I know about your book stash you ain't slick."

"Boy if you even think about burning my books

we will fight! Those are fighting words honey you do not mess with a woman's novels that consist of words written about fine ass men. My, my, my you have a lot to learn baby. I would hate to make our kids fatherless because he couldn't keep his hands off my books. Tuh...Tuh!" they stared each other down for a minute not saying anything before they bust out into laughter. Kalil kissed Chanae's forehead, nose, and then lips.

"You a crazy ass woman you know that?" he asked looking deep into her eyes while she stare up at him and smile.

"And that is why you love me so much."

"Yeah I guess if you say so." She punched him lightly on the arm.

"I am just kidding with your violent ass. We are going to have to get you some anger management classes as soon as we get back home." They laughed and held each other tighter as the stars danced around in the night sky.

"I love you so much Kalil Barber."

"I love you too Chanae Barber and I always will." Their lips connected as one forever sealing their everlasting love for one another.

The End

Altar'd

To My Supporters

I am thankful and blessed to be given a talent that I can share with others. To me writing is a way that I can create my own experiences and outcomes in a situation. I can give someone else a way to get away from their everyday life. Escape to a place where they can read about others' problems and maybe even see a message that can help them relate to their own lives. I have to start with thanking the man above for this gift without him none of this would be possible.

Each and every person that has supported me from the start and continuing to do so I just want to say that I truly appreciate you. Without you in my corner pushing me to farther my journey in this writing world I can honestly say that I would have probably thrown in the towel. This journey has not been an easy task but because of the continued support it forces me to keep coming. For that I am forever thankful, and grateful for you (my supporters). You all know who you are... ♥

To keep in touch with me here are my contacts.....

Email: dnicolegrant@yahoo.com

Facebook: https://www.facebook.com/danielle.grant.96

Altar'd

An Excerpt From My Upcoming Novel "Mama Didn't Raise Me"

Enjoy...

"Mikel you can't just barge in someone's house like this" Symone said in a shaky voice.

Mikel walked up and grabbed his sister around the throat. "That shit you pulled today could have killed my fucking son!" he spat through clenched teeth.

"It wasn't my fault she started it" cried Symone trying to loosen his grip from her neck.

"Hold the fuck up who you think you are coming in here grabbing on my bitch like that?" Rob said slamming the front door and walking over to Mikel.

Mikel let go of Symone's throat and watch her collapse on the floor. He turned to face Rob who was now standing two feet away from him. "You hard of hearing huh? Didn't I tell you to shut the fuck up?" Mikel spat.

"I want my uncle!" Mikel heard Jamila cry out and started banging on the door.

"Oh you must be her brother huh? Nigga I heard about your soft ass. You need to take that little smart mouth bitch back there with you so I can enjoy the rest of my game" Rob smirked at Mikel not knowing that he hit a nerve. The wrong one at that.

Before he could react Mikel fist were pounding into his face at rapid speed. The blows were so loud it knock Symone out of her thoughts on the floor. She stood to her feet but didn't move. She could see the blood spilling from Rob's face. Mikel stood up straight and looked over at his sister. He kicked Rob in the face for good measure. Symone found herself so scared she pissed on herself. She knew she really fucked up this time.

"Where the fuck is my niece Symone and I don't want to hear none of that bullshit you be talking" Mikel said trying to catch his breath.

Symone pointed to the backroom too scared to open her mouth and speak. Mikel walked to the back and when he made it to Jamila's room door he became pissed all over again. He looked back at Symone who was still standing in the same spot.

"You have a lock on the outside of her door? You locked my fucking niece in this damn room? Bitch have you lost your fucking mind? Come and open this fucking door before I be the only child my mother still have walking this earth!" He shouted at the top of his lungs. His voice was so deep and powerful Symone jumped. She fumbled around in her pocket for the key as she made her way to the door.

"Walk faster I don't have all damn day!"

She unlocked the door and stepped back. Mikel twist the knob and pushed the door open. Jamila now stood in the middle of the room with her face covered in tears. When she saw her uncle she ran to him at full speed.

"Uncle Mikel don't leave me please take me with you" she cried into his chest.

"Dollface that is exactly what I plan on doing. Do you have anything here that you want to take with you?" Jamila ran over to her bed and pulled a journal out from under her mattress. She walked back over to her uncle and took his hand.

"Let's go" Mikel and Jamila walked out of the room and he stopped in front of Symone. "I don't want you anywhere near my niece. If I find out that you had any contact with her, Symone I swear to you on daddy's grave I will bury you next to him. As far as I'm concern you are dead to me." They started walking towards the door when he turned back to face his sister.

"Let your man know if he know what is good for him he won't even think about calling the police or coming at me on some revenge shit. You should really stop lying to people about me being soft maybe he would have at least been prepared for that ass whooping." He said nodding over towards where Rob lay unconscious in a puddle of his own blood.

Mikel and Jamila hopped in his car and pulled off. Jamila eyes were red and puffy from crying for hours. She leaned over with her head against the window and dozed off to sleep. She felt safe now and not afraid of what her future may have planned for her.

Coming Soon 2014!!!!

Altar'd

An Excerpt from "Precious Gems"

By Monique Chanae and Danielle

Grant!!!

While everyone enjoyed the party Garcelle and her boyfriend Xavier were at one of the tables trying to keep their hands off of one another. It was not working for them. He had his hands under the table rubbing them up and down her leg through her dress. She was rubbing her hand down the side of his face. His skin felt so smooth on her hands. Garcelle could not take the teasing anymore.

"I am going to the bathroom" she announced standing to her feet and winking at Xavier before walking off.

Xavier looked around before getting up and

walking in the same direction she just went. Gabriel and Israel where on the other side of them room cracking up at them. They knew exactly what they were up too.

"Those two cannot get enough of each other" Gabriel giggled.

"Just like I can't get enough of you" he said kissing her soft lips. "Come dance with me gorgeous" he grabbed her hand and led the way to the dance floor. They dance with big smiles on their face while staring in each other's eyes.

"Yeah he definitely getting it tonight" she said to herself laying her head on his chest.

Xavier caught up with Garcelle a few feet away from the women's bathroom. He grabbed her around the waist and turned her around to face him. Their tongues become intertwined as they started a heated make out session right outside of the bathroom. Lucky for them no one could see them unless they came all the way around the corner of the hall. Garcelle broke their kiss and grinned at her man. "Damn I love this man" she thought.

She looked around him and them behind her before grabbing his hand and guiding him into the women's bathroom with her. They didn't even check to see if anyone was in the bathroom before they continued their lip locking make out session. Garcelle could feel the heat radiating off of their bodies. She also could feel Xavier's member start to grow through his pants suit.

"Are you sure about this someone might walk in on us? I am not trying to disrespect your parents in anyway shape or form by getting it in with their daughter at their party. And I definitely respect and love you too much to have sex with you in a bathroom. No matter how nice and clean it looks" he said looking around the bathroom. It was a fancy bathroom with all types of soaps and perfume sitting on top of the counter.

Garcelle just fell in love with Xavier even more after what he just said. He was always thinking about her and what her parents think of him especially when it comes to how he treats her. "We can wait until we get back to your place" she pecked him on the lips before turning to go into one of the bathroom stalls. She really had to use the bathroom.

"My place?" he thought before realizing what she meant. She was coming home with him tonight.

"Ahhhhhhhhhh" Xavier was broken out of his thoughts by Garcelle's screams. He ran over to her to see what she was staring at. When he saw what it was he grabbed her. She was standing there with her hands over her mouth with tears running down her face she looked as if she was about to throw up at any second. Before Xavier could lead her out of the bathroom she ran to an open stall and emptied out the dinner she had just eaten tonight into the toilet.

When she was done he pulled her out of the bathroom blocking her view from looking back at the disturbing sight. When they came be to where everyone else was Gabriel and Gavin was the first to see them. They ran over to Garcelle and she fell into her brother's arms crying on his shoulder. By this time other guest noticed the disturbed Garcelle. Her parents made their way to her to see what was going on with their daughter.

"Celle what is wrong talk to us" Gabriel encouraged her sister to tell them what is wrong but she only cried harder.

"Xavier what is wrong with my sister?" she asked looking him in the eyes he looked as if he was in a daze.

"She dead Gabriel. She was covered in blood, someone had killed her" a dazed out Xavier said he had seen some dead bodies before but that one was a bloody mess. Someone had stabbed her several times in the throat. You could see her tongue hanging out through her neck.

"What are you talking about Xavier" before he could respond there was another scream from someone that was running from the bathroom area.

"Someone killed Sue!" they screamed out. Causing all the guest to gasp and look around now scared for their own safety.

Who killed Sue and what role do

Altar'd

the *Precious Gems* play?

Gabriel and *Garcelle* just inherited more than the family business; they just inherited a murderer too...

Coming soon 2014!!!

CPSIA information can be obtained
at www.ICGtesting.com
Printed in the USA
LVOW04s1852040416

482086LV00020B/953/P